RED SUN OVER AFRICA

An International Financial Thriller

JAMES E. MERRIMAN

Red Sun over Africa
Copyright © 2023 by James E. Merriman

All rights reserved. No part of this book may be used or reproduced by any means, graphic, electronic, or mechanical, including photocopying, recording, taping, or by an information storage retrieval system without the written permission of the author except in the case of brief quotations embodied in critical articles or reviews.

This is a work of fiction. All the characters, names, incidents, organizations, and dialogue in this novel are either the product of the author's imagination or are used fictitiously.

ISBN: 9798386611088

ALSO, BY JAMES E. MERRIMAN

Blood & Diamonds

Blood & Money

Borderland Ranch

Missing in Bocas

Bad Blood

Push Back

GateKeepers

Always for Fay

CHAPTER 1

TINY CRYSTALS OF SLEET slammed into the windows of Luc Johannes's corner office on the top floor of 425 Park Avenue, combining with its chrome and glass decor to create the illusion of a sparkling ice cave. There were no family photos, no mementos of his forty-year career building Consolidated Diamonds, PLC, into a rival of De Beers. The sterile, impersonal environment was interrupted by a massive sunset photograph of Ayers Rock in the Australian Outback and another equally large black-and-white photograph of wildebeests and zebras crossing Tanzania's Mara River during the Great Migration.

The only paper on the glass-topped desk was a folder marked CONFIDENTIAL in bright-red letters. In the folder was the death sentence for Consolidated. According to the engineers, the company's Australian mine, the Golden Wattle, would play out in less than five years at the current rate of production. Without its main source of diamonds, Consolidated would no longer be a rival of De Beers, and Johannes would have to preside over the liquidation of his life's work.

The Skype meeting with Consolidated's Amsterdam office flickered on the computer screen and disappeared. It did not matter. Johannes knew enough for now. There was a sliver of hope. Botswana, a landlocked African country roughly the size of Texas with a population of about 2 million people, had just announced that it was going to sell its 50 percent interest in the Debswana Diamond Company, Ltd., the world's largest producer of diamonds by value. Unfortunately, De Beers owned the other 50 percent. Outmaneuvering De Beers would be no small feat.

There was a perfunctory knock on his door, followed by the entry of a tall, trim, biracial woman who strode across the office like the long-distance runner she was. Short, black hair in a layered cut accentuated a heart-shaped face with high cheekbones and full lips that a model would kill for. Emerald-green eyes were set off with naturally long lashes and a touch of mascara. It was Sarah Taylor-Jones, Consolidated's CFO, who had not been hired for her looks. A Duke undergrad and top of her class at The Wharton School, the woman was a financial genius who could easily match wits with anyone on Wall Street or Canary Wharf. She had been on the Skype call in her office.

"Well, Luc, are we going after Debswana?" Sarah asked.

Johannes's ice-blue eyes focused intently on her. Sarah was familiar with business valuation and control premiums. That was her job, but she let him think aloud.

"Of course. I'm not about to throw in the towel without a fight, but it's going to be messy and, frankly, our chances are not good. In a normal situation, De Beers would add a premium to its bid to get full control of the most valuable diamond mine in the world. Our bid would be less because fifty percent is not control. That said, we will try to match the De Beers control premium because we need the diamonds to survive. This is going to be a very expensive undertaking, and I'm not sure we can get the financing to outbid De Beers."

"Agreed, and it gets worse if De Beers finds out we need the diamonds to survive. They will pay even more to put us out of business and reduce competition," Sarah said.

"That's where you come in, Sarah. Our offer must be about more than money. We need to come up with something outside the box. To do that, we need as much information as we can get.

"I want you to start by pulling De Beers apart. Their financials are important, but I want to know who will make their decisions on something of this magnitude. Who are their shareholders? Who are the shareholders' shareholders? Who are their bankers? Who makes the final decisions for those bankers? I want to know all we can about the real decision makers for De Beers. In my experience, in major matters, they often are not the frontline executives but those behind the scenes who have ultimate control. You may find something we can use."

Sarah nodded. "I'll get started right away." Relishing the challenge, she left the office as quickly as she had entered.

Building Consolidated Diamonds into a multinational powerhouse that was nipping at the heels of De Beers had not been easy. Today, Johannes's longish gray hair was professionally styled, his dark-blue suit and light-blue shirt custom made on Savile Row in London, his shoes handmade, but it had not always been that way.

After serving in Vietnam with the army's Long Range Reconnaissance Patrol, he used the G.I. Bill to attend Brooklyn Law School at night, where he met the son of Forty-Seventh Street's biggest wholesaler jeweler. After graduation, Johannes was unable to catch on with the type of law firm that interested him and found himself a single practitioner in a Brooklyn second-floor walkup office struggling to pay the rent. When the jeweler's business ran into trouble, his friend called, and Johannes devised a way out of the mess. The grateful jeweler offered Johannes a job, and he joined the restructured company renamed Consolidated Diamonds, PLC.

Now sixty-eight with four decades of corporate warfare behind him, along with three ex-wives and three estranged children, he was tired and ready to retire. He wanted to live his dream with a new woman: sail the Mediterranean in the summer and the Caribbean in the winter. He envisioned himself deeply tanned, with his gray mane of hair swept over his ears, barefoot, in a well-used white linen shirt and worn blue shorts at the helm of a fifty-foot sailboat, a beautiful blonde soulmate at his side and a gin and tonic in his hand. The money, the sailboat, and the gin would not be a problem; the blonde—well, that might be, given his track record with women.

The deal to buy Botswana's stake in the Debswana Diamond Company would save the company and cement Consolidated's future. A fitting end to his career. Or, if he failed…well, he was not going to think about that. He was going to think about how to outwit De Beers.

To atone for how he had treated his ex-wives, Johannes wanted his successor to be a woman. He had spent the last few years grooming Sarah for the job. On paper, she was a perfect choice. Her job performance was outstanding. Her one drawback was youth. One could argue that at forty she did not have enough experience, but Johannes was not worried about that. After working with her for five years, he knew she was brilliant. His concern was elsewhere. He sensed that there was an emptiness in her that she filled by working ungodly hours and running. To his knowledge, she had no love interest, and her social life was limited to a few running buddies.

If she had an exploitable weakness, rivals would use it against her, against Consolidated. The contest for Debswana would give her an opportunity to prove that she had the strength and ruthlessness that was necessary to run a multinational company in a brutal industry.

Sarah returned to her office pumped up with the challenge of the coming battle with De Beers. For the first time in months, she was excited about something. Her job had become mind-numbingly routine. Day after day, the same issues and problems arose, only with different names.

Her frustration had led her to accept calls from a couple of headhunters with opportunities at Fortune 500 companies. That had been a disaster. The recruiters had said a black woman with her background could name her price. Boiled down the companies were looking for black skin to check the diversity box. It infuriated Sarah, who refused to self-identify as black rather than of mixed race. The recruiters could not understand why she did not want to trade on her skin color—everyone who could did exactly that. They pointed out the senator who claimed to have a drop or two of Native American blood to get a teaching job at Harvard University, and the school got to check the diversity box. Sarah told them to call back when they were looking for a CFO based on qualifications, not skin color.

As usual, her social life sucked. As the CFO of Consolidated, she was one of the company's senior officers, and fraternizing with subordinates could cause all sorts of problems. Her skin tone was a touch too dark to pass for white and not dark enough to be a so-called authentic black. Due to refusing to self-identify as black she had never been comfortable dating black men and had not fared particularly well with white men, as evidenced by her brief failed marriage that had left her with the last name Taylor-Jones.

Now, praise the Lord, she felt the adrenaline pumping like it had not for several months. This was the kind of challenge she had been waiting for. If Consolidated could pull this off, it would show the world that she was more than a check-the-box affirmative-action hire.

Sarah called one of her running group friends to let her know she would be out of action for a while, got a fresh cup of coffee, and began her research.

CHAPTER 2

UNDER AN INCREASINGLY CLOUDY sky, a twenty-knot wind barely rocked the three-hundred-and-twenty-eight-foot yacht moored at the Lantau Yacht Club in Discovery Bay, Hong Kong. Owned by a Russian oligarch through a myriad of shell companies, it was leased to Chinese billionaire Wendall Chun. In the ultra-modernist salon, Wang Jin, son of the leader of the Chinese Communist Party, used a yuan banknote to inhale a line of cocaine off a small mirror.

Frowning at his childhood friend, Tommy Chun asked, "When did you start with the coke?"

Wang Jin jumped up and began pacing around the room.

"A while ago. I just use it occasionally when I need to get my head straight. It's not a habit or anything like that. It just helps me deal with the pressure I am under after the Bank of China fucked me on the Debswana loan request. They bitched that the company was undercapitalized. Idiots. I liquidated everything I had to set up and fund Eastern Enterprises, but everything I have wasn't enough for the bank. They refused to see that the diamonds will be plenty of security for the loan. I couldn't convince them.

"Now I'm going to have to go to my father…again…and listen to his lectures about how I need to make something of myself. What does he think I've done? I'm on three corporate boards and have half a dozen consulting contracts. He refuses to see what is right in front of him."

"I know, I know, you've told me a hundred times," Tommy replied, not quite hiding the boredom in his voice.

Wang Jin stood. "When are the girls getting here?"

"Not for an hour, and maybe not at all if the weather gets much worse. The launch from the dock will not be safe for babes in cocktail dresses and heels."

Wang Jin walked to the back door and looked out. "Do we have to pay them if they can't get out here?"

"I paid Sung when I ordered the girls. Weather is our problem."

Wang Jin uttered a Chinese curse. "I might as well get it over with and call the old man. How much more can you put in the company?"

Without hesitation, Tommy replied, "You already have all I can spare."

Wang Jin punched keys on his cell phone and walked out of the room. He did not want to share his humiliation with Tommy.

Tommy lifted a bottle of Cristal champagne from the ice bucket on the bar and opened it, holding a towel over the cork. He might as well enjoy the good stuff if he had to keep putting up with the insufferable Wang Jin. He took a small sip, savored the taste, and moved to the back of the lounge to watch the weather.

In grade school, Wang Jin had been a normal kid. But by the time he had gone to the University of Oxford, he had a full appreciation of what it meant to be the only son of the chairman of the CCP. As one would say in English, he had grown into a narcissistic, entitled ass. He was also a handsome ass and had a way with women until they got to know him.

The coke bothered Tommy more than he had let on. Wang Jin had a vile and vindictive temper. If someone did not show him respect, it would bother him for days while he plotted revenge. Tommy had paid off several men and even a few women who had been victims of Wang Jin's retribution for causing him to lose face. He was obsessed with this pillar of Chinese culture. He acted shamelessly but obsessed over his reputation.

Tommy refilled his glass as rain began to spit from the sky in large drops. The only good thing about Wang Jin from his perspective was that he had become Tommy's major source of income. Tommy's father stayed in the good graces of the party as his fortune grew by having his son keep an eye on Wang Jin. Tommy was paid quite well to make regular reports to his father on Wang Jin's activities. His father passed the information along to Wang Jin's father.

It was a weird deal. Wang Jin's father doted on his son but had enough sense to know that the reckless young man could get into trouble that would reflect poorly on him. Tommy was not proud of spying on Wang Jin, but it paid him quite well, allowed his father's fortune to grow and, more importantly, let him move a major portion of his wealth offshore, out of the grasp of the CCP. In China, one's status and freedom were at the mercy of the party. His father was prepared if he fell from favor.

Later, Wang Jin returned with a smile on his face and went directly to the champagne. The rain had stopped, and the wind had dropped significantly.

"The old man said he would take care of things. I think that is the launch coming with the women."

CHAPTER

3

AT THREE IN THE morning, a fine mist blanketed a dimly lit Park Avenue. The imposing dark facade of the massive buildings lining the avenue was randomly broken by light from a few windows. Behind one of those windows, Sarah sat at a desk cluttered with notepads, computer printouts, Chinese take-out cartons, and empty coffee cups. Without air circulating at that hour, the smell of Kung Pao chicken lingered in the air. Sarah herself needed sleep, a shower, and clean clothes, but she was typing up the results of her research on De Beers.

She was amazed by the multiple layers of business entities formed in the Cayman Islands, Panama, Singapore, and elsewhere that she had to work through to find where the ultimate control of De Beers resided. It had been easy to find that Anglo American, PLC owned 85 percent of the De Beers Group and that the government of the Republic of Botswana owned 15 percent. It had been a good deal harder to trace the ownership of Anglo American. Small stakes were held by several US asset managers and a South African pension fund. However, almost 60 percent of Anglo American was owned by a group of companies formed in the aforementioned tax havens that were ultimately controlled by Vulcan Investments, a Singapore holding company, which was itself owned by a Panamanian trust called the Patel Family Trust, which had an Indian billionaire as trustee. When she finished her box diagram of the various shareholders, the top box contained the name Bharat Patel.

Sarah could not be certain that Patel was the man who controlled the trust. Although named a family trust, the beneficiaries were secret, as were the terms of the trust. There was no way of knowing for sure if all the beneficiaries were Patel family members. It was possible that someone, even another family member, was a major beneficiary of the trust with the power to change the trustee at will. Sarah had no way to uncover that information from public databases. It would take an investigator with a lot of money for bribes, which might not work and could be dangerous, depending on the identity of any undisclosed players.

The pale light of dawn was creeping over the eastern horizon as Sarah stretched and yawned. The whites of her eyes were red and felt full of small pieces of gravel. It was time to go home and get a few hours' sleep. She had followed the ownership trail as far as she could. She had no idea what Johannes would do with the information in her report, which she put in the middle of his empty desk on the way out.

Back in her Sutton Place apartment, Sarah opted for a quick nap, followed by a hot shower, a change of clothes, and a big breakfast at a hole-in-the-wall diner. Just after nine that morning, she pushed her way through the heavy glass doors of 425 Park Avenue. She had not pulled an all-nighter since she had left Goldman Sachs over a decade ago. Part of her felt she was too old for a night without sleep, but a larger part was excited. She had unraveled De Beers's ownership as much as possible.

When she got to her office, she was pleased that the debris of last night had been removed and the air purifier had dissipated the Kung Pao-infused air. Her assistant handed her a note that Johannes wanted to see her. She hurried to his corner office.

"Good work, Sarah," Johannes said, smiling. "This may be very useful."

"How so?" Sarah asked.

A knowing smile creased Johannes's face.

"There was a time many years ago when the world was awash with blood diamonds. They were illegally mined or stolen by some African warlords to finance insurrections in several African countries. The Kimberley Process has helped immensely in cutting down the trade in illegal diamonds, but it persists in some dark corners of the world. Back in the day, there was an Indian company in Cape Town that was rumored to buy illegal diamonds and ship them with Kimberley certificates to a related company in India that processed the diamonds and sold them in the legal trade. The man who still runs that company is named Patel. An odd coincidence, don't you think?"

"An interesting one, to be sure," Sarah said.

Johannes's secretary arrived with coffee.

"Luc, I have been thinking about how to deal with De Beers. I think we can get financing up to a certain point, but if De Beers bids one dollar more, we are done. What if we went to Patel and offered to withdraw from the bidding in exchange for a long-term take-or-pay contract?"

Johannes slowly set down his coffee cup. "Explain."

Sarah could see she had his full attention.

"Oversimplified, we agree to take a certain quantity and quality of diamonds for twenty to thirty years with an agreed-upon pricing mechanism. If we don't take the diamonds, we have to pay anyway. This would solve our supply problem without having to own part of the company, and it could work to De Beers's advantage also."

Johannes got up from the coffee table, returned to his desk, and began to make notes. Sarah followed him and sat across from him.

"How could this work for De Beers?"

"From my research, I found out that the Debswana mines are going to need a billion or so dollars to expand the mines and improve them. Debswana is going to have to borrow for that with a guarantee from De Beers. They are also going to need some heavy financing to buy Botswana's fifty percent. If we are in the bidding, the price will be higher than they might otherwise have to pay."

Sarah held up her hand, raising her fingers one at a time as she made her points. "Debswana will have a guaranteed stream of revenue free from future price competition. Their lenders will be more likely to approve financing for the project because of the stable revenue. Some of the market risk of diamond prices is transferred to us, and their budgeting process will be easier."

"What about all the unknowns, like disasters and market disruptions?" Johannes asked.

"All things to be negotiated: force majeure, prices, and contract review every so often. It's doable if both parties see the benefits," Sarah replied.

Johannes was quiet for several minutes while he doodled on the pad in front of him. Finally, he put down his Montblanc pen and looked up.

"I like it, Sarah. There is no need to get into the weeds unless De Beers is interested. I'm going to try and set up a meeting with Mr. Patel. Be sure your passport is current."

Sarah left the room walking on a cloud.

CHAPTER 4

AFTER A NINETEEN-HOUR FLIGHT, including a three-hour layover in Amsterdam, Sarah's town car pulled up in front of the Taj Mahal Palace in Mumbai, India. A porter in a white, gold-braided jacket wearing an elaborate turban took her carry-on suitcase. As usual, Sarah held on to her briefcase.

The iconic Taj Mahal Palace sat on the Mumbai waterfront opposite the famous Gateway of India arch. The hotel, constructed in 1903 in the Saracenic Revival style complete with arches, domes, and minarets, had hosted kings, dignitaries, and famous personalities since it had opened as India's first luxury hotel.

Sarah checked in and, once in her room, showered and changed for her 5 p.m. meeting with the billionaire Bharat Patel. Immediately after their conversation on Monday, Johannes had contacted Patel, who had agreed to a meeting. Johannes and Sarah had decided that she would conduct the initial meeting because she had a better grip on the financial issues. He would remain in New York dealing with a myriad of other matters. It was now late Wednesday afternoon in Mumbai. The shower helped, but she was running on adrenaline.

Sarah applied a touch of mascara and studied her face in the mirror. Amazing. Here she was, an orphan from Chicago's South Side, jetting around the world to meet with an Indian billionaire regarding a high-stakes business deal with the future of her company riding on the outcome. She frowned briefly, thinking that it was beyond sad that her grandmother had not lived to see what had become of the little girl she had taken in and raised.

Sarah sighed deeply and pushed the memory aside. It was time for business. She picked up her briefcase and headed downstairs.

She had read what little, bland public information was available about Bharat Patel and had seen a ten-year-old picture of him. Other than that, she did not know what to expect when she entered the hotel's Wine & Malts Lounge at precisely 5 p.m. The room was wood-paneled, incorporating arches upon which were painted intricate designs. Music played softly in the background, the furniture was classical, the lighting warm and soothing—all in all, a warm and inviting ambience. It seemed a strange choice for a business meeting.

A waiter approached. "Are you here for Sahib Patel?"

Sarah was escorted to a corner table, where Bharat Patel stood to greet her with an outstretched hand. This handsome man was probably in his mid-fifties, shorter than Sarah, with dark, wavy hair and a typical dark Indian complexion. He wore a white linen suit with a navy-blue open-collared shirt. He was quite comfortable with himself and his surroundings, exuding a sense of calm authority. He held on to Sarah's hand while he spoke.

"Ms. Taylor-Jones, you are an unexpected delight for the weary eyes of this old man," Patel said with a twinkle in eyes.

"Flattery will get you everywhere, but not today, I'm afraid," Sarah replied, smiling and withdrawing her hand. No need to be offended if he was flirting. Sarah had learned years ago that almost all men underestimated a beautiful woman, usually in direct proportion to her beauty. A sexist construct? Perhaps, but it had worked to her advantage many times.

They sat and a waiter materialized.

"Ms. Taylor-Jones, a beverage?" Patel asked.

"Yes, thank you. Bottled water."

Patel ordered a glass of Sancerre. Out of the corner of her eye, Sarah saw two formidable-looking men a short way across the room. One was watching the entrance and the other watched her. Bodyguards? Probably.

"Ms. Taylor-Jones, first time in Mumbai?" Patel asked, perfectly relaxed and smiling.

"Please call me Sarah."

"Very well, I am Bharat. We are off to a good start."

"Yes, it's my first time, but unfortunately, this is a business trip, so I will only have time to see the airport and this hotel. There is usually an office to visit, but meeting here is very convenient."

"I find it beneficial to keep those with whom I do business uncomfortable, a little off-balance, so I chose this hopelessly romantic spot for our rendezvous to put you a little off-balance," Patel said, still smiling.

"What makes you think I'm 'off-balance'?"

"One does not usually conduct a business meeting with a woman he has never met in a place like this. Because of the surroundings, you are undoubtedly wondering if I am going to try to seduce you. I am sure others have tried, but now that I am in your presence, I am sure they failed. But no matter, that is not my intention. Please explain what you have in mind."

The waiter returned with their drinks.

Sarah didn't know what to make of this man. She *was* a little off-balance—not because of a possible attempt at seduction but because he had told her about his purposely trying to unsettle her. What was his intention? Sarah could not help herself; she chuckled. Yes, he had her a little off-balance.

"You succeeded for a moment, but now my balance is fine." She reached under the table for her briefcase.

"Please, no papers. I understand De Beers. I had some research done on Consolidated and I know what take-or-pay contracts are, so tell me as succinctly as possible why De Beers would want to enter a long-term contract to supply diamonds to one of its competitors?"

Sarah pulled her chair a little closer to the table and put her elbows on the table with her hands under her chin. She looked directly into Patel's eyes and began.

"Debswana needs to borrow a billion or so to expand and improve its mines for the future. De Beers is going to have to borrow almost all of what it will take to buy Botswana's interest in Debswana. That is one heck of a lot of borrowing.

"Like the energy markets, diamond prices fluctuate for all kinds of reasons that are out of your control, like the COVID-19 pandemic. The contract we propose will give Debswana a secure, consistent, and predictable stream of revenue that will protect the company from market fluctuations and will give lenders a key reason to lend you and Debswana the money you need.

"Finally, if Consolidated is out of the bidding, there is no one other than Russia that might bid for Botswana's interest. Russia is still screwed up because of Ukraine and, with its shattered economy, has other uses for its money. In essence, you will be able to negotiate the purchase for less money than if we were to bid against you."

Sarah sat back and took a sip of water.

Patel clapped his hands silently. "Excellent presentation, Sarah. Now, if you would be so kind, please tell me how Consolidated would benefit from this contract."

That's none of your business, Sarah thought.

"Bharat, with respect, you cannot expect me to share Consolidated's confidential business plans and trade secrets with you."

Patel took a sip of his wine. "Excellent wine. You should try some." He put his glass down. "That is what I asked, but you do not have to do that. Your problem is the Golden Wattle. It is running out of diamonds, or at least your engineers think so. Debswana is your solution, but you don't yet have financing to become an owner—but you can afford to buy diamonds forever if the price is right and avoid the perils of ownership. Did I miss anything?" Patel smiled, enjoying himself immensely.

Sarah was stunned, momentarily speechless. How did he know that? Only a handful of people in the company had access to that information. Was he guessing?

"We have plenty of diamonds coming our way, but we want to expand, so we need more," Sarah said too quickly.

"Then please tell me why De Beers should provide Consolidated with the means to expand and increase its competition with us?"

She had made a mistake, thinking too fast for her own good. One of the rules she had learned the hard way at Goldman Sachs years ago was when you find yourself in a hole, quit digging.

Sarah forced her most charming smile and thought frantically for something to say. But Patel spoke first.

"Sarah, the reality is that De Beers is going to own all of Debswana. Another fact is that De Beers has no interest in helping it competitors. That said, as you know, when possible, we like to control the supply of diamonds on the world market to maintain prices. Consolidated owns the Golden Wattle and a few other minor diamond mines."

He paused, and Sarah waited, not sure where this was going.

"What we will do for your employer is buy your mines at their appraised value, according to our engineers and appraisers."

Sarah was stunned. Patel had dropped this offer out of the blue.

"Frankly, Bharat, I don't know what to say," she said truthfully.

"I think your best response is that you will take the offer back to Mr. Johannes. If Consolidated accepts our offer, I would like to hire you to handle the transition and take charge of our New York office. We can negotiate your contract, but I assure you that the salary would be multiples of what Consolidated is paying you. Would you like to stay for dinner and talk about it?" Patel suggested.

Sarah pushed back from the table and stood.

"Thank you, but I have a lot to digest. Another time, perhaps."

She turned to leave, and Patel said, "Don't forget your briefcase.

CHAPTER 5

SARAH'S MIND WAS BLANK as she walked out of the bar and stopped momentarily, forgetting which way to turn for the elevator. She quickly regained her bearings and returned to her room.

When she could not get her thoughts to turn over, she took a half bottle of white wine out of the small refrigerator, opened it, poured a glass, and took a healthy swallow. Ugh, it needed to breathe. She unceremoniously dumped a tiny bottle of vodka into a glass and took a swallow that burned all the way down.

The man was trying to bribe her. It was outrageous. Insulting. Another swallow and the vodka was gone.

Buy Consolidated. Unbelievable. She sat down uncomfortably. Stood up and paced the room. *Calm down, girl; you really are off-balance now. Six-thirty p.m. here means 9:30 a.m. in New York.*

She called Johannes's cell phone. Sarah explained what had happened in detail to Johannes, who listened in silence.

"Interesting," he said when she had finished.

"'Interesting'? Is that all you can say? The man is trying to bribe me to get you to sell him Consolidated," Sarah said, raising her voice.

"Now, Sarah," Johannes replied soothingly. "Think. Why does he want our diamonds? Reduce competition and get more control over pricing is what he says, but is there something else? Are we are missing something? One other thing—be careful throwing around accusations of bribery. He could have engaged a headhunter to call you and offer you a job at an increased salary if the deal went through. Would that be bribery or just a good business practice to retain your services and have a smooth transition? Maybe you should be flattered."

"Are you seriously going to consider his offer?" Sarah asked.

"What we have is an expression of interest. Remember that we answer to the Hess family, which owns ninety-one percent of the stock and controls the board of directors. It's not just our little playpen. Do this: send him a text that you spoke with me and that I requested a written offer. If we get one, we will take it from there.

"What I am concerned about is how he knew about the Golden Wattle problem. Two engineers prepared the report. One of them typed it on his personal computer. The report was not stored on the internet or forwarded in an email. You and I got the only printed copies, which came by FedEx. You and I didn't leak the report, so it must be one of the engineers. I'm going to investigate that while you fly back.

"You're booked on an early-morning flight, so get some sleep. As soon as you get back, I need you to get to work lining up financing for the Debswana bid."

Johannes disconnected the call with Sarah and had his secretary place a call to the headquarters of the Golden Wattle Mine in Australia. Half an hour later, he stood looking out over the Manhattan skyline, marveling at the shameless corruption of human beings. He had just fired an engineer who had spent twenty years with Consolidated and had a defined retirement benefit package that would vest in five years. The man had just taken title to an oceanfront home in Fiji that was clearly beyond his means. A shell corporation had purchased the home and deeded it to him. Johannes didn't need to find out who was behind the shell corporation. Bharat Patel was a demonstrated master at using multinational corporations to conduct his business.

The only unknown was who approached whom. Most likely, the engineer had thought the Golden Wattle was going to die before his pension vested, so he had reached out to De Beers to sell confidential corporate information.

As a practical matter, there was nothing Johannes could do about the engineer's treachery or De Beers. But experience had taught him that for those with shoddy business ethics, it was often the case that what goes around comes around.

CHAPTER

6

WAITING ON SARAH'S DESK when she returned from Mumbai was a packet of Debswana's financial information provided to qualified bidders. For the next two days, she barely slept as she digested the data, transferred it to spreadsheets she created, and worked on earnings projections. She spent most of the time projecting how the $1 billion cost of upgrading the mines would affect the value of Debswana for bidding purposes. When she finished, she sent her analysis to Thomas W.J. Watson III, Consolidated's account manager at J.P. Morgan, with a request for a meeting to discuss putting together a syndicate to finance Consolidated's bid.

Watson had the Consolidated account when Sarah had joined the company and had done a satisfactory job. They spoke on the phone from time to time, but she and Watson had never met in person. He had invited her to lunch, drinks after work, and dinner on the grounds that since they were working together, they should get to know each other better. Sarah always politely declined. Now she regretted what had seemed the right choice at the time. If they knew each other better, it could help her finance the biggest deal of her career.

Watson called after reviewing Sarah's analysis and expressed some reluctance to get involved in what would be a complicated transaction. Consolidated had never taken on this much debt. Multiple currencies might be involved, and there were international implications of putting together a syndicate of banks to come up with the money.

Having anticipated these objections, Sarah had good answers ready, but she didn't want to give them over the phone. She could be more persuasive if they met face-to-face. Watson had a full day with a dinner meeting that night at The Harmonie Club on Sixtieth Street just off Fifth Avenue. He said he could give her an hour at 5 p.m. if they met at The Plaza Hotel, which was almost across the street from The Harmonie Club. Sarah readily agreed. As she walked from her office across Fifty-Sixth Street to Fifth Avenue and up to The Plaza Hotel, the invigorating fresh air pumped her up for the meeting.

Sarah had checked out Watson on the bank website and had reviewed his professional profiles on LinkedIn and Facebook. He looked and, on the phone, sounded exactly like what he was: a man from a Boston Brahmin family. Prep schools had been followed by Harvard University. His entire career had been at J.P. Morgan. Mid-fifties, handsome, athletic-looking with thinning brown hair showing streaks of gray. Sarah thought that at his age, he should have advanced further up the corporate ladder by now. If she had to bet, his family connections had gotten him the job, and he had done well enough to keep it but had been no rising corporate star.

Sarah entered The Plaza Hotel's ornate lobby and checked her coat before heading into The Champagne Bar, where Watson had made them a reservation. As she approached the table, Watson glanced up but then back down at his phone. She stood at the table waiting for him to look up.

He punched a few keys on his phone, put it down, and looked up with an appraising eye.

"I'm afraid I can't help you, miss; I'm meeting someone shortly. Good luck, though." Watson smirked and picked up his phone.

What the fuck? Sarah thought. *This asshole thinks I'm a hooker.*

She was tempted to turn and walk out, maybe throw a drink in his face and create a scene. But this was business. He obviously did not know what Sarah Taylor-Jones looked like and had made assumptions based on her hyphenated last name, the only thing she had taken from her failed marriage, and her unaccented voice. He obviously hadn't bothered to check her picture on the Consolidated website or in its annual report that the bank got every year.

A hooker. The muthafucka.

Sarah had escaped Chicago's South Side by luck and hard work, but she retained the kick-ass, don't-fuck-with-me attitude that had been necessary for survival. Her mother, who had turned tricks for drugs, had died of an overdose when Sarah was two years old. All she knew about her father was that he must have been white. She had been raised by her invalid grandmother who, by the time Sarah was ready for school, required her full-time attention. The former schoolteacher homeschooled Sarah but insisted she take ballet classes three times a week to have some social contact. When she reached high school age, running with a local track club replaced ballet. One benefit of her grandmother's discipline and her cloistered environment was that she had escaped the notice of the street gangs that ruled the South Side. Another benefit was that her homeschooling had been a first-rate education. She had topped the lists in college and business school admission tests and had had her pick of scholarships.

Sarah pulled out the chair opposite Watson and beckoned the waiter who was standing nearby.

Sarah smiled. "Pappy Van Winkle bourbon, neat, please."

Watson dropped his phone and looked around the bar like he didn't know what to do. Before he could say anything, Sarah spoke calmly in a businesslike voice.

"I'm Sarah Taylor-Jones. A pleasure to finally meet you in person," she said. *You uptight entitled patrician asshole.*

Sarah could see that Thomas W.J. Watson III did not know what to say or do after making such a horrendous mistake about the CFO of his largest account. Sarah wanted to call out and squash this racist pig, but she was a businesswoman with an objective in mind. She now had a choice: She could embarrass him even more and make him squirm, or she could ignore what he had done and leave him feeling that he owed her for the kindness. His faux pas might work in her favor. She chose option number two.

"This is such a lovely bar. Much more intimate that The Palm Court." Sarah smiled again.

She could see the man breathe a sigh of relief as she let him off the hook. "Yes, yes, you're quite right," Watson said with an uncomfortable upturning of the corners of his mouth. "It is a pleasure to be able to put a face with your voice."

Idle chitchat followed until Sarah's drink arrived, then Watson moved the conversation to business, asking, "Could you share some more of your thinking about a Debswana bid?"

After a few minutes, the undercurrent to the conversation ebbed, and they discussed what Sarah had gleaned from the Debswana documents. As the 6 p.m. witching hour approached, Watson turned on a radiant smile.

"Sarah, I see what you mean. I like it. We will have to put together a syndicate to cover a transaction of this size, but I don't see any problems. There will be some back-and-forth on terms, participation percentages, the loan fee—the usual things. But I don't see a problem with three billion if the bidding goes that high."

Sarah stood and Watson hurried to his feet.

"Excellent, Tom. I will need positive indications of interest by the end of the week."

They shook hands, and Sarah headed for the coat check room, having forgotten about Watson's opening insult. He was confident that he could pull together five or six lenders to finance the Debswana deal. Sarah was pumped up. Consolidated could get the money.

Watson slipped down into his chair, thinking he had dodged a bullet. In his wildest dreams, he had never supposed that Sarah Taylor-Jones was black or a person of color. Black women were not named Sarah Taylor-Jones. They had names like Xandria or Shanice or Jasmine, not Sarah, for God's sake. Sarah Taylor-Jones was a British type of name. Black, white, or whatever, she was one intelligent woman. This Debswana deal could be the push he needed for finally stepping up the ladder. He knew just who to call at Citi and Wells Fargo to get the ball rolling.

He left for his dinner meeting with a spring in his step.

CHAPTER 7

THE CRYSTAL-CLEAR DAY IN Hong Kong sparkled with the promise of fortunes to be made and lost as Zhang Chun, president of the Bank of China, stepped off the elevator on the seventy-second floor of the Bank of China Building, the most noticeable skyscraper in a city of skyscrapers. He had moved there from Beijing when China had regained control of Hong Kong and was making a fortune for the bank as well as a smaller fortune for himself. As the Italians liked to say, he put his beak in the trough from time to time. Often enough for a young mistress and a large colonial home on Victoria Peak with a spectacular view of the harbor.

The first thing he noticed was that Mae Ling, the stunningly beautiful receptionist that he had personally hired, looked terrified.

"C-C-Chairman W-W-Wang Chen is w-w-waiting in y-y-your office," she stammered.

Zhang hurried to his corner office and found Wang, chairman of the Chinese Communist Party, standing, hands clasped behind his back, looking out the floor-to-ceiling window toward Victoria Peak.

Without turning around, he said, "You know, Zhang, with this office and a home on Victoria Peak, you live very well."

The tone of Wang's voice made Zhang acutely aware of the century-old silk rug he was standing on, the museum-quality art on display, and his desk from the Zhou dynasty. However, he knew when to keep his mouth shut. The silence lingered as sweat dampened the underarms of his Turnbull & Asser shirt beneath his custom-made pinstriped suit. He wanted to remove the pocket square from the breast pocket of his suit and wipe the dampness from his forehead, but that would give away his nervousness and spoil the carefully crafted look of the pocket square.

He knew the interrogation technique: create a silence and wait for the person being questioned to fill it. The chairman's unexpected visit could only be about one thing. The bank had turned down a request to finance a business venture proposed by the chairman's son, Wang Jin.

The young Wang's only business experience was trading off his father's name. He had wrangled a few corporate board seats for which he was obviously unqualified and served as an intermediary for foreign investors that needed access to the Chinese government. Hong Kong gossip had him as a ladies' man with a vindictive temper who never let a perceived slight go unpunished. The man had left a string of jilted lovers and angry business associates in his wake.

Wang Jin had learned that the government of Botswana was considering the sale of its 50 percent interest in Debswana. Botswana was going to privatize its interest and use the capital to help diversify the country's economy that was dependent on tourism, diamonds, and some agriculture, particularly cattle. He had approached the bank to finance his purchase of the Botswana interest. At the time, Zhang had been amazed at the audacity of Wang Jin. The ink was still wet on the formation documents of the Panamanian company Wang Jin had created to be the purchaser. This new company had no assets and precious little capital, yet he wanted the bank to issue his company, Eastern Enterprises, an open-ended financing commitment. The only security for the loan would be the Debswana interest.

Out of respect for Wang and fear of the CCP, Zhang had sent Wang Jin's business plan to the Risk Management Committee for evaluation. Unsurprisingly, the request was rejected unanimously. Off the record, the committee members complained to Zhang about wasting their time with an obviously ridiculous loan request.

Wang turned from the window and gestured for Zhang to sit in his desk chair. Zhang sat.

"I would like you to explain why my son's company was turned down for a loan to purchase fifty percent of the world's largest diamond producer."

Wang's face was inscrutable except for a tightness around his narrow eyes that emphasized the crow's-feet embedded there, but otherwise, the request seemed without anger, just a straightforward request for information. That said, Zhang sensed a dangerous undercurrent. It was well known that Wang had an impenetrable blind spot when it came to his son. If anyone else shamelessly peddled access to the government the way the boy did, they would have been jailed years ago without the formality of a trial.

Zhang reached for a bottom drawer in his desk. "Let me show you the Risk Management Committee's rationale for turning down the request."

"No. You run this bank. I want your…" Wang made quotation marks with his fingers. "rationale for turning down the request."

Zhang started to speak.

"Don't you dare tell me you just followed the recommendation of the committee. This is my son we are talking about."

Zhang's mouth was so dry it was difficult to speak. He made a few unintelligible sounds, stood quickly, and walked across the room, where he poured a glass of water. He sighed deeply and resigned himself to the inevitable.

"Mr. Chairman, most importantly, the request had no loan limit. Your son simply wanted to pay whatever it took to buy the interest and secure it with the interest itself. He offered no other security. We would not have known what the bank was committing to until the bidding was complete. Without that information, we had no idea whether the projected income could repay the loan in timely fashion."

Wang crossed the room, took the glass of water out of Zhang's hand, and placed it on his desk. Then he put his hands on Zhang's shoulders and squeezed lightly.

"I looked at the business plan and do not see any problem. My son is not stupid enough to overpay for the company. He will hire professional management. The diamonds are good security. I am mystified why China's bank refuses to help acquire one of the world's most valuable assets."

Zhang began, "But…"

Wang squeezed his shoulders hard.

"Silence. You will agree to make the loan." Wang stepped away. "Give Jin what he wants. I will take steps to be sure he does not overpay. If you refuse, there are many who would like to have this magnificent view."

Wang turned and strode briskly out of the room.

Insanity, Zhang thought. The bank was to rely on Wang to keep his son from overpaying. How was the esteemed chairman, a politician, to know the value of Botswana's interest? This was not how banks operated. It was highly likely that the Bank of China would put its future into the hands of Wang Jin, an accomplished idiot and semi-criminal. De Beers was one of the most sophisticated companies in the world. It would not commit financial suicide to acquire the half of Debswana it did not own.

He had also heard that Consolidated Diamonds, PLC would enter the bidding. De Beers could drive the price higher to increase the value of their own interest, and once Consolidated realized that there was no limit on Wang Jin's bid, they would drive the price so high that he would never be able repay the loan and be bankrupted very quickly. Then Consolidated or De Beers would get the interest out of bankruptcy.

Zhang's first call was to his stockbroker, from whom he purchased a put option on his Bank of China shares. He would have shorted his shares, but he could not be certain Wang Jin would fail.

CHAPTER

8

ON A CLOUDY, MISTY morning on Queen's Row in Hong Kong, Wang Jin and Tommy Chun stepped off the elevator into the offices of McFadden & Billings, an international law firm. They were in China, but with Turkish rugs scattered about in a seemingly random pattern on a shiny wooden plank floor, wingback chairs, and the mahogany and brass touches, one could be forgiven for thinking they had stepped through a time warp and arrived in London, England.

Wang Jin, a handsome man a little over six feet tall with slicked-back black hair and a wispy moustache, was a well-known ladies' man in the social set comprising the children of senior Chinese Communist Party officials. A student of art history in college, he stopped before an old master oil painting of a woman with a vase next to a traditional Chinese landscape done in the Xieyi style from the Song dynasty.

He whistled softly and whispered to Tommy, "These guys have spent a fortune decorating this place."

Tommy whispered back, "Clients like us paid for it."

Sitting at an elegant leather-topped desk was a young man in a dark three-piece suit with a plain-burgundy tie whose rimless spectacles gave him an owlish look. There were no papers or electronics on the desk. He held up one finger and spoke softly in Mandarin. An unseen device picked up his voice, and a moment later, a mature woman in a silk kimono appeared and led them to a windowless conference room with a table for twelve, a credenza for refreshments, and a half dozen large computer screens on the walls.

The man standing on the far side of the table had a full head of gray hair with a matching Van Dyke goatee and mustache. He spoke in unaccented English.

"Gentlemen, I am J. Walter Billings. Please be seated." He gestured to the chairs on the opposite side of the table.

"Thank you for signing the retainer agreement and sending the check. Since you are paying us by the hour with an additional fee in the event you successfully purchase the Debswana interest, I won't waste your time with idle chitchat.

"We have already begun to gather information in connection with the Debswana sale. Besides yourselves, the only other serious bidders are De Beers and Consolidated Diamonds. On your behalf, we have engaged Morgan Stanley investment bankers to conduct a thorough valuation of Debswana and an analysis of your competitors' finances to understand their bidding strength."

Wang Jin impatiently drummed the table with the fingers of his left hand.

"Look, Billings, we have a blank check from BOC; with that, we can bid anyone into oblivion. We don't need investment bankers, and I don't want to pay their exorbitant fees. Yours are more than enough."

Billings's left eyebrow arched, and he eyed Wang Jin like an errant child. He let the silence linger until it became uncomfortable. He took a cell phone from his pocket and entered a string of numbers before handing it to Wang Jin.

"Play the video."

Wang Jin hit the button, and his father's face appeared on the screen.

"Son, I want you to know that I support your plan to acquire the Debswana interest. It fits neatly into our Belt and Road Initiative.

"That said, we are Chinese not stupid. Your bid must make economic sense for the Bank of China based upon the value of Debswana. I know the loan commitment is a blank check, but that is not what you have. The commitment was structured that way so that you can use access to unlimited funds as a technique to discourage other bidders. They will fear your financial strength.

"I have directed you to McFadden & Billings because we have used them successfully in other endeavors. Listen to them. They will exploit multiple pressure points to discourage your competitors and allow you to acquire the Debswana interest at a very reasonable price.

"Goodbye and good luck."

While his father spoke, Wang Jin's eyes narrowed and his jaw tightened, reminding Tommy of a boiling tea kettle about to whistle. He had seen that look many times, and things never ended well for the object of Wang Jin's anger. But this time, the fool was going to have to swallow all that outrage. Careful to remain inscrutable, Tommy enjoyed the comeuppance being delivered to his friend.

Wang Jin handed the phone back to Billings without looking at him. Then he looked at Tommy, who shrugged and offered a faint smile.

"All right, I guess we're stuck with Morgan Stanley. What are the pressure points my father referred to?"

Billings nodded and explained, "First, you must understand business valuation. Anything less than fifty-point-one percent of a company is a minority interest and cannot exercise control of the company without the consent of someone else. Therefore, in a monetary sense, a controlling interest is worth more than a minority interest.

"De Beers, with fifty percent of Debswana, will pay more for the other fifty percent than it would make sense for you to pay because it gives them control of the company. There is also an unconfirmed rumor that Consolidated Diamonds has supply problems. If that is true, they would be willing to pay up for the fifty percent to get the supply they need in the future.

"This situation puts you at a decided disadvantage in trying to acquire the Botswana interest. The fifty percent is worth more to your competitors than it is to you on a valuation basis."

Wang Jin and Tommy looked at each other, trying to digest this upsetting news.

"OK, OK, I get it, but you haven't answered my question about pressure points," Wang Jin snapped.

A smug smile tugged at the corners of Billings's mouth.

"If the object of the exercise is worth more to them than it should be to you, the only way to avoid overpaying is to remove your competitors from the bidding. That is why your father sent you to us. Our job is to exert pressure on your competitors to abandon bidding."

Wang Jin sat forward eagerly, intrigued by the idea that implied illegality. Billings continued.

"First, we have engaged the Andrews law firm in Gaborone as local counsel. I was surprised they were not representing Debswana or De Beers. Andrews is very well connected with the government, so that is a huge plus. To solidify the

Andrews advantage, we engaged the other two law firms of any consequence in Botswana on phantom matters to create conflicts of interest so they are unavailable to De Beers and Consolidated. De Beers can probably find South African lawyers admitted to practice in Botswana, but Consolidated may have to use second-tier lawyers. The Andrews firm has notified both De Beers and the Botswana government that your company will enter the bidding and gave them a not-so-subtle hint that the Chinese government is behind you.

"Now it is time to apply pressure to sideline De Beers. I have a job for you. I want you to speak to friends in the Chinese press and drop a story that the Chinese government is considering imposing a massive tariff on imported jewelry made with De Beers diamonds. The rationale is that it will improve the market for Chinese synthetic diamonds. People will only pay so much for real diamonds when synthetics are so inexpensive in comparison."

Tommy smiled. Wang Jin, looking confused, spoke to Billings like he was the village idiot.

"Why would we do that? We don't want tariffs on our diamonds, for God's sake. De Beers diamonds come from Debswana. We would be shooting ourselves in the foot," he said.

"I think Mr. Chun understands; would you explain it to Mr. Wang, please?"

Tommy turned toward Wang Jin.

"It's a shot across De Beers's bow. If they outbid us and take away a Chinese opportunity, China will respond with massive tariffs on their products, killing their Chinese business. That would be much worse for them than continuing the status quo with a Chinese instead of a Botswana partner. The threat obviously goes away if we own the Debswana interest."

Wang Jin nodded slowly as the idea sunk in. This kind of tactic was what his father had meant when he had talked about exploiting pressure points.

"Got it. No problem. We will get started on it today," Wang Jin said as if he had understood the strategy from the outset.

"Do you have any ideas for dealing with Consolidated?" an obviously impressed Tommy asked.

Billings pushed back from the table, signaling an end to the meeting.

"The investment bankers are working on that as we speak. Consolidated will need financing, which may prove difficult to get. Who knows what motivates lenders?" Billings said enigmatically.

Wang Jin and Tommy rode down in a crowded elevator. In Hong Kong, everything was crowded. As they pushed out the door, Wang Jin spoke.

"The Peninsula is just around the corner. How about a drink? I could use one."

"Best idea of the day," Tommy replied.

The colonial-themed Peninsula Hotel, opened in 1928, overlooked the harbor and was touted as the Grande Dame of Far East hotels. The friends crossed the vast lobby with its vaulted ceilings and ornate corniches and entered The Bar, where they found a quiet corner in the dim mahogany-paneled room.

After ordering their drinks, Wang Jin took a small vial out of his suit coat and emptied some white powder on the glass-topped table. Ignoring Tommy, he used a credit card to make a small line, rolled up a yuan note, and snorted the line. Wang Jin's head jerked up. He wiped his nose and sighed contentedly.

Tommy was stunned. The moron was doing a line of coke in the middle of The Bar in the poshest hotel in Hong Kong.

"I thought you only snorted that poison when you were stressed out. You just got the best news imaginable that, in essence, the government is going to back our play for Debswana. You have got to get a handle on this!" Tommy hissed, mustering as much disapproval as possible.

Wang Jin gave his friend a silly smile. "I deserve a little coke to celebrate. It won't hurt me."

The waiter arrived with their drinks, interrupting them. Tommy surreptitiously wiped up a few flakes of the cocaine visible on the table. This was turning into trouble. If he reported Wang Jin's drug use, it was possible that, given the chairman's blind spot for his son, he might blame it all on Tommy. That would not be good. But if he didn't report it and Wang Jin spun off the rails, he would definitely be blamed for not reporting it. He was in a corner. Fuck.

Wang Jin took a sip of his expensive scotch, smoothed his thin moustache, and asked, "What are you thinking after that meeting?"

Tommy forced a smile. "We are playing in the big leagues, my friend. Without your father's backing, those snotty lawyers would not give us the time of day."

Wang Jin did not take issue with his friend. "I don't like that *gweilo*, but he does seem to know his business. You can speak with your cousin at the *South China Morning Post* and get him to mention the possibility of a tariff on De Beers diamonds in his business column."

An attractive Chinese woman in a short white sundress walked into The Bar alone and sat at the bar by herself. Wang Jin stood and picked up his drink. "While you're doing that, I'll see if I can buy that beauty a drink."

CHAPTER 9

SARAH WAS ON A roll. Watson was close to putting together a syndicate that would provide up to $3 billion in financing for the Debswana bid. Adding Consolidated's currently strong cash position, they could bid close to $4 billion.

A little after ten in the evening, she was finishing up replies to emails that could not wait until tomorrow when a soft beep emanated from her computer, followed by a small blinking light on the bottom panel, which indicated her customized Google data feed had delivered news about the diamond industry to her inbox. Sarah stifled a yawn and clicked on the icon. The headline read: "Chinese Considering Large Tariff on De Beers Diamonds."

She skimmed the article from the *South China Morning Post*. It quoted only one anonymous source for the information about Chinese synthetic diamond manufacturers pushing for a tariff. *Interesting timing,* Sarah thought. No manufacturers of Chinese synthetic diamonds were named. Synthetics had been on the market for several years. The Chinese market for real diamonds was huge. Why a push for a tariff just as the Debswana stake was coming to market, and why only De Beers diamonds?

It did not make sense, but she was just too tired to try and figure out what the Chinese were up to. She dropped a copy of the article on Johannes's desk and headed out.

Sarah was rested when she arrived at the office at nine the next morning. Johannes wanted to see her.

"What do you think about this possible Chinese tariff on De Beers diamonds?" he asked.

"I was too tired to think about it last night, so I left you the article."

"Well, now that you've had a little rest, see what you can find out," Johannes said as he reached for his phone, dismissing Sarah.

Daylight was deserting Manhattan as a harsh wind sent leaves, debris, and paper items tumbling down the cross streets of Midtown. Workers buttoned their coats and turned up collars as they emptied office buildings and rushed to buses, subways, and trains for the journey home. Sarah, carrying a thick binder, pushed her way through the escaping staff on the way to Johannes's office.

He disconnected a telephone call as she entered, smiling contentedly as if he had heard an amusing story. It was close to six in the evening. Johannes's tie was firmly snugged to his collar, his shirt looked crisp, and he was wearing his suit jacket. He had looked the same at nine that morning. Sarah, wearing black slacks and a white blouse with the sleeves rolled up, looked like she had unwelcome news, which she did.

"That Chinese tariff article didn't make any sense at first. It seems there is a Panamanian company that has indicated an interest in bidding for Botswana's partnership interest," she said, taking a seat in front of Johannes's desk and holding the binder in her lap. "And I think it is going to be a big problem for us."

"Relax, Sarah. Business is about solving problems. That's why it's so much fun." Johannes smiled in a kindly way.

Sarah did not open her folder. She did not have to.

"This is not going to be fun. First, this Panamanian company, Eastern Enterprises, was formed just sixty days ago by the notorious Panamanian law firm that specializes in hidden ownership and offshore tax evasion. You read about them in the Panama Papers exposé a couple of years ago that caused the prime minister of Iceland to resign."

Johannes seemed unconcerned. "Yes, I remember that. Your point?"

"Botswana forced the company to disclose its ownership. The majority owner is Wang Jin, the asshole son of the chairman of the CCP."

"Interesting, but again, your point?"

Sarah, becoming irritated, said, "Just let me finish, please."

Johannes nodded and settled back in his chair. He steepled his fingers and locked eyes with Sarah. Outside, the wind swirled around the building.

"Last year, Botswana signed a memorandum of understanding with China on the Belt and Road Initiative. China is promising to help Botswana grow its digital economy by sharing technology and experience. As part of the deal, China is also promising to encourage Chinese enterprises to increase investment in Botswana and actively explore cooperation in industrial parks, special economic zones, and regional development belts.

"You know how this goes. China will make loans on flexible terms that the West would never offer to build roads and rail lines so that it is easier to access the minerals and natural resources that it wants. The technical jobs will go to Chinese and a few menial jobs to the locals. China has an outlet for cement and steel that is in oversupply in China. The minerals and natural resources are security for the loans. If Botswana does not pay attention, over time, a debt trap will be created, which ends with China owning the minerals and natural resources, with Botswana having paid for the infrastructure to exploit them."

Sarah paused to organize her thoughts. Johannes loosened his tie and sat forward in his chair with his forearms on his desk, listening intently. His contented smile was a thing of the past.

Sarah breathed deeply and continued. "The Chinese will claim that the Debswana acquisition is the beginning of implementing the Belt and Road Initiative and put pressure on the government to accept their bid or face loss of future projects."

Johannes steepled his hands under his chin, lost in thought. "Where does De Beers fit in? Surely they will bid for the half of Debswana they do not already own?"

"The way I see it, China has immense leverage over De Beers. First, China is the world's second-largest consumer of diamond jewelry. The article in the *Morning Post* about potential tariffs on De Beers diamonds is a not-so-subtle threat that if De Beers outbids the Chinese, China will impose tariffs to make De Beers diamonds uncompetitive in China. Second, China has perfected the technology to create synthetic diamonds that are so good, one needs special equipment to tell the difference between a synthetic one and a real one. It could flood the market but would not shoot itself in the foot if it gets half ownership of Debswana. So bottom line, if China leans on them, which it looks like they are doing, I think De Beers will step aside."

Johannes stood, removed his suit coat, tossed it on his chair, and began to pace around his office. He did so for a full minute before returning to his chair and carefully draping the suit coat over the back of the chair.

"Sarah, the flaw in your presentation is that you are conflating Eastern Enterprises with the Chinese government. Eastern Enterprises has no leverage without the government. Why would the government help them?"

Sarah stood up to emphasize what she was about to say.

"It's Wang Jin and a few of his contemporaries—scions of the Chinese Communist Party rulers. Wang Chen has a blind spot as big as Manchuria where his son is concerned. According to my sources, the Bank of China is providing the funds for their bid."

Johannes sighed deeply. "So you're saying that we are going into a bidding war with China."

"Yes, sir."

Johannes returned to his feet and walked across the room to a bookcase, where he pulled a particular volume partway out. The bookcase opened outward, revealing a wet bar.

"I have scotch, vodka, gin, and bourbon. Your choice," Johannes said, reaching for a bottle of vodka.

"Bourbon, neat," Sarah replied, joining him at the bar.

Johannes moved his hand to a bottle of Pappy Van Winkle Special Reserve 12 Years Old and poured each of them two fingers of the nectar. They clinked glasses and sipped.

"Do you know who gave me this bottle?"

"No, but it must have been a good friend."

"Mokgweetsi Masisi, the president of Botswana. A good friend indeed."

Johannes walked across his office to a sofa and two chairs surrounding a chrome-and-glass coffee table, followed by Sarah. Johannes chose a chair and Sarah the sofa across from him.

"I had no idea," she said.

Johannes sipped his bourbon and settled back into his chair in a contemplative mood. "I have known Mok for almost fifty years. It's an interesting story, at least to me.

"After college, I enlisted in the army to save the world from communism and stop the dominoes from falling. After some perfunctory training, I was sent directly to Vietnam. It was not an experience I remember with fondness. Someone more erudite and literate than me said, 'We the unwilling, led by the unqualified to kill the unfortunate, die for the ungrateful.' Anyway, you could say I was disillusioned when I came home. It didn't help when I saw the reception vets were getting from the public we were supposedly protecting. I just wanted to get as far away from that environment as possible."

What he chose not to tell Sarah was that he returned from Vietnam with the Distinguished Service Cross, the Silver Star, and the Purple Heart. He, like most combat veterans, never spoke about that part of his service.

"I was used to backpacks, so I loaded up another one and headed to Southern Africa with no destination or plan in mind. The backpacking life was getting old by the time I got to Bulawayo, Zimbabwe, looking to buy a pair of Selous safari boots at the Courteney boot factory. One of their salesmen recommended a bar across the street, where I went for a drink. I had a couple of beers and chatted with a guy who filled me in on the history of Southern Africa. He left, and I decided it was time to go. Outside, I found two goons trying to rob my new friend. They were working him over pretty good, so I joined in, and they ran off empty-handed. The man I helped was Mok Masisi.

"This was back in the seventies when his family operated a safari company where he was a guide. He invited me to come on safari with him for a week, so I grabbed my backpack and was off. When the week was up, his family offered me a position doing general maintenance around their camps."

Johannes took another sip of bourbon, and his face softened with pleasant memories.

"I stayed a year bouncing back and forth among their five camps. Frankly, it was one of the best years of my life. The army showed me what kind of man I was, but Africa…Africa taught me a love and appreciation of nature and animals that has followed me through life. I have been back many times both on photographic safaris and business. Consolidated and I have put a lot of money into conservation efforts in Africa. Mok was best man at my first wedding, and we stay in touch."

"Wow, that should give us a leg up in the Debswana fight," Sarah said eagerly.

"They will listen to us, but Mok is a hard-headed businessman who will put his country first every time. Never forget that." Johannes stood, bringing an end to the conversation. "Now get to work with our bankers at J.P. Morgan on financing the Debswana purchase."

CHAPTER 10

SARAH FELT ON TOP of the world as she sat in the guest chair across the desk from Johannes and finished filling him in on the good news that Watson and J.P. Morgan had finished putting the syndicate together.

"The lawyers are completing the paperwork. Morgan brought in Citi, Wells Fargo, Bank of America, and Goldman Sachs. The banks figure Botswana's percentage value at around three billion. As syndicate leader, Morgan is sending a team to Gaborone to conduct a due diligence review of operations. I think I should go with them," Sarah suggested.

"Of course you should. Get me the travel dates. I think you should go a week or so ahead of the bankers and meet a few people before the suits get in the act. I don't want them to be the first impression the Botswana officials get of Consolidated."

Sarah just stared at Johannes as her blood began to boil. She began to rise from the chair. Johannes could see the anger in her eyes and had no patience for it.

"Sit down, Ms. Taylor-Jones," he snapped.

Sarah sat.

"Yes, I want you there before the white guys in suits because you are half black. We are going to use what we must to get this deal done and will trade on your race without apology. The government will choose between the Chinese, who claim to be helping them with their Belt and Road Initiative, and white guys who ruled them as colonials. That does not get us off to a good start in the psychology of the deal, and you can bet the Chinese will work that angle.

"Botswana is Africa's most successful democracy in part because there is not that much ethnic diversity in the black population, most of whom are Tswana. The tribe preaches respect for all humanity. It is a concept known as *botho*, which means that everyone is connected to the larger community as if it were an extended family. Less than five percent of the population is white, but there is little racial animosity. Interracial couples are commonplace.

"You are a symbol of *botho* while the Chinese are among the worst racists in the world. I want you to be the face of Consolidated, not some white guys in suits. In the final analysis, it may make a difference."

Sarah sat quietly. She had dealt with the question "What are you?" for her entire life. She wasn't black enough to be accepted by many blacks and not white enough to be accepted as white by most whites. What box to check on forms turned her stomach to acid.

Her dream was to be just Sarah.

She got the J.P. Morgan travel dates for Johannes, and two days later, he called her to his office.

"Sarah, I have lined up a special treat for your trip. You will fly to Joburg and take a bush plane to the Vumbura Plains Camp, where an old friend of mine will guide you around the Okavango Delta for a couple of days. Then you will hop another bush plane to Gaborone, where you will have lunch with Mok Masisi and a few government officials. The bankers will arrive a couple of days later and deal with some lesser functionaries in the Department of Mineral Resources and Energy."

Sarah put on her biggest smile. The last thing she wanted to do was go to some safari camp and look at wild animals. If she wanted to see animals, she would go to the zoo. But Johannes thought this would be a special treat for her, and he was, after all, her boss.

"Great, Luc. A business trip with something to see other than an airport, a hotel room, and an office. I can't thank you enough."

Sarah looked at the clothes strewn across her bed and cursed. This was the biggest deal of her career and probably the last for Johannes. She should be in the office going over balance sheets and income and expense projections for Debswana. But no, here she was, picking out a safari wardrobe. Christ. Sarah was a city girl to the core. Her idea of the great outdoors was a stroll through Central Park on a quiet Sunday morning, followed by brunch at Tavern on the Green. Why was he insisting on her spending a couple of days riding around in an open jeep looking at wild animals? If Consolidated could win the bidding, the future was wide open. If they lost, it was probably the end of Consolidated. Making matters worse, the Chinese company had the backing of the Bank of China.

She picked up a long khaki skirt, held it up in front of the full-length mirror, and threw it back on the bed. She was wasting money on clothes she would never wear again. She hated wasting money, but she had learned early in her career that in corporate life, one wanted to fit in, to look and dress like you belonged wherever you were. Khaki was not a good color on her, but she would grit her teeth and wear it. What she would not do is buy a pair of clunky boots. She was going to wear her running shoes instead.

CHAPTER

11

It was seven in the morning on a crystal-clear day when the Qatar Airways Airbus A350 touched down in Johannesburg, South Africa. Sarah stood in her business-class cubicle and stretched, smoothing down the front of her mid-calf khaki safari skirt that was nicely complemented by a khaki short-sleeve shirt covered by a light cashmere vest. Her clothes did not look like she had slept in them or been wearing them for twenty-eight hours of travel time because she hadn't. She had worn designer jeans on the New York-London leg of her trip and, after an interminable layover in London, changed into the pajamas handed out by Qatar Airways for the London-Johannesburg leg. She had brushed her teeth, washed her face and hands, and applied a little makeup before changing into her safari clothes twenty minutes before landing.

Sarah got her Red Oxx backpack from the overhead compartment, slung it over her shoulder, and picked up her briefcase. Her only worry was whether the duffel bag with the rest of her safari clothes and her big suitcase with her business clothes had made the trip safely. Her big suitcase would continue to Gaborone, Botswana, where it would be delivered to her hotel. Her backpack, duffel bag, and briefcase tipped the scales at forty-four pounds, the maximum allowed for the small bush planes.

Just inside the terminal, Sarah saw her prearranged greeters, a smiling woman and young man stood holding a sign printed with her name. The woman took Sarah's passport and visa and led her to a VIP waiting area while her documents were processed. A short time later, she reappeared along with the young man, who now had Sarah's duffel bag on a pushcart. He added her backpack to the cart and reached for her briefcase. She shook her head no and carried it to the waiting van, which a few minutes later delivered her to Air Link International's FBO terminal for the next leg of her flight to Vumbura Plains Camp in the far north of Botswana's Okavango Delta.

The Air Link plane had seats for twelve passengers, with ten occupied for the flight to Maun, Botswana. There she changed into what she considered a toy plane that held only four passengers and one pilot, a young black woman. She and an older couple were the passengers.

Sarah had done her homework. Thirty-eight percent of Botswana's land mass was dedicated to national parks and other wildlife preservation areas. However, this book learning had not prepared her for the flight over the Okavango Delta, the largest inland river delta in the world where the Okavango River sunk into the dry sands of the Kalahari Desert, forming a lush, waterlogged oasis with lagoons, channels, and flood plains. Dubbed the river that never finds the sea, the delta it created covered almost six thousand square miles. Her initial nervousness quickly faded as the plane passed over elephants, giraffes, hippos, and a myriad of other animals Sarah could not identify except that they had horns. Unseen, waiting for nightfall, were the predators: lions, leopards, cheetahs, hyenas, jackals, and wild dogs.

The plane banked and lined up with a dirt airstrip. Sarah held her breath as the young woman brought the plane down flawlessly.

The Vumbura Plains Camp was built from wood, glass, and canvas on raised decks above grassland that often flooded. Upon arrival, Sarah was met by the smiling camp manager and a woman with a glass of champagne and a cool towel for Sarah's hands and face. After a brief introductory explanation of how the camp operated, Sarah was escorted to her tent, where the attendant unzipped the netting that covered the entire front and ushered her inside.

Sarah had trouble believing what she was seeing. It was definitely not what she had been expecting. The tent, with a twelve-foot ceiling, was the size of a two-bedroom apartment in New York. There was a wooden floor, scattered rugs, plush stuffed furniture, and a king-size bed draped in white mosquito netting. She also found electric lighting, an indoor bathroom with a flush toilet, and an indoor/outdoor shower. Hi-speed Wi-Fi connected her to the outside world.

After wandering around her accommodations, she marveled that here in the middle of Africa was a tent more luxurious than any hotel room she had ever seen.

Sarah could not help herself. The city girl got to work with her phone camera and recorded the entire interior of the tent and the outside deck with an oversize sunken tub euphemistically called a plunge pool. She tested the water. It was very cold despite the lingering heat of the day. She wouldn't be doing any plunging it that.

As she enjoyed a long, hot open air outdoor shower to wash off her travel, she was again amazed. A short distance away, she could see zebras, a herd of cape buffalo, an elephant, and some animals that were probably in the antelope family. There was no fence. These animals could walk right up to her tent.

Sarah, drying herself, stepped inside from the shower and then jumped back, dropping her towel like she had seen the proverbial ghost. Thirty feet from where she stood, dripping wet, a massive elephant had its trunk in her plunge pool, slurping away. Naked, she grabbed her phone to record this magical introduction to an African safari. Forgetting the towel and clothes, she watched the elephant from safely inside the tent until it wandered away. Then she quickly pulled on shorts and a T-shirt and spent a half hour with the tent binoculars watching the nearby wildlife. She couldn't help but wonder if a lion would visit the camp and, if so, was she safe?

At cocktail time, she donned fresh clothes and headed to the dining tent, where she was to have a drink before dinner with Johannes's friend who had come to camp to be her personal safari guide for two days. The sun had set, but there was still enough light for her to walk unescorted. At orientation, she had been told that after dark, she had to be escorted from and to her tent, and it was very important not to come out on her deck once she had returned after dinner since animals could and often did wander into camp and walk among the tents.

Halfway to the dining tent, a deep, guttural grunting sound she had never heard before shattered the quiet. It seemed to come from a large pond twenty yards from the walkway. Sarah's heart missed a beat as she frantically looked around but saw nothing. She quickened her pace to a very fast walk.

Uproarious laughter filled the air as Sarah approached the bar area, where a tall white man in khaki safari clothes and a light-brown slouch hat stood with his back to her in the middle of a group of camp staffers, all of whom were doubled over in laughter. One of the group pointed toward Sarah, and the laughter subsided. The man turned, saw Sarah, and excused himself from the group.

"You must be Ms. Taylor-Jones. Luc's description didn't do you justice," the man said with a heavy Afrikaans accent, sweeping off his hat and offering a big smile full of white teeth. "I'm Aiden Bekker." They shook hands.

"Well, Luc said you were a tall Afrikaner with a great sense of humor."

"Didn't he say I was intelligent and good-looking with a great head of hair?"

Sarah smiled. "He said you always wear a hat."

"OK, enough of this foolishness. What can we get you to drink?"

One of the staff materialized at their side and took Sarah's drink order. They sat in overstuffed chairs looking out over the endless grassland as the deep-red horizon highlighted the dark forms of antelopes, zebras, and elephants.

"Mr. Bekker, I don't want to sound frightened, but on the way here, I heard something grunting, a kind of guttural sound. But I could not see where it was coming from."

"Probably a hippo. There are a couple that hang around in that pond not far from your tent. It probably made the sounds you heard and submerged. Nothing to worry about."

"But the hippo could walk up to my tent. That's something to worry about. An elephant already stopped by to drink from my plunge pool," Sarah said tentatively.

"Yes, he could, and he may, but there are gaps in the walkway that he can pass through. The animals don't bother the tents. You are perfectly safe if you stay inside after dark. You may hear the hippo or a cape buffalo munching grass outside your tent tonight, but don't worry about it."

"Don't worry about it? I don't want to be too girly, but that would be terrifying," she said with concern.

"You'll get used to it."

Sarah decided to keep her uncertainty to herself and changed the subject. They chatted about Johannes for a while. When they sat for dinner at their own table slightly apart from the other guests, Sarah's curiosity got the better of her.

"Mr. Bekker, since I am supposed to trust my life to you for the next two days, perhaps you should tell me something about yourself."

A big smile lit up Bekker's face.

"First, please call me Aiden. You may have surmised from my accent that I am a proud Afrikaner. My grandmother told me the family is descended from Jan van Riebeeck, the Dutch surgeon who led the Dutch East India Company expedition that founded Cape Town. We Dutch controlled South Africa until the early 1800s, when the British took over. My ancestors and many others did not cotton to the British way of ruling, and many of them picked up and trekked north into what is now Botswana. My family's ranch is on the northern rim of the Kalahari Desert, not too far from here."

Sarah was fascinated that this man could trace his family back as far as the 1600s. Bekker paused while dinner was served.

"As a young man, I worked as a safari guide and ran into your boss. We hit it off, and on return visits, he always arranged for me to guide him. I quit guiding maybe fifteen years ago and have been running our cattle ranch since then."

"A cattle ranch in Botswana?" Sarah questioned.

"Of course. Botswana is the largest cattle producer in Africa and number five in the world."

"Are you saying I'm having dinner with a real African cowboy?"

"Yes, ma'am, you are."

Dinner was served, and one of the staff filled their wineglasses. Sarah nervously poked the main course, which appeared to be some kind of stew, with her fork.

Bekker grinned. "Don't worry, Sarah. It's Seswaa, the national dish of Botswana. It's quite good."

Sarah tentatively took a small bite. Her face relaxed and she nodded. "Yes, quite good."

"Now tell me something about Ms. Sarah Taylor-Jones."

"Well, I had a white father—" she uncomfortably began.

Aiden interrupted her. "Sarah, that tells me what you are, not who you are. You didn't choose the what, but you did choose the who. That's what interests me."

Bekker's comment had a relaxing effect on Sarah, and she gave him a quick, sanitized version of her life story, including the fact that her hyphenated last name was the only thing she had kept from her failed marriage to an American. "I only mention that because, given your family history and the Boer War, I don't want you to think I have any connection to England," she said, chuckling. "It might not be safe."

"Very wise, young lady. Very wise," Bekker said with mock seriousness. "Since you have spent so much time sitting on a plane getting here, how about tomorrow morning we use an open Toyota to cruise around looking for animals and, in the afternoon, we do a walking safari?"

As if on cue, a deep-throated, terrifying roar assaulted them from the darkness. Sarah's eyes widened and she looked to Bekker. "What was that?"

"Your neighborhood lion just letting other lions know this is his territory. If he was hunting, he wouldn't be making all that noise."

Sarah looked around uneasily. "OK, but you have to be kidding about walking around in the middle of all these animals."

"Not to worry. Wild animals are usually not a serious threat unless they feel threatened or their food is at risk," Bekker said.

She looked and felt uneasy.

"Sarah, this isn't some jungle movie with animals hiding and waiting to pounce on unsuspecting humans. Usually, they just want to be left alone. I will be armed, and we'll be followed by a park ranger who'll also be armed. We do walking safaris all the time."

"What worries me is your use of the word *usually*, but OK," Sarah said, not sure what she was getting herself into.

CHAPTER 12

Dawn was damp and chilly. Dressed in heavy fleece, Sarah joined Bekker for a quick breakfast on the dining deck. Afterward, in the faint dawn light, they climbed into a modified Toyota and spent the morning observing herds of antelope, zebra, and cape buffalo.

Just before lunch, the radio crackled with a call from another guide who had come across some wild dogs. Bekker floored the Toyota and headed in the direction the other guide had given him, splashing through marshland while Sarah held on for dear life. Sadly, they arrived too late. The dogs had vanished in the thick brush.

During lunch, Sarah lost her big-city, seen-it-all-attitude and animatedly marveled at what she had seen.

"Aiden, what a morning! No one will believe that we got so close to those animals. I mean, they acted like we weren't even there. I could have reached out and petted that lioness."

"Good thing you didn't," Bekker said. "With rare exceptions, they don't bother with the vehicles or anyone inside them."

"Rare exceptions?" Sarah questioned.

Bekker chuckled. "Well, once a cheetah was chasing a gazelle, which jumped into the vehicle amid the guests. The cheetah gave up the hunt, and the gazelle jumped out and went on its way. But don't worry. It's a very rare event."

"I thought for sure that baby leopard was a goner when it sat there and watched those two hyenas come up the hill toward it and then, at the last minute, scampered up a tree in the blink of an eye. My friends won't believe it. Now I can begin to understand why Luc keeps coming back here," Sarah opined as they finished lunch. "I mean, the animals are always doing something different. Some time, I would like to see cheetahs chase their prey at full speed, maybe even see the Great Migration."

Bekker smiled and encouraged her enthusiasm. It wasn't the first time he had seen Africa capture part of someone's heart.

After lunch, Sarah left her fleece in her tent.

"Ms. Taylor-Jones, are you excited? Ready for a walking safari?" Bekker asked playfully.

Sarah, Bekker, and a park ranger walked out of camp under the hot African sun. Bekker carried a Dakota 76 rifle, and the ranger had an AK-47. Rather than give her comfort, the need for such high-powered weaponry made Sarah more nervous.

They walked through an ocean of knee-high grass that awaited its seasonal inundation by the Okavango River. Single acacia trees stood in splendid isolation interspersed with occasional random piles of granite boulders called kopjes.

Sarah's new khaki safari shirt was dark with sweat and stuck uncomfortably to her body as she followed Bekker. She was nervous. Who in their right mind went for a walk where lions and leopards roamed freely and there were herds of elephants and cape buffalo? In this case, a woman who had climbed the corporate ladder and was intent on the top rung. Her faux self-confidence was shaken when they gave wide berth to several hippos and Bekker told her that the massive beasts killed more big-game hunters than any other animal in Africa.

About a mile from camp, they were almost at a kopje. Sarah had listened patiently as Bekker enthusiastically explained about the birds, grasses, and tiny creatures that inhabited the grassland. Maybe a walking safari was not about the big animals, but Sarah sensed that they were under constant surveillance by unseen wild creatures.

They reached the kopje, and Bekker began his spiel about how kopjes provided habitat for many animals because of the presence of a variety of plants, shade, and water holes for small creatures. He had just mentioned that they also provided a vantage point for many predators when they stepped around a huge boulder and came upon a massive male lion enjoying a meal of fresh zebra about one hundred feet away.

Sensing their arrival, the lion stood, muzzle smeared with bright-red blood, amber eyes wide open and glowing in the sunlight, focused intently on those interrupting his meal. Sarah was sure the lion was eight feet long. He opened his mouth full of blood-stained teeth and roared with such ferocity and volume that her chest shook.

Sarah's head swiveled, and she took a step, looking for an escape route. Without turning, Bekker reached behind himself and grabbed her shirt.

"Stand still or die," he hissed.

Sarah struggled briefly before the ranger stepped forward and put his hands on her shoulders. More than anything she had ever wanted in her forty years, Sarah Taylor-Jones wanted to run. Through the fog of terror, she remembered that Bekker had told her that should there be such an encounter not to run, or the lion would assume she was prey. She didn't care. Every bone in her body, every fiber of her being, told her to run.

The lion began to trot toward them in a zigzag pattern, growling. She struggled, and the ranger grabbed her around her arms and chest, immobilizing her. She remembered that a lion could run fifty miles per hour. The fastest human, only twenty-seven. No contest. Run and die.

The lion picked up speed and then stopped about twenty feet away. In unison, the men moved her against the boulder so the lion had all avenues of escape. The animal started back toward his kill and suddenly spun and charged again, stopping a little closer this time. When the lion stood still and started pawing the ground, tail moving back and forth, the men began backing up with Sarah securely between them. Three more backward steps, and they were around the boulder and the lion was out of sight.

One more ear-shattering roar brought tears to Sarah's eyes. Were they safe?

The walk back to camp was a blur. Bekker spoke in a calm, reassuring voice about how rare such an encounter was and how brave she had been. She knew it was all BS. The only thing she could take pride in was not wetting herself. Nothing in Sarah's prior life had prepared her for the sheer, mindless terror evoked by the roar of the blood-soaked lion moving toward her.

When they reached camp, the ranger disappeared, and Bekker led her to the bar, which was adjacent to the dining tent.

"White wine?" he asked as he guided her to a chair overlooking the savannah below.

"No, not after that. Bourbon neat." Sarah sighed and collapsed into the chair, feeling fortunate that the other guests were out on a game-viewing drive that included lunch in the bush.

The bartender handed her a crystal glass with three fingers of Bushmills, and Sarah took a healthy swallow. She was beginning to pull herself together now that she was out of the bush and safe. Sarah took a deep breath and exhaled very slowly.

"Aiden, first, thank you and that ranger for saving my life. If you two hadn't held me, I would have run. I remembered what you told me, but I couldn't help myself." She slowly shook her head. "I was raised on the South Side of Chicago. Despite the best efforts of my grandmother, I saw men, women, and children shot dead in broad daylight by gangbangers. I have competed against ruthless men throughout my business career. But nothing I've seen or done prepared me for that lion. I just don't know what to say. I don't think of myself as a coward but, well, you were there. I was terrified."

Bekker smiled softly. "Sarah, no one, *no one*, is prepared for the first time they encounter a lion on foot in the wild. It's counterintuitive to stand there. I have a lifetime of experience with lions, as does the ranger. Each time we encounter one on foot, it's one time too many and may be the last. I don't get a rush out of it. I just deal with it.

"I'm quite certain that should you have a similar encounter in the future, you'll handle it quite well. You're not a coward. You just encountered something unexpected and totally foreign to your experience. Now it isn't."

Sarah nodded and sipped some more whiskey.

The camp manager approached them. "Ms. Taylor-Jones, there is a call for you from New York on the satellite phone in my office."

She hurried behind the manager to the office and picked up the phone.

"Sarah, it's Luc. J.P. Morgan and the syndicate have pulled their financing commitment. I don't know why. They won't give me a straight answer. I've arranged for a private plane to pick you up at nine in the morning and take you directly to Gaborone. Once you're there, we'll figure out what to do."

CHAPTER 13

WANG JIN HAD DELIBERATELY failed to tell Tommy that he was meeting with Billings at the lawyer's office. He would keep his old friend around for the time being for appearance's sake, but now that he had lawyers like Billings and would soon own half of the world's largest diamond producer, he was playing in the big leagues. He would make new friends—important ones. Tommy would think he was somehow important and just be in the way as Wang Jin's power and influence grew exponentially.

Finally, Wang Jin had arrived on the world stage. Like his father, he was born to have power and influence people and governments. He would prosper in business until it was time for him to step into his father's shoes and run China. The Debswana deal would cement his future. It would be the beginning of his triumphant march across the global business world. Nothing would stand in his way. His destiny was there for the taking.

The same kimono-clad woman as before ushered him into Billings's office, which continued the Englishmen's club decor of the reception area. Billings rose and came around his desk to shake hands. He was not nearly as standoffish as he had been at their first meeting. He had a slight smile tugging at his features. Or was it a smirk?

"Sit down, Mr. Wang," Billings said as he returned to the other side of his desk and settled into a big, high-backed leather desk chair. Wang Jin thought that if the old fart had worn a white wig, he could pass for a judge.

"I wanted to tell you in person that we are moving the Debswana transaction in the right direction," Billings announced in a tone that told Wang Jin he was quite pleased with himself.

Wang Jin nodded. "OK, what happened?"

"Consolidated's financing has collapsed," Billings revealed triumphally.

"Fantastic! Tell me about it."

"Our bankers at Morgan Stanley knew that Consolidated's primary bank is J.P. Morgan and found out—there are very few secrets on Wall Street—that it had put together a syndicate with Citi, Bank of America, Goldman Sachs, and Wells Fargo to finance Consolidated's bid for Debswana." Billings chuckled at a secret joke he was about to share.

"How ironic. You may remember that J.P. Morgan's chairman, that pompous ass with the white hair, made a joke not too long ago that Morgan had been doing business in China since 1921 when the Chinese Communist Party was formed and that the bank would outlast the CCP."

"Yeah, he apologized, didn't he?"

"Yes, sir. Less than twenty-four hours later, he groveled with an apology. That is a demonstration of the power China has over foreign banks wanting to do business in the world's second-largest economy."

"J.P. Morgan has twenty billion dollars of exposure in China. It and the rest of the syndicate are all trying to expand their business in your country. They want to run securities brokerages, help businesses raise money, broker transactions, and manage money for wealthy Chinese. These banks have no soul, no loyalty to anything except making money. They are so without conscience that your father has used the threat of their Chinese business licenses to turn them into lobbyists for Chinese interests with the US government."

Wang Jin did not follow politics beyond knowing who held what kind of power in the CCP. He was surprised, then pleased to hear that the US banks were so easily co-opted to serve China.

"I had lunch with Morgan's man—actually, it's a woman—here in Hong Kong and explained that your company had the backing of the Bank of China and the investment was being made as part of China's Belt and Road Initiative in Botswana with the approval of the Botswana government. 'Approval' was a slight exaggeration, but she got the point. Financing Consolidated would not please China. She couldn't wait to get out of there. The next morning, she called and said the financing was off and that she had explained things to the other participants in the syndicate, and that they were also out."

Wang Jin sat back in his chair. "No one would dare to cross my father. The European banks won't either."

"Probably not," Billings said. "The Debswana deal is now poison for the banks."

"Where are you with De Beers?"

"I have been letting the pot simmer since you planted that article about tariffs. But now that Consolidated is out of the way, I intend to travel to Africa and meet personally with a member of their board of directors and apply some direct pressure."

Wang Jin stood and began to pace around the office.

"What's the problem?" Billings queried, slightly irritated that this favored son was not gushing with praise for the firm's accomplishments.

"Things look great now, but Consolidated might be able to find financing somewhere else and De Beers might call our bluff. If I was sure they were both out, I could reduce our bid substantially and still get the diamonds. The stupid Africans will have to sell at our price if they want any Belt and Road projects."

Billings rose from behind his desk and took Wang Jin by the arm, gently guiding him toward the door.

"There is a reason that the CCP uses our firm for delicate matters, Mr. Wang. We plan for all contingencies. As it happens, the Botswana Minister of Mines has a son at school in London and a daughter living in Shanghai with a gambling problem. While in Africa, I will suggest that his financial problems would disappear if your company won the bidding. Just a suggestion, but cheese is irresistible to rats."

Wang Jin was floating on air as he rode the elevator back to earth. He was privy to the subtle exercise of raw power in the globalized business world. With Consolidated out of the picture, only De Beers stood in the way. He would soon know if their little news release conveyed the desired message.

He looked at his gold Rolex. It was almost five, so he headed directly to The Bar at the Peninsula Hotel, where he always had good luck with the ladies. Wang Jin took a seat at the end of the bar with a clear view of anyone entering and ordered a Macallan eighteen-year-old single-malt scotch.

How was he going to sideline his old friend Tommy without creating a dangerous enemy? They had been friends since elementary school. In high school, Wang Jin had copied Tommy's homework. He was smart like his billionaire father, but Wang Jin found him naive and gullible. That would be his downfall. Wang Jin could stick him in Botswana, nominally in charge of the diamond mining operation, while he stayed in Hong Kong and exercised real control of Eastern Enterprises's finances and searched for another company he could acquire by leveraging Eastern's assets and his father's name. China's Belt and Road Initiative was worldwide and would provide him entrée anywhere in the third world.

Two well-dressed Western women just entering middle age walked into The Bar and looked around before sitting at a table near the door. To Wang Jin's experienced eye, they were the bored wives of a couple of European business executives who had accompanied their husbands and were in search of some excitement in mysterious Hong Kong. Perhaps some afternoon delight while their tiresome husbands went about their business.

Wang Jin ordered another scotch, smoothed his thin moustache, walked over, and introduced himself to the ladies. With shy smiles and furtive glances at each other, they invited him to join them.

CHAPTER
14

WANG JIN AND TOMMY held warm bottles of beer as they surveyed the customers in Trekkers Night Club in Gaborone, Botswana just after ten at night. The floor was plain concrete, the roof corrugated metal, the furniture beat-up wood and plastic. The place smelled of heat, sweat, and stale beer under a canopy of cigarette smoke. The band's singer couldn't carry a tune in a bucket. Worst of all, these glistening ebony women were not in the same league as the fine Chinese women they were used to bedding.

The men had arrived on a China Airlines flight early that afternoon to observe the Morgan Stanley investment bankers pore over the Debswana books and question its executives while a team of engineers hired by them was in the countryside examining the mines. After a quick nap and a shower, Wang Jin had done an internet search of local hotspots. There wasn't much available, but Trekkers was listed as being frequented by local women.

"I can't get drunk enough for one of these cows," Wang Jin said.

Tommy breathed a sigh of relief. AIDS remained a significant problem in Botswana, and he didn't want to trust his future to a condom. He had a wife and two small children at home that he wanted to see grow up.

"Those street walkers hanging on the corners on the way here were better than this bunch," Wang Jin complained.

He fumbled in his wallet and found a folded piece of paper with a name and phone number. One of his friends was involved with the Macau branch of the

14K triad. When Wang Jin had told him he was going to Botswana, the friend had given him the name and number of the 14K boss in Gaborone. China and Botswana had established diplomatic relations in 1975, and over the years, China had been involved in major infrastructure projects for the government. The Chinese imported many skilled workers, and with them came all the components for a local Chinatown, including criminals.

"Come on, Tommy. Let's go back to the hotel and call this guy. If he's such a big shot, maybe he can send us a couple of hookers."

Back at the hotel, Tommy was able to disengage from Wang Jin and go to his room for a good night's sleep. Meanwhile, Wang Jin's 14K triad contact told him to go to the Avani Gaborone Resort & Casino and play blackjack. In an hour or so, he would send over a very fine woman who was in town from Zimbabwe.

"Why not my room?" asked Wang Jin, who was already feeling a little woozy.

"No one knows you. You must establish trust. The woman will have access to a room at the casino's hotel."

"How will she find me?"

"How many Chinese men of your description do you think will be playing blackjack at one in the morning?" the triad boss replied.

It was closer to one thirty when a short, overweight woman with a massive pillow chest tapped on Wang Jin's shoulder. By then, he was three double scotches down the road and was singularly unimpressed by her. While he had waited, he had lost $1,000 at the blackjack table, putting him in a foul mood further fueled by the scotch. He started off badly by complaining about her being late. On the way out of the casino, he roughly grabbed her arm. When she jerked her arm loose, Wang Jin slapped her.

A massive black man materialized from behind a bank of slot machines and wrapped his huge arm around Wang Jin's neck.

"Go away, woman," the giant growled.

When she was out of sight, he released Wang Jin, who spun around and faced him.

"What in the hell do you think you're doing? Do you know who I am?"

"You do not treat my women that way, and yes, I know who you are. You're an asshole. Now get out of here before I lose my temper."

By the time Wang Jin found a cab and got back to his hotel, the booze had hit him full force. He barely made it inside the lobby before collapsing on a sofa and passing out.

Just before six that morning, Wang Jin was shaken awake by Baruti Masisi, the hotel general manager.

"Sir, you cannot sleep here. Please go to your room."

Wang Jin mumbled incomprehensibly and stumbled off stinking of liquor, cigarette smoke, and sour sweat.

CHAPTER 15

SARAH WAS NERVOUS TO find that she was the only passenger on a tiny, single-propeller bush plane piloted by an Australian man who looked barely old enough to buy beer. Despite her misgivings, it was a smooth and uneventful flight to Gaborone, the capital and largest city in Botswana. Located in the southeast corner of the country near the South Africa border, the city was home to 230,000 people, about 10 percent of Botswana's population.

The city was clean, and the paved roads upon which her cab traveled to her hotel were excellent. When Botswana had gained its independence in the 1960s, it had been one of the least developed countries in Africa. Since then, it had transformed itself into a middle-income country where its GDP per capita was the fourth-highest in the continent. Not coincidentally, it was considered Africa's least corrupt country.

Sarah's cab dropped her at the ultra-chic room50two hotel located in the tallest building in Gaborone. As she was checking in and arranging for her big suitcase to be delivered to her room, she noticed a tall, attractive Chinese man with a wispy moustache staring at her with an appraising eye. The last thing she needed right now was to be hit on by a Chinese businessman. There was no one to carry her luggage, so Sarah slung her backpack over her shoulder, picked up her duffel bag and briefcase, and headed for the elevator.

The Chinese man moved quickly to cut her off.

"Excuse me, miss. May I have the pleasure of helping you with your bags?" the smiling man asked in flawless English with a British accent.

Sarah was bone tired after a fitful night tossing and turning trying to figure out what had happened to the financing syndicate. "No, thank you. I've got things under control," she managed to say politely.

"If I may be so bold, my name in Wang Jin, and I would like to ask if you could join me for a drink later?"

As Sarah pushed the elevator button, it hit her. Wang Jin. Was this the son of the Chinese Communist Party chairman and the man behind Eastern Enterprises?

The elevator door opened. She stepped inside, turned, and said, "Not today. Perhaps later."

The door closed on a smiling Wang Jin.

Why had she said that? Did she really want to spend time with her rival? Maybe she could elicit some information from him before he found out who she was? Maybe, but that was tomorrow's problem. Tonight, she needed to make some calls and get some sleep.

CHAPTER
16

JOHANNES PUT HIS GLOCK 19, ear protection, and shooting glasses in his personal locker at the Westside Rifle and Pistol Range, slipped on his suit jacket, and headed for the door accompanied by the faint smell of gunpowder.

He had picked up a love of guns in the army. He fully realized that it was an odd hobby for a man who wanted nothing to do with hunting wild animals. He understood and approved of the way hunting was conducted in the United States, as a means of controlling the population that was best for the overall species. But when it came to hunting in Africa, he rooted for the animals. He had abandoned association with a man who had invited him to his home to show off his trophy room prize, which was two stuffed giraffes' necks crossed in a fighting stance. Cape buffalo and big cats could put a hunter at risk, but giraffes? Johannes had wanted to beat the man about the head and shoulders. He hadn't, but he had excused himself as soon as possible and refused to have anything to do with him thereafter.

Johannes had killed more Viet Cong and NVA in Vietnam than he cared to remember. It did not bother him. It was war. It was simple: kill or be killed. From time to time, he remembered the giraffes and thought of the novel where a lunatic had a game preserve where he hunted humans. That would be fitting justice for the giraffe killer.

Johannes found the total concentration required in shooting to be an excellent stress reliever. Despite his age, he could match shots with most of the competitive shooters who frequented the club. He had one of the rare concealed-carry permits issued in New York City, which was a holdover from the days when he had personally delivered diamonds for Consolidated. Today, he rarely carried, but given the rising crime in the city, he was giving serious thought to packing a firearm.

After the terse email from J.P. Morgan that the financing syndicate had fallen apart, he had needed to clear his mind of anger and disappointment before deciding on a course of action. His time at the range had helped. He flagged down a cab and headed for home.

A short time later, Johannes hopped out of the cab and walked into the Dakota at One West Seventy-Second Street. His fourth-floor apartment was in the northeast corner. The landmark had opened in 1884 as New York City's first luxury apartment building. His third soon-to-be ex-wife had insisted he purchase the apartment in the mid-1990s, but he was the one who had worked extensively with the designer to remodel and furnish the nine-room old-world apartment in an elegant and sophisticated Spanish style rich with details and textures reminiscent of a bygone era. He loved the contrast with the icy coldness of his office. When his third ex had said goodbye, he had been too comfortable to move even though he didn't need all the space.

Johannes poured two fingers of Pappy Van Winkle and stood at the window observing darkness descend on Central Park across the street.

There could be numerous reasons for the syndicate to fall apart, but J.P. Morgan had not offered any plausible justification. His call to the bank's CEO had not been returned. He had to know that the bank's behavior was likely to cost them Consolidated's business, so whatever the reason, it was obviously more important than Consolidated. Stranger still was that the other members of the syndicate had abandoned the transaction without looking for a replacement member.

Johannes finished his drink, turned from the window, and said one word aloud to the empty room: "China."

Under the circumstances, that was the only reason that made sense. It fit with leaning on De Beers. The fucking Chinese were trying to bully the competition out of the bidding. There were other lenders but not many with the sophistication for a transaction of this size with its international ramifications. Any bank that wanted to do business in China would bend over for them whenever and wherever asked.

His phone vibrated in his pocket. Sarah must have arrived in Gaborone.

"Hello, Sarah. Are you in Gaborone?"

Sarah was at the small desk in her room, wrapped in a robe with her hair in a towel. "Yes, I just finished washing off the safari dust. One of the most interesting days I have ever spent. Do you know what happened with the financing?"

"I called the chairman, but he hasn't returned my call. I'll leave Watson to you. J.P. Morgan has substantial exposure in China and is looking to expand there. It makes sense that China leaned on them, and they rolled over along with the rest of the syndicate."

"Isn't there something we can do? The State Department, Senator Cortez?"

"It was a private business decision. State won't get involved, and there isn't much Cortez could do even if she wanted to help."

"What about the Treasury Department? Maybe this kind of pressure is illegal or something?" Sarah asked, grasping at straws.

"The banks would say they reevaluated the credit risks and changed their mind. Nothing funny going on here."

"Maybe some European banks?" she offered.

Johannes poured himself another drink. Hadn't he told Sarah a short time ago that solving business problems was fun? This surely was not.

"I want you to try. Start with HSBC. But to save them and us a lot of time and wasted effort, be candid about what happened with Morgan."

"OK, I'll get on it in the morning. Maybe we could get some private equity firms interested? They wouldn't care about China," Sarah said.

Johannes knocked back a healthy swallow of his drink.

"Sarah, private equity is just that. They might put up money for a big piece of Consolidated. They aren't in the business of making loans. At the least, they would want preferred stock with a healthy dividend convertible into common stock a la Warren Buffett."

She was quiet, thinking. Johannes was silent while he managed another sip of his drink.

Sarah offered tentatively, "Maybe giving up a piece of Consolidated is the price for the diamond supply we need to stay alive?"

"It would be a big piece with which they would want at least one seat on the board. They wouldn't care about Consolidated long term. As soon as they settled on the board, they would shop Consolidated, logically to De Beers, maybe even China. Private equity does not invest long term. So, to answer your question, if one or more of them would put up the money, it would only prolong the inevitable.

In any event, it would require the Hess family to give up some of its stock, and I don't see that happening."

Sarah sighed, knowing Johannes was right. "Patel still hasn't responded to my text about putting his offer in writing."

"I imagine he's busy trying to figure out if China is serious about a tariff on De Beers diamonds," Johannes replied.

"Yes, probably so," Sarah said. "Before I forget, you won't believe who offered to carry my bags to my room this afternoon."

"Brad Pitt?" Johannes joked lamely.

"Almost as unlikely. Wang Jin himself. He's here in Gaborone. He even hit on me for a drink."

"He didn't know who you are?"

"Apparently not."

"Sarah, be careful. If he knows who you are, he's up to something. If he doesn't, he'll find out soon enough," Johannes said with a note of caution in his voice. "See if you can drum up some interest with European banks. I have a couple of ideas that I want to consider."

The call ended.

CHAPTER 17

SARAH CHECKED THE TIME. Six p.m. in Gaborone was 11 a.m. in New York. Thomas W.J. Watson III answered his phone.

"Tom, what in the hell happened to our syndicate?" she snapped without any preamble.

"S-S-Sarah, what a s-s-urprise. I d-d-didn't recognize the ph-ph-phone number," Watson stammered.

Fool. Of course you didn't. It's my cell. If you had seen a Consolidated number, you would've ducked the call.

"Really, what did you expect when the bank sends an email to Johannes, not me, calling off the financing without any explanation? Diamond won't answer Johannes's calls. We need to know what's going on."

"I'm sorry, Sarah, it's complicated. Way above my pay grade. It wasn't my decision. I'm sorry."

Sarah's first instinct was to tear this pompous ass a new rectum, but that feel-good moment wouldn't get her anywhere except Watson hanging up. She needed confirmation of what she and Johannes suspected. China was applying the pressure. He had probably been told to keep his mouth shut, but rather than volunteer anything, he might confirm what she already suspected.

"Tom, we know that Eastern Enterprises, one of the bidders, is a Chinese company. Did China lean on you guys to get out of the deal?"

Silence. Sarah let it linger.

More silence. Then Watson filled the emptiness, saying, "Come on, Sarah, there's a difference between Chinese companies and the Chinese government."

Stalling but talking. So Sarah pushed. "That may be true, but in this case, Eastern Enterprises is owned by Wang Jin, the son of the head of the Chinese Communist Party, and the company is being financed by the Bank of China. Neither you nor I are naive. Eastern may be privately held, but it clearly has the imprimatur of the Chinese government."

Another pause. She waited.

"Sarah, it's just business. J.P. Morgan has a lot at stake in China, and we're applying for some new licenses, including retail brokerage. The market is huge. The bank cannot afford to irritate the Chinese."

"J.P. Morgan is an American company. Consolidated is an American company. How can you dance to China's tune? It's blackmail," Sarah said incredulously.

Watson, no longer on the defensive, interjected, "No, Sarah. Understand this: J.P. Morgan is a global company operating in a global market. Second, as I said, it's just business, not blackmail. Theoretically, we don't have to do business in China and, in fact, they do not have to let us do business there. That said, if we, as a global company, want to do business in the second-largest market on the globe, we must play by their rules and keep China happy. It's not rocket science."

Sarah started to say something, but Watson cut her off. "The fact is that even if we provided financing to Consolidated for its bid, you would lose because Eastern Enterprises has unlimited financing from the Bank of China. I saw a copy of the commitment letter. No matter how much you bid, Eastern has the resources to bid one dollar more. You were going to lose anyway, so why should our group piss off the Chinese for no reason? It makes no sense."

Sarah wanted to argue, but the die was already cast. There were no minds to change. "Well, Tom, I would like to say it was nice doing business with an upstanding American company, but it wasn't, and J.P. Morgan is American in name only—and oh yes, by the way, my assistant will be in touch with you about moving our accounts."

"Wait, wait. It wasn't my fault, but I'll make it up to you on another deal. You need to stay with us."

"No, *you* need us to stay with you because we're your largest account. Did you really think J.P. Morgan could screw us over and we would just take it? How arrogant. Good luck at bonus time. Goodbye."

Sarah needed to cool down and clear her mind, so she turned on the television and found the evening news. Russia's war with Ukraine. China flying fighter planes in Taiwan's airspace. North Korea firing missiles over Japan. Houthis sending drone bombs into the United Arab Emirates. Millions of unvaccinated, untested, and unidentified illegals from across the globe being allowed to pour across the US/Mexico border and being flown secretly in the dead of night to cities around the country. Inflation running wild. Supply-chain chaos. Student performance in standardized tests abysmal and getting worse. The FBI targeting parents who complained about woke school curriculums and sending fully armed SWAT teams to arrest harmless Christian ministers in predawn raids. She turned off the television in disgust, took a sleeping pill, and went to bed.

Things did not get any better the next morning. Four hours on the phone with European banks got her nowhere. Initial interest evaporated when she explained how China had leaned on the US banks.

She changed into athletic attire and went for a run along the Notwane River. After five miles at a seven-minute-mile pace, Sarah, head down, skin and clothes damp with sweat, pushed through the door to her hotel and almost bumped into Wang Jin. He was elegantly attired in an open-collared white shirt, blue blazer, gray slacks, and Gucci loafers. He jumped aside to avoid contact.

Recovering quickly, Wang Jin spoke before she could get past him. "The lovely lady with the big backpack. We meet again."

Sarah stopped, still drawing deep breaths to slow her heart rate. She noticed him eyeing the rise and fall of her breasts.

"Perhaps a drink later?" he asked.

Having decided after her conversation with Johannes to see if she could get some information from Wang Jin, she replied, "I'll be at the rooftop bar around five."

"Excellent. See you then."

They both continued on their way.

Wang Jin climbed into a waiting Lincoln town car for a short ride to join his accountants at the Ministry of Mines. The woman was beautiful and likely a biracial mixture of black and white or maybe even triracial. She would be something new.

CHAPTER 18

SARAH SAT AT THE desk/dressing table in her smallish room decorated in several shades of gray. So ultra modern and chic. *Johannes would love it,* she thought. She had never been in his apartment at the Dakota.

Hair done, she applied just traces of makeup like she usually did. This wasn't a date, and she was not going to seduce this entitled prick. Her plan was to get him talking. Narcissists loved to talk about themselves. She hadn't planned on social activities when packing, so she had only business and safari attire. She chose khaki slacks with a short-sleeve safari-style shirt in pale green and her white cashmere vest. Double purpose: casual and no hint of business.

At 5:05 p.m., Sarah walked into the table50two bar/restaurant on the twenty-eighth floor and found Wang Jin sitting at a table for two against the glass pony wall with a bottle of champagne on ice. The dining venue was in the tallest building in the country, and the view of Gaborone as lights flickered on across town in the growing darkness was spectacular.

Wang Jin leaped to his feet and held out his hand in greeting. They shook hands, both cool and firm. No hint of nervousness on his part. He pulled out her chair, and they sat.

"I hope you like champagne," Wang Jin said, smiling.

"Of course," Sarah responded, smiling in return.

Wang Jin snapped his fingers at the waiter, who opened the bottle and poured them each a glass. She took a small sip.

An engaging smile creased Wang Jin's face. "Sarah, I admire your multiracial beauty. Tell me, what races are you?"

Sarah wanted to scream but chose to change the subject.

"The champagne is excellent. What brings you to Gaborone, Mr. Wang?" Letting him know she knew the difference between Chinese first and last names.

"Business. I'm here with my accountants, who are looking into the finances of a diamond mine I want to buy."

He doesn't know who I am unless he's very clever. Straight to the point; impress the woman with diamonds. She didn't want to lie—she just preferred selective disclosure until the cat got out of the bag.

"How exciting. Are you from China? Do you plan to live in Botswana?"

"Hong Kong, actually. I am involved in several businesses around the world. I'm often my father's eyes and ears where we have Belt and Road Initiatives."

Now I'm supposed to ask him who his father is, be suitably impressed, and drink a lot of champagne before he beds me. Time to throw him off so he tries harder to impress me.

Sarah launched into a monologue about the view, the hotel, the city, and how great Botswana was. Wang Jin hid his boredom and appeared to listen while draining his glass and signaling the waiter to pour more. Finally, he couldn't remain quiet.

"Yes, I'm enjoying what little I have been able to see of the country. A lot of moving parts in buying the largest diamond producer in the world."

Sarah sipped her champagne, then said, "Fascinating. What's the company's name?"

"Debswana. It's owned by the government of Botswana and the De Beers diamond company. It's a huge deal."

"Are you competing with others for this Debswana?"

Wang Jin smiled enigmatically. "Yes. But I have the inside track. With the Belt and Road Initiative, China may do a lot of business with Botswana, so they should smile on our offer, particularly when the others step aside."

Sarah took another sip of champagne and caught the waiter's eye. "My friend's glass is empty."

The waiter dutifully filled Wang Jin's glass. "Another bottle?" he asked.

Wang Jin looked at Sarah, who smiled demurely. "Of course," he said, smiling broadly. Sarah was halfway through her first glass. "Some dinner?"

"Not now, I had a big lunch," she replied, patting her flat stomach.

"Where did you go on safari?" asked Wang Jin, watching the waiter open the new bottle and refill his glass.

"Okavango Delta. I'm curious: what makes you think your competitors will step aside?"

"I have my ways. De Beers wants to sell diamonds in China, and the other company lost its financing."

"Surely there will be other bidders?"

"Doubtful. No one wants to go up against China," Wang Jin replied somewhat pompously.

"I can see that. China must be very powerful in world trade," she said, putting a hint of wonder and respect in her voice. "I bet you had something to do with that company losing its financing." She did her best to look awestruck by this powerful businessman.

He finished his drink and smirked. "We Chinese work in mysterious ways."

Sarah figured that was all the confirmation she was going to get, but it was enough. He moved to refill her glass, and she covered it with her hand. "No, thanks, I've had enough.

Wang Jin's disappointment was written on his face. His conquest was in trouble without alcohol.

"Sarah, I apologize, but I've forgotten your last name."

Truth time. She had deliberately mumbled her last name when they had sat down while he had once again fixated on her breasts. "Taylor-Jones."

It took a moment for her last name to sink into Wang Jin's alcohol-muddled brain. Then it hit him.

"Bloody hell, woman! You're the Consolidated CFO!" he exclaimed, obviously flustered. "Why didn't you tell me?"

"I wanted to see what you would say," Sarah replied matter-of-factly. She could see him replaying their conversation in his head, trying to remember if he had disclosed any secrets. "Thank you for the drink," she said, then stood and walked away.

Wang Jin sat there, speechless. What had he told her?

Sarah returned to her room and ordered dinner from room service. She hadn't learned anything new except that Wang Jin appeared to relish dirty tricks. She had no idea how far he would go to get what he wanted, but until she and Johannes came up with the financing, it didn't matter.

CHAPTER 19

WANG JIN SAT STUNNED while rage built within him. He had lost face to that nigger *gweilo*. She was probably laughing at him and would soon be telling others how she had made of fool of him. Got him to buy her champagne. He picked up the nearly empty bottle with the idea of throwing it at the pony wall, but he could feel people staring at him. Tommy materialized table side and calmly took the bottle out of his hand. A stream of Chinese epithets exploded from Wang Jin. Now people at several surrounding tables were furtively looking at him.

Tommy sat down, snapped his fingers at the waiter, and requested a fresh glass. "Quickly, I'm thirsty."

Wang Jin and Tommy had been at the hotel for three days while the Morgan Stanley investment bankers conducted the required due diligence of Debswana, and the staff was tired of their imperious manner and assumption of superiority. Those who did not know about the arrogance and racism among privileged Chinese were getting a firsthand crash course.

"I will make that woman pay for humiliating me if it's the last thing I do," Wang Jin fumed.

After all their years as friends, Tommy was used to Wang Jin's volcanic temper. He sipped the excellent champagne, which was a little too warm, and let his friend cool down before broaching what had sent him looking for Wang Jin.

"Those *gweilo* bankers are about finished. I was with them all day. To be honest, their valuation is going to be very conservative. They are applying a considerable discount to future cash flows because the company needs to expand one of its mines at a cost of somewhere around a billion dollars. The result will extend the life of the mine significantly, but one must get from here to there, and COVID-19 has already disrupted the mining and trading of diamonds."

Wang Jin was still seething.

"You're not listening. BOC won't let us bid more than the Morgan Stanley valuation, and I'm afraid that both De Beers and Consolidated can easily outbid us. We've got to force them out of the bidding."

Wang Jin replied with self-satisfied smugness, "Consolidated is out. Billings wrecked the syndicate that was going to finance them. He'll be in Johannesburg in a day or two to meet with a De Beers director. He'll confirm the story about potential tariffs and sweeten the guy's bank account. De Beers will fold.

"Look, Tommy, without any competition, we can lie about the Morgan Stanley valuation and offer less. If they don't accept, I'll tell them the Belt and Road Initiative is down the drain. They'll have no choice but to accept our offer if they want to sell. We'll be seen as business geniuses back home, and finally, my esteemed father will have to shut the hell up."

CHAPTER 20

SARAH JOINED MOKGWEETSI MASISI and his wife, Anne, for lunch at the Mahogany Restaurant and Bar at the Avani Gaborone Resort & Casino. With its white tablecloths and somewhat masculine decor, she was reminded of a US steakhouse. She was surprised to find that Anne was Belgian. Johannes hadn't mentioned that when he had filled her in about the luncheon, which was intended as a social meet and greet. Her business would be conducted with the Minister of Mines and others in his department.

After the initial pleasantries, Masisi regaled Sarah with stories of his and Johannes's adventures when Johannes had worked at his family's safari camp. Sarah and Anne shared smiles and sidelong glances with each other at the antics of the twentysomething men.

Masisi ordered Seswaa, and the ladies selected salads, water, and iced tea. While they waited for lunch, Masisi shifted gears. "Sarah, do you know anything about the history of Botswana?" he asked.

"I must confess that my entire focus has been on Debswana. To say I am embarrassed would be a vast understatement."

"I think you'll find our country's history very interesting for reasons that will become obvious. In the 1880s, Botswana became a British protectorate called Bechuanaland, which was governed from an office in South Africa. Our George Washington was Seretse Khama. He was born into the royal family of one of our major tribes in 1921. Both his grandfather and father died by the time he was four, and he became hereditary king.

"After World War II, Khama went to England and fell in love with a white woman named Ruth Williams, whom he married in 1948. The next year, he came home and held several meetings with thousands of tribal members because he had to convince them that his marriage to a white woman who was not royal wouldn't interfere with his leadership. His tribe agreed and accepted the marriage.

"However, South Africa, which had banned interracial marriage in l949, was outraged to have a black-and-white ruling couple on its border and complained to England, which wanted to maintain its access to South African minerals. British Parliament commenced an investigation that was kept secret for decades. It found Khama fit to rule. But Britain had to do something, so they forced Khama into exile in England from 1950 to 1956."

When the waiter served lunch, Sarah felt that a fascinating story was being interrupted. "Please continue, Mok. This is so interesting."

"In 1956, Britain agreed Khama could return to Bechuanaland if he abdicated his claim to chiefdom. Khama moved back with his wife and children, and entered politics. He became the voice of the independence movement and was elected prime minister in l965."

Sarah's lunch sat untouched as Masisi continued the fascinating history lesson.

"First, he convinced Britain to move the capital from South Africa to Bechuanaland. Then in 1966, he secured independence from Britain and became the new country of Botswana's first president."

"That's amazing," Sarah said, finally taking a bite of her salad.

Masisi smiled contentedly as a professor would to a promising student. "But there's much more. In the 1960s, Botswana was the third-poorest country in the world with per-capita income of about eighty dollars annually. It was landlocked, bordered by white minority regimes in South Africa, present-day Namibia, and present-day Zimbabwe. Our main trade route was through South Africa. We had no army and were overly reliant on British aid. To say our viability was questionable and threatened by South Africa is an understatement."

Sarah nodded. "It's a wonder South Africa didn't take over."

"Fortunately for Botswana, that country had enough to worry about as it installed apartheid," Masisi replied. "Khama had faith in our people and our country. His vision was security and prosperity in a nonracial democracy where all individuals were entitled to political freedom and individual protection without racial discrimination. Khama persuaded the West that Botswana stood as a counterpoint to apartheid and deserved aid with which to succeed, and with success, Botswana's example would undermine apartheid. It got the country up and running.

"The discovery of diamonds, Khama's insistence on the rule of law, and his free-market economic policies ushered in phenomenal growth. We had the fastest-growing economy in the world from 1960 to 1980 without falling victim to the corruption and conflict that enveloped our neighbors. Today, our per-capita income is over sixty-seven hundred dollars, and we are the fourth-richest country in Africa by GDP per capita."

Sarah was overwhelmed. "Such an amazing success story. It should be taught in schools around the world."

"Perhaps," Masisi mused, "but it does not fit the Western narrative of Africa as the Dark Continent riddled with poverty, corruption, and disease."

"That may be the narrative, but Botswana stands for what Africa could do if it had more leaders like Seretse Khama," Sarah said emphatically.

Both Mok and Anne smiled broadly. "Darling, you have made another convert," Anne said, chuckling.

"I hope so. Sarah, moving on to the point of your visit: I have instructed Obdura Leballo, the Minister of Mines, to open the Debswana books to you and show you whatever you wish to see, starting tomorrow. The Chinese will have finished their review. Luc told me that you were having some trouble lining up financing and I am sorry about that, but we must proceed with the sale next month regardless of Consolidated's ability to participate."

"I understand," she said, "but I do have a question. Diamonds are about seventy percent of your export earnings, twenty-five percent of GDP, and one-third of government revenue. Why are you selling an asset that's central to your economy?"

Anne jumped in. "My husband, like Seretse Khama, is a visionary. Diamonds are a finite resource and do not provide enough jobs. We want to transform Botswana into an information economy where we educate electrical engineers, software developers, and people who know how to use information. Enough with the shovels—we need computer operators and developers of information technology."

Masisi reached over and patted Anne's hand. "As you see, I have converted my wife. Now I must convert our nation to prepare it for the future. As she said, diamonds are a finite resource, but they can provide a springboard to the future."

"Enough politics," Anne said. "Sarah, I have a favor to ask."

Sarah nodded. "Sure, anything."

"Our son, Baruti, is the general manager of room50two. He has been tentatively offered a job with Marriott International in New York City. He wasn't looking for a job in the United States, but a recruiter found him, and a Skype interview with the HR department went well. They have invited Baruti to New York for an in-person interview. If it goes well, it will result in a formal offer. Our son is forty and has traveled quite a bit but has never been to the United States. He has a lot of questions, and I was hoping you'd be willing to answer some of them."

"Of course, but I don't know anything about the hotel business," Sarah said, wondering where this was going.

"That's not his concern. Baruti is obviously biracial. He thinks he can do anything he puts his mind to. He is Botswanan, so race is never an issue here, but I have been following the US news for some time and am concerned how he would fit in business wise and socially. Here, no one cares about the color of one's skin, but Americans seem to obsess over it."

Sarah was momentarily speechless. This had come out of the blue. What could she say? Out of the corner of her eye, she could see Mok shifting uncomfortably in his chair.

"Anne, darling, what you're asking is very personal. Sarah, Anne is first and always a mother who worries about her children."

"No, no. That's all right. I'll try to answer his questions, but it's just one woman's opinion. Anecdotal. But if he is interested, I would be willing to share my perspective," Sarah answered, trying to keep the uncertainty out of her voice.

"Good," Anne said. "Baruti has never married and has no children, so it would be fairly easy for him to move, but he would be giving up a successful career here and moving to a foreign country. If things don't work out…well, he could find himself in a mess."

"Like I said, always the mother hen," Mok said, chuckling.

Anne lightly punched Mok's shoulder. "Sarah, how about dinner tomorrow night?"

Sarah floated back to her hotel on a wave of inspiration. What wonderful people. What an untold story—at least to her. But what would she tell Baruti?

CHAPTER 21

A CLEAR, SUNNY DAY filled Johannes's Manhattan office with light as he sat at his desk reviewing his options for financing. Any bank with enough size to fund Consolidated's bid was or would like to do business in China, making them susceptible to Chinese economic bullying. Private equity in the United States or sovereign wealth funds like the Saudis and the United Arab Emirates might loan the money, but they would undoubtedly want convertible bonds, which would mean giving up a major equity position if things went well. That would not fly with the Hess family. He needed another approach.

Even if he could persuade the family to give up a significant piece of its stock, the investors would request seats on the board of directors and, in short order, push to take the company public, what private equity called a liquidity event.

He had told Sarah that they would have to think outside the box, and here he was beating himself up with the usual approach to acquisitions. China's size, economy, and massive economic marketplace gave it a huge advantage in the business world. OK, nothing he could do to change that economic power.

His secretary knocked and delivered a roast beef sandwich and a diet soda from the deli around the corner from the office. Johannes opened his computer to *The Wall Street Journal* and began to read while he ate. When his eyes reached a headline, "Pension Funds Chase Returns in Private-Market Debt," he stopped eating. It seemed public pension funds had been scaling back on bonds, bank loans, and other types of publicly traded debt as yields dropped to near zero. According to the article, pension funds were crying for income to meet annual investment return projections. There were quite a few money managers that handled private credit investments for the pension funds.

Johannes called to his secretary, "Hannah, please get Sarah on the phone."

An hour later, Johannes and Sarah had a plan of action. They had identified three major money management firms that handled many private market debt investments for pension funds. It was agreed that Sarah would make initial contact with the managers whom, as luck would have it, she knew from her days at Goldman Sachs. If she got an expression of interest, her staff would provide any financial information that was needed and hand off the contact to Johannes and the lawyers to work out the terms. They hoped that the lure of higher interest rates secured by diamonds would prove irresistible.

CHAPTER 22

A LOVELY YOUNG EURASIAN woman handed J. Walter Billings a crystal glass of scotch as soon as he was settled in his first-class seat on the Qatar Airways flight from Johannesburg to Hong Kong. He inhaled the aroma of the amber liquid before taking a small taste. Excellent.

His trip to Africa had exceeded his expectations. Obdura Leballo, the Botswana Minister of Mines, had met him in Johannesburg at one of the Saxon Hotel's private villas set on a lush hillside among courtyards, fountains, and gardens. The opulent surroundings of the hotel had the desired effect on the minister, who was on the first trip of his life outside Botswana.

Leballo's recruitment had begun when two massive debt collectors for Shanghai's Hang Seng Casino had escorted his daughter from the blackjack table to a private room in the bowels of the casino where the walls and floor were concrete and a large drain was positioned in the middle of the floor. A garden hose was attached to a spigot on one wall. The only other furniture in the room was a well-used wooden chair with restraints on the arms and legs. The chair was covered with irregular dark stains.

The young woman who had been nervous walking with the men was clearly terrified when they had showed her into the room and closed and locked the door. Then silence. More silence. Tears began to leak, and she wet herself, which dribbled down her leg. Finally, one of the men told her that if she did not clear her gambling debts in one week, they would bring her back to this room for another conversation. After she was escorted back to the main floor of the casino, she left immediately for her apartment.

The incident had had the desired effect. She did not know her frantic phone call to her father was being recorded when she first asked for and then hysterically demanded help. As expected, Leballo did not have the free cash to cover her gambling debt but said he would figure something out and for her not to worry. This series of events had been carried off as predicted.

Billings let Leballo experience a sleepless night of worry. The next day, a messenger delivered a note to Leballo's home before he left for work asking him to call a phone number with a Shanghai prefix about his daughter's debt. The call was to be made from a public telephone in the Gaborone bus station. The call was forwarded to Billings in his Hong Kong office.

Billings told Leballo that he represented a party that would cover his daughter's debt if Leballo would meet with him in Johannesburg about the Debswana auction. Leballo asked no questions and readily agreed. He was told a date and flight number and that a ticket had been purchased in his name.

After a couple of scotches, Billings spun his line. China would in fact impose crippling tariffs on De Beers diamonds if the company bid against Eastern Enterprises for the Debswana interest. Therefore, it made sense for Leballo to act in the best interests of De Beers. He should tell the board that he had verified the truth of the rumor and that it would be best for De Beers to withdraw from the bidding. If he did this, Billings told Leballo his client would be grateful to the tune of $50,000. That money, along with the gambling debt, was being advanced by Billings' firm and would be added to the Eastern Enterprises invoice.

Leballo again asked no questions and readily agreed. Billings showed him how to open a numbered Swiss bank account and seeded it with the $50,000, along with the promise of another $100,000 if De Beers withdrew and the Eastern Enterprises bid, which would be supported by a Morgan Stanley appraisal, was accepted.

As the flight attendant served Billings his second scotch, Leballo's substantial bulk was stuffed into a front-row seat on a twelve-seat Air Botswana plane. He was completely unaware that three seats behind him was Baruti Masisi. Baruti knew enough about the sale of Debswana to realize there was no reason for the minister to be in Johannesburg by himself. He would mention it to his father.

CHAPTER 23

A FEW DAYS LATER, Mokgweetsi Masisi's secretary handed him the early edition of the *Botswana Guardian* with the headline "De Beers Withdraws from Debswana Auction." He could not believe what he read. No one had told him about this decision. His government owned 15 percent of De Beers. Obdura Leballo was a board member. How could its board make such a decision without consulting with the government? Without De Beers and with Consolidated's financing in doubt, the Chinese company had the upper hand in the bidding. Masisi understood quite well that competition between De Beers and Consolidated would drive up the price for Debswana.

He told his secretary to track down Leballo. Five minutes later, he was on the line. Masisi punched the blinking button on his phone. "Leballo?"

"Yes, Mr. President."

"What in the hell is going on with De Beers? Why do I have to read about them dropping out of the bidding for Debswana in the newspaper? Why didn't you give me a heads-up?" Masisi was breathing heavily.

"I had no idea the board would take such an action at yesterday's meeting. It wasn't on the agenda. I argued against it, but the consensus was that De Beers could not risk losing the Chinese market. We would be better off as partners with the Chinese."

Masisi was stunned, almost speechless. There was silence on the line.

"What are you talking about? Lose the Chinese market?

"I thought you knew. There was an article in a Chinese newspaper that China was considering a tariff on De Beers diamonds and jewelry. The board was afraid that if we outbid Eastern Enterprises, China would impose the tariff as punishment. If the Chinese bought the Debswana interest, there would be no reason to impose a tariff."

"You, the Botswana Minister of Mines, voted to deprive our country of the bidder that was likely to pay the highest price for our interest," Masisi said incredulously. "You did this knowing that Consolidated was having trouble obtaining financing. You are trying to hand our interest to the Chinese…"

"No, there was no vote. There was a discussion, and a consensus was reached. I did not vote to withdraw. I argued against it, but the others did not want to risk the Chinese tariffs."

Masisi disconnected the call. He was having trouble believing this was happening to his country in the twenty-first century. It wouldn't surprise him if the Chinese were behind Consolidated's financing difficulties. They were taking the competition off the board. No one would bid against them. He couldn't sell under these conditions, but without the proceeds, his plan to restructure the economy of Botswana for the future was in jeopardy.

Mokgweetsi Masisi was not naive. The Chinese were playing him for a fool. The promises of the Belt and Road Initiative included loans for infrastructure that would give better access to exploit the diamond mines, which they would half-own now, then determine how to squeeze De Beers out. Then they could go after the gold mines. They were using their playbook from the Congo, where they owned or financed fifteen of nineteen cobalt mines that produced two-thirds of the world's production of the metal used in lithium ion batteries for computers, cell phones, and electric cars.

He should just cancel the sale and tell China to strangle itself with its Belt, but could he afford to do that? He needed to plan for the future of his country.

Sarah slowly folded her copy of the *Botswana Guardian*. The Chinese had pulled it off. De Beers was out of the bidding. She had been on the phone and on countless Skype conference calls with pension funds and their private debt managers. A letter of intent was being drafted, but there were still several sticking points, particularly the definition of an event of default and what immediate remedies the lenders would have. It was looking good, but you never knew with lawyers.

She called Johannes, who was fixing his first cup of coffee at 6:00 a.m. in New York.

"Good morning, Luc. Big news: It's official. De Beers is out of the Debswana bidding. The tariff threat must have worked."

"Where is the announcement?"

"Today's *Botswana Guardian*. Apparently, the board of directors decided to withdraw from the bidding. The article said that Morgan Stanley is doing an appraisal of Botswana's interest and, according to an unnamed source, are going to lowball the value because the mines need to spend almost a billion dollars for improvements that will prolong the life of the mines and because—get this—De Beers is dropping out of the bidding. It looks like our Chinese friends are getting a made-as-instructed appraisal to justify a lowball bid. Botswana will get screwed six ways from Sunday."

Johannes was silent for a moment.

"Sarah, we need to think about this. It's looking like the pension funds will put up enough money to get the deal done if they approve the price. No one knows that yet."

"Mok isn't a dummy. He knows what China is up to by killing our bank financing and forcing De Beers out of the bidding. Remember how certain Patel was that De Beers would get Botswana's interest? I didn't care for his business ethics, so China using dirty tactics to force him to give up the interest is certainly ironic. As they say, turnabout is fair play."

"I am going to push the lawyers to close the pension fund commitment. Ask around and see what you can find out about what buttons the Chinese are pushing. Maybe call the *Guardian* reporter and see if he has any more information. If he has an inside source, he might give us some useful information about what went on at the De Beers board meeting if you promise him a scoop once we close the pension fund financing."

"Will do. By the way, the Masisis have invited me for dinner Friday to talk about their son, who has a job opportunity in New York. Should I mention that we may be back in the bidding?"

"Call me before you go. Maybe we'll have it buttoned up by then."

CHAPTER 24

SARAH HAD BEEN NERVOUS before her lunch with the Masisis, but they had been so gracious and friendly that her nervousness had dissipated quickly. For dinner at their personal residence, she was nervous for a different reason. She had done some online research and found that their son, Baruti, was an unmarried forty-year-old who had attended the University of Oxford and was well known in the hospitality industry. A trade publication had named him as one of the top twenty up-and-coming African businessmen in the industry. The photographs also revealed that he was well-dressed and handsome. For the dinner, Sarah selected a conservative black pants suit with a white blouse and low-heeled shoes.

To her surprise, the Masisis lived in a modest, tree-shaded two-story house just outside central Gaborone surrounded by an eight-foot wall that had been erected after Masisi was elected president for security purposes. A guard opened the gate and directed her to the house, where the couple greeted her at the door and led Sarah into the living room furnished in the same style as the so-called tent she had inhabited at the Vumbura Plains Camp.

Anne offered Sarah a glass of wine and said, "Mok's family may have sold their camps to Wilderness Safaris, but the safari camp decorating style is in his blood. Baruti should be here shortly. Something came up at the hotel with some guests."

A short time later, Baruti arrived. He was about Sarah's height and wore a dark suit, with a white shirt with a red tie snuggly against his collar. Sarah, like most women, checked his shoes: tasteful black and polished to a high gloss. The photographs hadn't done him justice. He had piercing blue eyes that jumped out of his café au lait-colored skin.

Baruti saw Sarah, and a big smile appeared on his face. Their gazes locked, and she noticed that his eyes stayed on hers. Most men to whom she was introduced gave her a head-to-toe glance. Not Baruti.

Holding out his hand, he said, "Ms. Taylor-Jones, a pleasure to meet you. It is very kind of you to join us. You will find that my mother, although Belgian by birth, has mastered African cooking."

After a few more pleasantries, Baruti said, "Dad, I saw De Beers isn't going to bid on Debswana. That's quite a surprise. I thought we had a seat on their board."

"We do. Obdura Leballo is our representative. This whole thing came as a surprise to us as well."

"Speaking of surprises, I saw him on a flight from Joburg the other day. Did he have government business down there?"

"Not that I know of."

Sarah saw an opening. "If it's any consolation, Luc wanted me to tell you that Consolidated signed a letter of intent with several US pension funds that want to provide financing for our bid, so we are back in the game," she said. "The Chinese won't be the only bidder."

"Fantastic," Masisi answered with a huge smile.

"Hear, hear, enough of business. It's time for dinner," Anne announced. She had prepared an African-style chicken stew and a salad of fresh greens and tomatoes.

"This is marvelous," Sarah said, savoring the rich flavor. "Will you share the recipe?"

Anne pointed to her temple. "It's all in here, but I'll write down the ingredients for you to work with."

It turned out that Baruti was quite a raconteur. Much of the dinner was taken up with his stories about weird hotel guests. Once he started to talk about the Chinese, his father artfully changed the subject. From time to time, Masisi appeared distracted. Sarah got the feeling that the revelation about Obdura Leballo was bothering him.

With dessert, Anne got to what was on her mind. "Sarah, since Baruti was contacted about the Marriott job, we have been paying attention to current events in the United States. It seems that your people of color are being oppressed by white people. We—no, I mean, I—am concerned that my son might have a hard time fitting in at work and making friends. What is it like for biracial people in the States?"

Sarah was not comfortable with the topic, but she had crossed that bridge when she had accepted the dinner invitation, knowing the subject was the primary reason for the invite. She should have politely declined, but she hadn't. Maybe after forty years, she finally wanted to talk about it with some people who did not patronize her.

Three sets of eyes were on her. She knew that whatever she said was going to have a significant impact on whether Baruti accepted the job. Anne had asked the question, so she focused on her as she began after a sip of water.

"The first thing I would like to do is dispel the idea that white people in the States are oppressing people of color. The proposition is preposterous on its face. Americans elected Barack Obama, who identifies as a black man, president. Our current vice president is of mixed race. The mayors of our four largest cities are black. Black and brown people are CEOs and senior officials of Fortune 500 companies. Major athletes and entertainers are people of color and earn millions of dollars. And, closer to home, I am the CFO of a major corporation. This new victim/oppressor construct has been developed solely for political purposes.

"The simple answer to your question is that there is no limit upon what biracial people can accomplish in the United States. Both Obama and Kamala Harris are biracial. Having said that, Obama is called our first black president, and Harris is touted as our first black woman vice president. The question is, why aren't they identified as biracial or of mixed race?"

Sarah took a sip of water, breathed deeply, and tried to answer her own question.

"Frankly, being of mixed race is not comfortable for many people. The clinical description is racial imposter syndrome. They don't know where they fit in. They are not black enough to be black or white enough to be white. People are forced by society to choose one race or the other, usually determined by their skin tone or the curl in their hair. While it's no longer the law, for many years in the States, if you had one drop of black blood, you were considered black.

"What race are singer Mariah Carey's children? Her father is half black and half Venezuelan. Her mother is white of Irish descent. Her children's father is African American seasoned with a drop or two of Mexican blood. Our obsession with skin color as a form of diversity is absurd. Diversity should be based on heritage and culture, not skin color." Sarah looked directly at Baruti. "Having heard all of that, if you move to the United States, do you want to identify as black or white?"

"Both," Baruti said with conviction. "I am white and black, but it's not something I think about."

"That is your power, but there will be pressure to make a choice. With your skin tone, you can go either way."

"That's horrible. No one should have to make that choice," Baruti said, shaking his head. "It forces one to deny one's heritage, to be less than a whole person."

Anne looked like her worst fears had been confirmed. Ever the politician, Masisi's face was inscrutable.

"Sarah, are you happy?" Baruti asked.

Sarah felt the three pairs of eyes on her again. Here was the bottom line.

"I have benefited from affirmative action, but it's a curse that taints everything I've accomplished. Colleges and employers considered me black. My fellow students and coworkers assumed I was less qualified than they were and wouldn't have been in the school or have the job if I hadn't been black. I want and expect to be judged by what I do, not the color of my skin, but it does not always work that way."

There was a brief silence.

"Thank you, Sarah. You have given me a lot to think about," Baruti said, looking at his watch. "Sorry, I've got to get back to the hotel and calm down a few people before they create an international incident." He pushed back his chair.

"What's going on?" his father asked.

Baruti looked at Sarah and back at his father. "Just the usual. The Chinese are being their usual rude selves, and some of my staff are fed up. Say, Sarah, can I give you a lift back to the hotel?"

She had hoped to stay a while longer and discuss Debswana, but it would be up to Masisi to suggest, and he seemed disturbed by something—most likely Obdura Leballo taking a strange trip to Joburg just before the De Beers board decision to drop out of the bidding.

"Sure, that would be great," Sarah said.

CHAPTER 25

BARUTI DROVE AN OLD but clean and well-maintained Lincoln town car. Sarah was surprised when he opened the passenger door for her. This handsome, intelligent man was also a gentleman. He had intrigued Sarah since he had walked into the house.

"Baruti, I appreciate the ride. We didn't get a chance to talk about you at dinner. What is it like being the son of the president of Botswana?"

He smiled and replied, "My father casts a long shadow, and it can be difficult to step outside it and just be myself. It's analogous to what you were saying about not being black or white. People judge me, expect me to have certain political beliefs, want to use me for their own purposes and so forth. I just want to be Baruti, not Mokgweetsi's son. Based on what you said, I think you want to be Sarah. Not black or white Sarah, just Sarah."

Sarah nodded and looked away. "Are you considering moving to New York to get out of your father's shadow?"

"It's one of the reasons at this moment, but my father has four years left for this term, and then he is out. He's not interested in being president for life like Mugabe over in Zimbabwe was. I imagine things will be different then. I know what you told my folks, but what do you think I should do?"

"I don't know enough about you to give you a meaningful answer. I read you are smart, an up-and-comer, as we would say. You are certainly presentable. Being biracial may help you get some promotions as you move up the corporate ladder, but it will also cause a lot of resentment from people who think you took their job because you're black, not because you performed better than they did or are more suitable for the position.

"More importantly, I don't know what you want out of life. You are a single, handsome, successful professional with a great future, but you aren't married and have no children. Nothing wrong with that, but if family life isn't for you, what do you want? A bigger car, a little more money? What?"

Baruti was silent until they pulled into the hotel and he stopped at the front door. "A hard question, Sarah. If you have time for lunch tomorrow, perhaps you can give me your answer to that question."

Sarah was surprised by both the question and the invitation. The doorman opened her door, and she got out. Turning and looking through the passenger window, she said, "Lunch sounds good. Maybe we can exchange answers." She handed him her card. My cell number works here. Call me in the morning to confirm. Thanks for the ride."

Sarah turned and walked into the hotel. What an interesting man.

CHAPTER 26

WANG JIN, TIE ASKEW, flung his suit coat carelessly on the sofa of his hotel suite. He poured himself a scotch before leaning back in a plush chair and propping his feet on the coffee table, oblivious to the scuff marks that his shoes, badly in need of polishing, were leaving on the shiny wooden surface. Tommy stood silently until Wang Jin was settled and then opened a bottle of water.

"Tommy, we've got these bushmen by the balls, and I'm getting ready to squeeze," Wang Jin said after a healthy swallow of his drink.

Tommy waited for more. They had just returned from a meeting with the Morgan Stanley bankers. They had almost finished their appraisal—which, as forewarned, was substantially below the numbers that had been bandied about when the auction had been announced.

"I must admit those *gweilo* lawyers put the hurt on Consolidated. No bank will finance them. Can you believe they bought Leballo? Together with him and the tariff threat, we own the De Beers board. These Botswana bushmen are fucked."

"Our offer will be based on the Morgan Stanley appraisal. They have no choice and will have to sign a letter of intent tying them up like a Uyghur on the way to interrogation. Then we start to negotiate and drop the price by fifteen percent, stringing out payment over five years. We'll pay the idiots with their own money."

Tommy drifted to the window and looked down at the street below. Wang Jin was on a roll. When he got full of himself like this, it was best to let him run on.

One thing Tommy had learned through the years was that business deals weren't over until they closed and the money hit his account.

The suite phone rang, and Tommy dutifully picked it up. He listened for a moment and handed it to Wang Jin, wearing a frown. "It's Johnson from Morgan Stanley."

Wang Jin listened for a moment before leaping to his feet and screaming, "Not on the hotel phone, idiot! Call me back on my cell!"

He downed the last of his scotch and refilled his glass as his cell phone rang from the pocket of his suit coat. Wang Jin angrily grabbed the coat and fumbled for his phone, dropping it in the process. As he picked it up, he spilled some of his drink and accidentally disconnected the call. A string of Chinese curses followed before the phone rang again. "OK, damn it. Start from the beginning."

Wang Jin listened for several minutes, during which time Tommy saw his knuckles growing white from squeezing the phone.

"All right, listen, you will just have to up your valuation so we can get more money from BOC…What? You work for me. You will value the company as I instruct!" Wang Jin said, barely in control of his temper. He listened for almost a minute before angrily answering, "You'll hear from Billings about this. You don't get it. If you want to do business in China, you will do what I say."

Wang Jin threw his phone toward the sofa, but it hit the arm and landed on the floor. He made no move to pick it up.

"Calm down," Tommy soothingly said. "What happened?"

Wang Jin dropped into the overstuffed chair but did not put his feet on the table this time. "Consolidated has gotten financial backing for its bid from some US pension funds. If BOC won't give us more than the Morgan Stanley appraisal, Consolidated could easily outbid us. Those fucks have got to raise their valuation."

Tommy sat across from his friend. "Why not get Billings to lean on the pension funds like he did the banks?" he asked calmly.

"What's wrong with you? US pension funds don't do business in China. There is no leverage. I'll call Billings and find out if he can do anything. If he can't, I'll call my father and see if he can lean on BOC to loan us more than the Morgan Stanley appraisal." Wang Jin leaped up and began pacing around the room. "The *gweilo* bankers have already shared a draft of their appraisal with BOC. They would have to find some reason to raise their valuation now."

Tommy stroked his thin goatee thoughtfully. "The bankers said one of the reasons for a low appraisal was the absence of other bidders. Now that Consolidated is back in the game, maybe they can use that to up the valuation."

"It's possible," Wang Jin replied. "Why don't you go talk to the *gweilo* bankers and see if they'll up their appraisal? I'll call Billings and see if he has any leverage with the US pension funds."

CHAPTER 27

IT WAS BARELY ABOVE freezing when Masisi arrived at the Presidential Palace just after sunrise. The echo of his rapid footsteps in the deserted marble-tiled hallway chased him into his office, where he was going to confirm his suspicion that Leballo had betrayed him and the country.

His administrative assistant, who had been advised to show up early and be ready for a long day, hung his topcoat on the rack in his office and handed Masisi a cup of freshly brewed coffee. The first call of the morning was to Arthur De Jong, an old friend and De Beers board member.

After the call, Masisi had to use all his will power to control his anger. According to De Jong, the board had previously discussed the newspaper article about a possible punitive tariff but dismissed it because there was only a single unnamed source. They wanted confirmation from named governmental sources before taking it seriously.

Leballo had told the board that he had recently spoken with several of his Chinese counterparts, and they had told him the Chinese government was behind Eastern Enterprises. If it didn't win the bidding, the Chinese would not only slap punitive tariffs on De Beers diamonds, but would withdraw from its Belt and Road Initiative in Botswana. There was a lot of back-and-forth among the board members. However, Leballo told them that Masisi felt so strongly about the potential for the Belt and Road Initiative that perhaps it would be best if De Beers withdrew from the bidding.

Masisi was beyond furious. Leballo had lied to him and the board. That was a fact. What he didn't know was why. His next call was to the Ministry of Mines, where the travel office had no record of Leballo traveling to Johannesburg on government business. Then he called the Ministry of Defense, Justice and Security for a check on the minister's personal credit cards. They confirmed that his cards had not been used to purchase air tickets to Johannesburg. Who had paid? A call to Air Botswana revealed that the ticket had been purchased by a law firm based in Hong Kong.

To Masisi's surprise, the security inspector told him that an investigation into the gambling debts of Leballo's daughter in Shanghai had been terminated because her debts had just been satisfied. All the security inspector was able to ascertain was that the debt had paid. How—be it cash or forgiveness—was said to be propriety information. This was all very strange since the woman had a low-level clerical job in the Consulate of Botswana in Singapore. There might be some other explanation for her debt suddenly disappearing and her father lying to get De Beers out of the bidding, but bribery was the obvious answer.

The money was probably hidden in Leballo's bank account somewhere in the world. Masisi did not think he was stupid enough to directly pay off his daughter's debt with money he couldn't explain. The Chinese must have taken care of it one way or another.

Should he confront Leballo? Did it matter? Had China really threatened to impose punitive tariffs, or was the unsourced story planted as part of the plot to sideline De Beers? Would the board have reached a different decision without input from Leballo, who had validated the threat?

The more he thought about it, he should have known better. The Chinese were all smiles, but they were in the world for themselves. The Belt and Road Initiative was a giant con job, and he had fallen for it. He could see the future: go along to get along, or China would pull the plug if they ever came through on any of their promises. What was he going to do?

Masisi called in his chief of staff.

"Robert, I want you to coordinate an assessment of the legal and practical consequences if China stops funding and/or participating in the Belt and Road Initiative projects. Also assess the same if we kill the projects. I want an answer in forty-eight hours."

"Yes, sir."

CHAPTER
28

SARAH WAS IMPRESSED WHEN Baruti pulled out her chair at the table50two restaurant and held it for her to sit. Men had stopped doing things like that in New York, and she had forgotten what it was like to be treated like a lady. They both ordered bottled water and chatted harmlessly about the view as Sarah perused the menu. She finally played it safe and asked Baruti to order for them.

Sarah noticed a Chinese man and two white men who had the look of American Wall Streeters across the rooftop restaurant. "It looks like your hotel is popular with those of us in the hunt for Debswana," she said, nodding discreetly toward the men.

"Yes. Those two Americans are from Morgan Stanley, and the Chinese guy is here with Wang Jin, the CCP chairman's son. Do you have any investment bankers coming for a due diligence review?"

"No. The Ministry of Mines provided the pension fund advisors with reams of data, and they are relying on us to do the on-site due diligence to keep the costs down."

Lunch arrived. While they ate, they talked about African food and international air travel after the COVID-19 pandemic. Sarah found the conversation effortless. She never had to reach for something to say. They were comfortably enjoying each other's company.

Over fresh fruit and coffee, Baruti said, "OK, Sarah, it's time for your answer. What do you want out of life?"

"Oh no, Mr. Masisi, I asked you first. How can I be your life coach if I don't know what you want to achieve?"

Out of the corner of her eye, she saw Wang Jin storm into the restaurant. Baruti also noticed the angry entrance. They both looked across the room, where Wang Jin jerked a chair away from an adjoining table and pulled it up to the table with his colleagues, blocking the aisle. He began virtually shouting at the two bankers. They could hear the anger in his voice but not the precise words. One of the bankers raised his voice in return. By now, everyone in the restaurant was watching what was turning into a confrontation.

Tommy put his hand on Wang Jin's arm, but he angrily shook it off. A waiter tentatively approached the men and tried to say something. Wang Jin shouted at him to go away.

Baruti looked at Sarah and said, "Excuse me."

Baruti walked up to the table and said, "Excuse me, gentlemen. Please lower your voices. You are disturbing the other guests. And you, sir." He looked directly at Wang Jin. "You must move your chair from the aisle. We can move you to…"

"Shut up and go away! Leave us alone, you ignorant bush bunny!" Wang Jin shouted.

Baruti took note of Wang Jin's dilated pupils and looked at Tommy. "I think it best if you take this man and leave," he said firmly.

Tommy nodded, and he and the bankers began to stand.

"Sit down, you fools! We are going to finish this," Wang Jin snapped.

The other men hovered between sitting and standing, clearly embarrassed. Wang Jin rose abruptly and moved menacingly toward Baruti. Sarah was afraid that he was going to hit Baruti. There was complete silence in the restaurant.

Baruti did not give ground. "Leave now, or I will have security escort you from the premises," he said in a voice as cold as ice.

Tommy took Wang Jin firmly by the arm and, with the help of the bankers, ushered him out of the restaurant. On the way out, Wang Jin looked back over his shoulder at Baruti with a murderous expression and mouthed a threat in Chinese.

Baruti faced the room. "My apologies for the interruption, ladies and gentlemen. For those who would like a dessert or perhaps another drink, it is compliments of the management," he said with a big smile.

The diners turned back to their meals and conversation about the rude Chinese visitor. Baruti returned to Sarah and apologized for the interruption.

"The other morning, I had to roust that man off one of the sofas in the reception area where he had passed out. Just now, his pupils were so dilated there was almost no color in his eyes. He must be on drugs."

Sarah nodded. "From what I've read about him in the press, he survives by trading off his father's name. He's a big, spoiled brat with a vile temper. I guess he just proved it," she said.

"He has certainly alienated most of staff. I have a lot of experience with unpleasant guests and from time-to-time unruly ones, but this Wang takes the cake, so to speak. He is wound so tightly I won't be surprised if he snaps. But enough about him. I must get back to work now, but let me take you to dinner tonight to make up for how this lunch was interrupted. I'll take you somewhere we won't run into that man or his friends. Very casual and lots of fun."

"Perfect," Sarah replied.

She spent the afternoon in her room catching up on what was happening with Consolidated in her absence. Occasionally, her thoughts wandered between the professional way Baruti had handled Wang Jin and the drug-fueled anger the Chinese scion had displayed. A man with an uncontrollable temper hopped up on drugs could prove very dangerous—even deadly.

CHAPTER 29

WANG JIN, TOMMY, AND the Morgan Stanley bankers were silent as the elevator descended to the lobby. When they exited, the lead banker said, "Tommy, step over here with me for a moment."

Wang Jin protested but seemed to be winding down.

"You, sir, wait here with Arthur," the banker said.

Wang Jin tried to follow Tommy, but Arthur stepped in front of him. Arthur Rock had been an All-Big Ten linebacker at Ohio State ten years ago and still spent a lot of time in the gym. When his six-foot, very solid, two-hundred-pound body blocked Wang Jin with the attitude of a man who would relish a confrontation, the message got through to Wan Jin's drug-addled brain. He turned and pushed the elevator button, saying he was going to his room.

The lead banker shook his head in disgust.

"Tommy, we've completed our work and are finalizing our appraisal. If that man goes off the rails one more time, I'm going to have to put something about him in the appraisal. He's not out client; we were hired by the Billings firm, who told us their client is the Bank of China, not your colleague. Arthur and I are right on the edge with that guy. He's trying to intimidate us. Morgan Stanley does not do made-as-instructed appraisals, and we are not going to change our opinion to accommodate him. I don't care if he's the son of the chairman of the Chinese Communist Party. Under no circumstances am I going jeopardize my reputation to make this guy happy. Am I clear?"

"Crystal," Tommy said. "Look, I'm sorry and apologize for Wang Jin. He's under a lot of stress with this deal."

"Tommy, I'm not sure, but given the way he was acting upstairs, he may be drunk or on drugs. Whatever—he's borderline out of control. Do you know that the manager of this hotel, the man who asked us to leave, is the son of the president of Botswana?"

Tommy's eyes widened in surprise. "No, I didn't know that. This is terrible. He's going to have to apologize to him. Grovel if necessary…but I don't know if I can get him to do that," he said in a voice full of uncertainty.

"It's not my problem, but you had better do something. You can be sure that Baruti Masisi knows who Wang Jin is. As I understand it, China is pushing hard with its Belt and Road Initiative here. Mr. Wang isn't helping anything. OK, enough. Our appraisal will be done shortly."

The bankers, who were staying at another hotel, left, and Tommy headed for Wang Jin's room. He didn't answer the door. Tommy went into his adjoining room and tried the connecting door. It was unlocked.

Wang Jin was passed out full length on the bed. He had not even taken off his shoes. His wallet was on the coffee table, where a credit card lay next to particles of white powder. Tommy did not have to guess what the powder was. He quietly returned to his room and locked the connecting door.

Tommy paced the room. He had to do something. Wang Jin was spiraling out of control. He needed to get him out of the country before something terrible happened.

CHAPTER 30

OUTSIDE MASISI'S OFFICE WINDOW, the setting sun splashed a palette of oranges, reds, and blues across wispy clouds, creating one of nature's gifts to mankind. The magnificent spectacle was completely lost on Masisi, who was sitting at his office desk reading the Belt and Road Initiative termination report he had requested.

Masisi was a linear thinker who preferred to make notes documenting his thought process. Pen in hand, he began to write on an empty pad. What was he going to do about the bribery of Leballo? He would send his information to the prosecutors. Leballo might be charged criminally, or he might reach a deal to resign without jail time. Either way, the justice system would grind him up.

The treachery of his minister was the least of his problems. The elephant in the room was China. Masisi had planned to use the proceeds from the Debswana sale together with the Belt and Road Initiative financing to align Botswana's economy with the Information Age. How would China react if he barred Eastern Enterprises from the bidding? Wang Jin would undoubtedly complain to his father that his company had been treated unfairly. Would that be enough for China to kill the Belt and Road Initiative in Botswana?

The report concluded that there was alternate financing available through the World Bank and various international development programs, but the rate of interest was higher, and time would be lost applying for the financing. Bottom line, if China pulled the Belt and Road Initiative financing, it would cost the country in money and time.

He drew a line across the page and began to make more notes.

What, if anything, to do about Eastern Enterprises? There was zero chance the prosecutors could prove the company was behind the bribe, even though it was obvious. Or was it? Eastern Enterprises could argue that it was equally plausible that Consolidated was behind the bribe because it also benefited from De Beers's withdrawal from the bidding. If both Eastern and Consolidated had a motive to bribe Leballo, what other evidence pointed to either of them as the culprit? The lawyer would never have disclosed the client behind the bribe to Leballo, who probably didn't care where the money had come from as long as he had gotten it. Regardless, he could not believe anything the man told him. He was likely to lie to protect the source of the bribe.

According to Sarah Taylor-Jones, China was behind the unwillingness of banks to finance Consolidated's bid. Bullying was the hallmark of China's dealings with foreign business entities wanting to do business there. The news article stating that China was considering punitive tariffs on De Beers was either true or had been planted by Eastern.

The Hong Kong law firm that had funneled the bribe to Leballo had a long history of working for the Chinese government and Chinese businesses. It had never worked with Consolidated. It would be a conflict of interest to work for Consolidated while it was representing Eastern and could jeopardize future Chinese business.

Weighed against all the evidence of Eastern's complicity, was Consolidated's naked motive without any supporting evidence sufficient to create a reasonable doubt as to the source of the bribe?

He was the jury and found the case against Eastern convincing, but there was another problem: politics.

If he barred Eastern Enterprises from the bidding, the only bidder would be Consolidated, which was run by his old friend Luc Johannes. His political enemies could allege a conflict of interest and spice it up with the fact that Masisi's son had been seen out on the town with Consolidated's beautiful CFO. Nothing like a little sexual intrigue to get social media and the tabloids in a feeding frenzy. It would be naive to think Wang Jin wouldn't claim that Consolidated had a motive to bribe the minister and Eastern was barred from bidding because Sarah had seduced his son.

Perhaps if Eastern Enterprises was barred from the bidding, De Beers would return and would in fact be the strongest bidder. That would blunt any conflict-of-interest claims. But he could not be sure De Beers would reenter the bidding and risk punitive Chinese tariffs. Would China really penalize De Beers and raise the price of diamonds to its citizens because the son of the chairman of the Chinese Communist Party got caught breaking the law? If the truth got out, it would not play well in China, and surely Chairman Wang had political enemies. The potential for a punitive tariff was De Beers's problem, but Botswana was a 15 percent stockholder in the company.

He was the president of Botswana. His decisions and actions had to be solidly grounded in what was best for his country, personal considerations aside.

It was full dark when Masisi's administrative assistant buzzed him that he was leaving if not needed any more that evening. Masisi now had three pages of handwritten notes.

For whom was the law firm acting when it had bribed Leballo? Eastern.

Should whomever the law firm was acting for be barred from the bidding? Yes.

Is there sufficient evidence that Eastern was behind the bribery? Yes.

If Eastern is barred, will China retaliate against Botswana by ending the Belt and Road? Unknown.

Can Botswana find alternate financing to restructure its economy? Probably.

Will De Beers reenter the bidding if Eastern is forced out? Unknown.

The only reason not to bar Eastern is the possible loss of China's Belt and Road financing. The financing is in the form of loans that must be repaid. Other financing is probably available at a somewhat higher price with more stringent terms.

Can I turn a blind eye and allow Eastern to acquire a half interest in Botswana's diamond mines as a result of unethical and illegal business practices?

As president, I represent my country. I have sworn to uphold our laws. Shall I sell our soul for a loan of forty pieces of silver that has to be repaid?

While Masisi was deliberating the fate of Eastern Enterprises, Baruti and Sarah were feasting on seafood in the romantic garden at Caravela Portuguese Restaurant located in a quiet neighborhood in northern Gaborone. There was perfect weather, party lights twinkling throughout the lush garden, a secluded candle-lit table, a fine bottle of crisp white wine, and a man who once again proved himself to be a gentleman as well as a gifted conversationalist. Sarah felt like she was the heroine in a romance novel. Not that she read romance novels, but this must have been how the writer set the scene.

When they returned to the hotel, Baruti left his car in the front drive, creating conflicting emotions in Sarah. If he wasn't going to try to sleep with her, she could relax, except down not very deep, she wanted him to try. It had been a long time since she had sex and a much longer time since she had enjoyed it. If they kissed, well, one could never tell.

She took his arm and held it close as the handsome couple crossed the lobby to the elevator. Out of the corner of her eye, Sarah saw the desk attendant watching them. What she did not see was Wang Jin also watching them from behind a massive planter full of ferns with a malevolent expression.

When they arrived at her room, Sarah slid her room card into the lock and opened the door. Then she surprised herself. "Would you like to come in for a nightcap?" she asked.

Baruti took her hands and kissed her on the cheek. "Very much so, but there are no secrets in this hotel. Let's do dinner tomorrow here. I want to talk to you about a quick trip to Victoria Falls."

He smiled softly, dropped her hands, and pushed the door open for her to enter. Then Baruti walked to the elevator with a spring in his step, humming his favorite tune.

Sarah closed the door and leaned back against it like a schoolgirl, closed her eyes, and softly touched her cheek. After a moment, she changed into a T-shirt and shorts before powering up her computer. In the search bar, she typed, *Victoria Falls*.

CHAPTER
31

THE NEXT MORNING, WANG Jin slept late in preparation for the seminal day in his life. The Morgan Stanley bankers would finally hand over their report, which would tell him how much he was allowed to bid for the Debswana interest.

As he was getting dressed, the local news was on the television in his room. The droning anchor tapped his earpiece and was silent for a moment. Then he announced, "We have breaking news. Obdura Leballo, the Minister of Mines, was arrested an hour ago on corruption charges." Turning to his teleprompter, he continued. "This shocking news comes as the government is entertaining bids for its fifty percent interest in the Debswana Diamond Company. President Masisi has issued a press release stating that the deadline for bids has been extended for thirty days. This is a developing story. We will continue to update it as more information becomes available."

Wang Jin's phone rang. It was Tommy, who had seen the same broadcast. They didn't know what to think about this development and agreed to meet in the lobby rather than talk on the unsecured hotel telephone line. They had just begun their conversation in the lobby when two official-looking men in dark suits and ties approached them.

"Mr. Wang, Mr. Chun, we are agents with the Botswana Ministry of Justice and would like to speak with you for a moment, if you please." Both men opened their wallets and showed the Chinese their credentials.

Neither Wang Jin nor Tommy spoke. They just looked at each other. After an awkward silence, Wang Jin answered, "We are very busy. What is this about?"

"Let's step into the hotel conference room for a little privacy," the taller man said.

They followed the agents across the lobby and down a carpeted hallway, which ended at a conference room where there was a large mahogany table, a flat-screen television on one wall, and a chalk board on the opposite wall. A credenza for refreshments was empty.

Tommy could feel his armpits oozing sweat that ran down his sides. There was no way this could be about anything but the bribery of Obdura Leballo. Somehow, the government had found out. How much did they know? Would he be arrested?

The agents motioned them to the far side of the table, where they took seats and waited expectantly. Both were well schooled in interrogation techniques and said nothing waiting for the agents to speak. The shorter agent removed a small tape recorder from his pocket and placed it in the middle of the table. He turned it on and spoke the agent's names, Wang Jin's and Tommy's names, the date, time, and location. He then asked, "Do you have any objection to this meeting being recorded."

"Do we have a choice?" Wang Jin snapped.

From long experience, Tommy knew that the tone of Wang Jin's response was a precursor to a full-fledged explosion.

"No," the unsmiling taller agent said.

Wang Jin started to reply, but Tommy squeezed his forearm in a vicelike grip. Wang Jin took the unsubtle hint and closed his mouth. Tommy relaxed his grip and sighed with relief. Maybe for once, the arrogant prick could control his temper.

The taller agent put his elbows on the table and steepled his fingers under his chin. He said, "As you probably know by now, this morning, we arrested Obdura Leballo, the Minister of Mines, on corruption charges; specifically, your lawyer bribed him to manipulate De Beers to withdraw from bidding for the Debswana Diamond Company. Your motive was to allow you to purchase our country's interest in the company at a reduced price, thereby defrauding the people of Botswana. That, gentlemen, is a very serious crime, for which there are serious penalties."

Both agents stared at Wang Jin and Tommy as the Chinese remained silent, staring back and maintaining eye contact.

"Including the death penalty," the taller agent said in a level voice.

Tommy broke eye contact and looked at the table. Wang Jin stared back angrily, then pointed at the tall agent and exploded.

"You can't prove anything! I am the son of the chairman of the Chinese Communist Party! You had better be very careful throwing around false accusations. China has multiple Belt and Road projects in development or under construction in this country. You are not going to do anything to us! It would be an affront to China, and my father will terminate each of those projects if we are detained for even one day on false, unprovable charges," Wang Jin spat, his insufferable arrogance infusing every ounce of his body language and tone of voice.

Tommy made no effort to control Wang Jin and continued to stare at the table with slumped shoulders. He slipped down in his chair in an unconscious effort to make himself smaller while wishing he was anywhere but sitting in this room with Wang Jin.

The taller agent had taken his elbows off the table to be farther away from Wang Jin's long, carefully manicured finger. "Do you have anything else to say?" he replied in a calm, level voice.

Wang Jin stood, putting one hand on the table and continuing to point at the agent with the other. "This is total bullshit! You can contact my local attorney if you wish to speak with me. Whoever sent you on this fool's errand should be fired. In fact, I am going to make it my mission in life to have both of you morons fired! You can't treat China and the CCP this way."

Wang Jin took a step toward the door, glaring at the taller agent, who removed a GLOCK 17 from under his coat and placed it on the table.

"Sit down, Mr. Wang."

Wang Jin stopped in mid-stride with his eyes focused on the gun, but he did not sit.

Tommy prepared himself to slide under the table.

"You are not leaving this room, Mr. Wang. This is Botswana. It is our country. It is not China nor are we under China's thumb. Now sit down or I will shoot you." The agent again spoke in a level voice, leaving no doubt that he was serious.

Wang Jin continued to walk. The agent's hand moved toward the GLOCK.

Tommy reached out and grabbed Wang Jin's arm. "Jin, sit down. He is serious."

Wang Jin sat slowly, not taking his eyes off the gun. When he was seated, the agent returned the GLOCK to its holster under his suit coat.

"Do you have any objection to our continued recording of this session, Mr. Chun?" the shorter agent asked again.

Tommy moved his head from side to side almost imperceptibly.

"Very well, gentlemen. President Masisi has graciously decided to allow you to save face by immediately announcing your withdrawal from the Debswana bidding and leaving the country tonight."

He removed a letter-size piece of paper from his pocket and handed it to Tommy. Still shaken by the appearance of the gun, he took it with a slightly trembling hand and opened it. He glanced at it, then handed it to Wang Jin, who read it and dropped it on the table.

The document stated: *In light of its other commitments, Eastern Enterprises has reevaluated bidding for Botswana's interest in the Debswana Diamond Company and has determined that it is in the best interests of Eastern Enterprises to withdraw from the bidding. We wish Botswana a successful sale.*

The taller agent said, "If you agree to withdraw voluntarily, we will release this statement to the press this afternoon. You will have no further comment while you are in Botswana. If you ignore this instruction, you will be arrested for corruption and held in the Gaborone Central Prison until your, trial which may take several years. We have made reservations on the 8 p.m. Qatar Airways flight to Doha for you."

Wang Jin started to protest, but the agent held up his hand and barked, "Silence! If you chose not to withdraw of your own accord, the government of Botswana will publicly announce in time for the evening news that Eastern Enterprises has been prohibited from bidding for Debswana due to its actual and attempted interference with the sale. I will arrest you and hold you in isolation until I deliver you to the Qatar flight in handcuffs, which will be filmed by local television stations and released on the internet. Do you understand your choices?"

Tommy nodded in the affirmative. Wang Jin seethed with anger.

"Each of you will answer audibly."

Tommy said yes immediately. Wang Jin said nothing until Tommy grabbed his arm and whispered furiously in his ear. Then he whispered, "I understand."

The taller agent nodded at them. "You are confined to this hotel until you travel to the airport to leave the country." He pushed up his sleeve and looked at his watch. "It's eleven now. You will give us your answer by noon. Stay in this room until you decide. We will wait in the lobby."

The shorter agent turned off the tape recorder and pocketed it. Both men left the room and closed the door.

An audible sigh escaped Tommy's lips. "We are so screwed," he said, leaning back in his chair.

Wang Jin jumped up and began pacing heavily around the room. "Fuck. Screwed doesn't begin to tell the story. This is a minor inconvenience for a rich guy like you. Daddy Bigbucks will replace the small amount you invested in Eastern Enterprises. I put everything I had into the company."

"How much is left?" Tommy asked tentatively.

"Not much. I spent the last of it on airfare and this hotel. BOC is supposed to fund some start-up money tomorrow. Fuck, fuck, fuck these bush bunnies to the eighteenth generation." Wang Jin was lying. He still had his credit cards and $70,000 in US currency under the false bottom in his suitcase for an emergency. He continued to pace. "It's those dog fucking lawyers. Big shots couldn't leave well enough alone. Consolidated was dead. De Beers couldn't risk Chinese tariffs. There was no need to bribe that guy. It's all their fault!" he shouted, slamming his hands on the polished table.

"Shut up! This room may be bugged," Tommy said.

Wang Jin dropped into a chair and put his elbows on the table and his head in his hands. "Quiet! I have to think," he snapped. "What am I going to tell my father? He'll ridicule me until the end of time. He'll say I caused him to lose face to the Africans. It'll be horrible."

Several minutes of silence followed. With his head still in his hands, he spoke as if to himself. "It has all been so wrong. Losing face to the cunt from Consolidated and the bush bunny hotel manager. It's all so unforgivable. They must pay, and I must get my money back. I will even the score. I will make them pay."

Tommy had had enough of Wang Jin. He had forgotten that Consolidated had gotten new financing, and he had approved approaching Leballo. While the lawyers had come up with the ideas, Wang Jin had condoned them. Yet he refused to take any responsibility and was hung up on Sarah Taylor-Jones and Baruti Masisi. This was not going to end well, and he wasn't going down with the ship.

It was time for a decision, but there was really no choice: they had to withdraw.

"Come on, it's time to tell them we will withdraw. There is no other choice."

"You tell them. I might punch the tall guy if he gives me that know-it-all look again."

"All right, I will. Suck it up. We are Chinese. We cannot give them the satisfaction of looking defeated, beaten by Africans."

The two men strode briskly down the hall, heads up, inscrutable expressions fixed in place. The agents stood as they approached.

Tommy said, "You may inform Debswana that Eastern Enterprises is withdrawing from the bidding."

"Very well," the taller agent said. "Be here in the lobby with your luggage at five. You may return to your rooms."

CHAPTER 32

WANG JIN AND TOMMY parted company outside their rooms, each lost in thought.

Wang Jin's inscrutable expression disappeared as soon as his door closed, replaced by outrage. This could not be happening to him. The Debswana deal was going to propel him onto the world stage. His plan to have Eastern Enterprises leverage the Debswana acquisition into a massive conglomerate that acquired control of the minerals necessary to manufacture electric car batteries was gone. When his father retired, or perhaps earlier, Wang Jin would have been able to grease the necessary palms to step into the old man's shoes and rule China. He would be the founder of a new dynasty.

Now it was all gone, destroyed. Gone was the seed money he had invested Eastern. Over $1 million.

He kneeled at the coffee table and poured some white powder on the surface, then formed it into a straight line. After rolling up a US dollar bill, he snorted the coke. His heart was off to the races as the drug kicked in, bringing an intense feeling of alertness, energy, and power. Less than a minute later, he rejected the humiliation of being escorted onto a plane out of Botswana like a common criminal. He would leave Botswana when he chose to do so. He would plan. He would have revenge, and he would get his money back. Then he would return to Hong Kong in triumph.

His wallet was lying on the table with the slip of paper that contained the phone number of the local 14K triad leader poking out. It was an omen.

Wang Jin took out his cell phone and dialed.

Tommy dropped into his desk chair and held out his hand. It still trembled. Wang Jin had almost gotten them shot. News of their withdrawal from the bidding would soon be on the internet. This was something his father had to hear from him first.

It took almost an hour for him to compose an encrypted email to his father reporting in detail about Wang Jin's increasing drug use and erratic behavior culminating in the ill-fated bribe of Leballo and the meeting with the federal agents. He did not fail to include the agent pulling his gun and threatening to shoot Wang Jin. Tommy was sure to write about how he had been a calming influence and had saved Wang Jin from being shot and Chairman Wang Chen losing face with his son's arrest for corruption. He had no doubt his father would forward the email to the chairman.

Tommy ordered a sandwich from room service and began packing. It was close to four in the afternoon when his iPad buzzed with an incoming message. His father requested that he check on Wang Jin and have him contact Wang Chen, who had been trying to reach him by voice mail, text, and email for over an hour without any success.

Tommy knocked on the connecting door. There was no answer. He tried the door. It was locked. He called Wang Jin on the room phone. There was no answer.

Something was seriously wrong. He went into the hall and opened the door to Wang Jin's room with his duplicate key card.

Wang Jin was not there. A few items of clothing hung forlornly in the closet. His big suitcase was open on the bed with its false bottom open.

Tommy went into the bathroom. All of Wang Jin's toiletry items were gone. He returned to the bedroom and searched for Wang Jin's backpack. It was gone too. His laptop computer and phone were gone. He looked carefully at the glass-topped table and saw a slight residue of white powder. He got a damp Kleenex, wiped it up, and flushed the tissue. No reason to make a bad situation worse.

Wang Jin was gone. Had he been arrested, kidnapped, or decided to run from the police? They had agreed to the government's demands, so there was no reason to arrest him. While kidnapping was always a possibility for the offspring of the chairman of the Chinese Communist Party, a kidnapper wouldn't have bothered with toiletries and packed clothes for his victim. Running made no sense. Where would he go? What did he expect to accomplish? Tommy had no idea why, but Wang Jin must have run.

Tommy returned to his room and finished packing while he considered his options. He did not like any of them. Finally, he sent an encrypted text to his father that Wang Jin had disappeared. He was being forced to leave Botswana that evening and could not search for him. If he found out anything else before his plane left, he would let him know.

It was a good choice. It was time to distance himself from Wang Jin. He needed to get out of Botswana before Wang Jin's cocaine-addled brain ran him off the rails completely. He closed his suitcase, shouldered his backpack, and headed for the lobby.

The agents were waiting for him. Tommy played dumb and said he had knocked on Wang Jin's door and called him but had gotten no answer. The shorter agent stopped at the front desk for a key card and headed for the elevator. He returned a few minutes later and spoke quietly to the taller agent, who turned to Tommy.

"Your friend has taken most of his things and disappeared. Where did he go?"

Tommy did his best to look surprised and confused, which wasn't too hard. "I have no idea. Perhaps he was kidnapped?"

The taller agent shook his head in disgust and looked at his watch. "All right. We'll find him, but you, sir, are still leaving. Come with me."

Tommy settled in the back of a black town car and heard the doors lock. He sighed with relief. In a couple of hours, he would be out of Botswana and away from Wang Jin.

CHAPTER
33

BARUTI WAS WAITING WHEN Sarah arrived for dinner at table two wearing her long khaki skirt with a white tank top covered by an unbuttoned short-sleeved light-green safari shirt. He jumped up and pulled her chair from the table for her to sit. He sat down and said, "You are absolutely stunning tonight."

Sarah did not feel stunning. She was exhausted after spending the day in her room on the phone with New York and Amsterdam, revising a draft of Consolidated's annual report and finalizing the company's bid for Debswana. She was tired of her clothes. When packing, she had not planned on romantically dining with a handsome African man. She only had conservative business clothes and her two safari outfits from which she could mix and match.

"Why, thank you. I didn't pack for wonderful dinners with a handsome man. I'm glad this works."

Baruti leaned across the table and whispered conspiratorially just loud enough for her to hear, "Have you heard what happened today?"

"I haven't heard anything. I spent the day working in my room."

"Then I have big, serious news for you. Obdura Leballo, the Minister of Mines, has been arrested for corruption. Eastern Enterprises has withdrawn from the bidding for Debswana. I haven't been able to speak to my father, but the rumor has it that Eastern bribed the minister to keep De Beers out of the bidding."

Sarah was visibly stunned and momentarily speechless. Then she said as if she could not believe what she was saying, "That means Consolidated is the only bidder for Debswana."

Baruti held up his hand. "Maybe, but my father has extended the bidding for thirty days. I imagine he hopes De Beers will reconsider and join the bidding."

Sarah's mind was jumping from issue to issue. "Baruti, we need to eat quickly. I must call New York."

Baruti flagged down the waiter, and they ordered salads. Then he said, "There's more. Wang Jin and his friend Tommy Chun have been ordered out of the country." He pushed up his sleeve and looked at his watch. "In half an hour, Chun will be on a plane, but you won't believe this: Wang Jin has disappeared. He left his business clothes and an empty suitcase in his room. He took a few casual clothes, electronics, and personal items in a backpack and left the hotel. An all-points order has been issued for his arrest."

"You should be able to find him by tracking his phone unless he pulled the battery."

"That's above my pay grade."

"This is unbelievable. I can't get my head around all the implications," Sarah said.

Their food arrived. Baruti ate in silence while Sarah picked at her salad, lost in thought. From time to time, she glanced at him without saying anything. As soon as he finished eating, Sarah pushed back from the table.

"I'm sorry, but I must get on the phone and talk this over with Luc. Is it all right if we reschedule talking about Victoria Falls until tomorrow night?"

"No problem. Let's go back to Caravela, if that's OK. Good food and great atmosphere."

"Fantastic. Thank you so much. I'm really looking forward to the restaurant… and you, of course," Sarah said, smiling. She stood and headed for the elevator.

Baruti remained seated, ordered coffee, and sat for a while thinking about Sarah Taylor-Jones. Here was an intelligent, beautiful woman who seemed interested in him. That was good.

Beyond good, but hold on to your heart. She's American and just visiting. But what if I took the Marriott job and moved to New York?

Back in her room, Sarah first searched the internet for any reporting on the day's events. She found less than what Baruti had told her. She wasted no time getting Johannes on the phone. They discussed what had happened and its implications for Consolidated.

"You could call Mok and ask him what's going on," Sarah suggested.

"I could, but then I would be using our friendship to further my business interests. It would put both of us in an awkward position. If the call was revealed, no matter how harmless, his political opponents could allege a conflict of interest and make Mok's life miserable. Our relationship seems to be off the radar for now, and I'd like to keep it that way as long as possible."

"OK, I get it. I think there is a real chance De Beers will reenter the bidding. Our current offer was put together with Eastern Enterprises as the only other bidder. If De Beers stays out, we could lower the bid significantly. In essence, it would be take it or leave it," Sarah said.

"Mok is no dummy. He will not take less than a fair price for Debswana. My guess is that one of two things will happen, or maybe both. De Beers submits a bid. If it stays out, I think Mok will set a minimum price for the auction. He has already required that bids must be all cash up front. I think we stay with our bid for the time being. If De Beers comes on the playing field, we can reevaluate."

"Do you think I should come back to New York? Things seem to be under control there but are rather fluid here."

"Stay a little while longer and let the dust settle on this Eastern Enterprises business. Wang Jin's father may try to pressure Mok."

"Before you go, I should tell you that I've been seeing Mok's son, Baruti, and we have been talking about a quick trip to Victoria Falls. Do you have any problems with either?"

Johannes's broad smile was reflected in the tone of his voice. "I have known Baruti for what seems like forever. He is a fine young man. I am sure Mok can handle any political fallout. Now, I have to say that you would be a fool to miss an opportunity to see Victoria Falls, and you are not a fool. Seize the moment and have a wonderful time.

"Keep me informed about our business matters."

Both disconnected the call with big smiles.

CHAPTER 34

THE DAY WAS FULL of sunshine and promise when Masisi arrived at the Presidential Palace. He smiled at the guards and the receptionist in his office suite before hanging up his suit coat and accepting a fresh cup of coffee from his administrative assistant.

He was expecting a difficult day. The press was now all over the arrest of Leballo and Eastern Enterprises's withdrawal from the Debswana bidding. His press secretary was drafting a statement that he would have to approve. More importantly, Wang Jin was still missing. Security Services Botswana had been unable to locate him by signals from his electronics. Apparently, the batteries had been removed or the devices destroyed. Masisi would not be surprised if he received a call from Wang Chen about his son's whereabouts. Any fallout regarding the Belt and Road Initiative would probably come after Wang Jin was safely back in China.

"What's going on this morning?" he asked his administrative assistant.

"The press is clamoring for a statement. They keep calling me and Security Services for comment. It would be helpful to get out an official statement to feed the wolves. Also, the Chinese ambassador's secretary called a few minutes ago asking if we know Wang Jin's whereabouts. I told him we did not. He said the ambassador wants to talk to you at your earliest convenience."

Masisi nodded. "Is that it?"

"So far, but it's early."

"I'll start with the press release, then the ambassador."

A few minutes later, his press secretary handed him a draft of the press release for the Debswana mess. Masisi revised and rerevised the press release before he finally turned it over to his administrative assistant for release. It stated:

"I have been informed that Obdura Leballo, the Minister of Mines, has been arrested for corruption. The arrest warrant alleges that Leballo accepted illegal payments to influence the bidding for Botswana's interest in the Debswana Diamond Company. I caution the press and others that under our law, the minister is presumed innocent until proven guilty. I will have no further comment on this matter during the judicial process.

"Yesterday, we received notice from Eastern Enterprises that it was withdrawing from the bidding for our Debswana partnership interest due to unforeseen financial issues. We are sorry to lose their participation. As a shareholder of De Beers, the government is calling on the De Beers Board of Directors to reconsider participating in the bidding for our Debswana interest."

Masisi asked his secretary to get the Chinese ambassador on the telephone. Thirty seconds later, he took a deep breath and picked up the phone. As with all diplomatic calls in Botswana, the conversation would be recorded. Both Masisi and the Chinese ambassador were aware of the protocol.

After brief greetings, the Chinese ambassador got right to the point. "President Masisi, Chairman Wang has been unable to reach his son by telephone, text, and email since yesterday afternoon. We understand he has checked out of his hotel, and he's not leaving an electronic signature from any of his devices. As I am sure you understand, the chairman is extremely concerned. Do you have any information about his whereabouts?"

The question was carefully limited to Wang Jin's whereabouts. Masisi assumed that the Chinese did not want to put anything about Eastern Enterprises on the record to preserve their deniability of involvement. The Chinese were a lot of things, but careless was not one of them.

"Unfortunately, we are presently unaware of his location. He left his business clothes at the hotel along with a suitcase. His toiletries, electronics, some casual clothes, and a backpack are missing. He left without checking out. His associate, Mr. Chun, told us he had no idea where Wang Jin had gone. We, like you, were unable to find an electronic signature for him. The National Police have issued a bulletin for him to be taken into custody when located. I will have you informed as soon as possible if we find him."

"President Masisi, do I understand that you have issued an arrest warrant for the son of the chairman of the Chinese Communist Party?"

"Mr. Ambassador, that is technically correct. But rest assured, he has not been charged with any offense at this time. The bulletin is a technical requirement giving police the authority to take him into custody so we can all be sure he is safe. Without the bulletin, we would have no basis to be looking for him until a missing person's report is filed, and it is too soon for that under our law. Should he come to your embassy, may I assume you will notify the police?"

"Of course. I understand your position, and China appreciates your help in trying to locate him. For your information, several of the embassy's security personnel will also be searching for him."

"Very well. We understand each other and will keep each other informed when the search is successful. Is there anything else, Mr. Ambassador?"

"No, thank you, President Masisi."

Masisi took a sip of his now cold coffee.

What in God's name is Wang Jin up to? Eastern Enterprises's activities in Botswana are dead and buried. There is nothing for him here. Why didn't he just go home?

Interesting that Chairman Wang had run his inquiry through the embassy. Smart. Given his relationship with his son, it was likely he was aware of the efforts to drive De Beers and Consolidated out of the bidding. Surely, the Chinese government was behind the pressure on banks not to finance Consolidated, and their government had not disavowed the news article about possible punitive tariffs on De Beers diamonds.

The best spin Masisi could put on things was that Chairman Wang was backing his son. If things turned out that China lost face on the world stage because of Wang Jin's mendacity, there would be trouble for the chairman within the party. There was no leader anywhere, in any form of government, who did not have political rivals waiting to pounce when the opportunity presented itself.

CHAPTER 35

CLOUDS PASSED INTERMITTENTLY ACROSS the moon as Sarah and Baruti pulled into the parking lot at Caravela Portuguese Restaurant. There was no valet, so Baruti parked as close to the front door as possible.

A moment later, a nondescript Toyota pulled into the lot and drove to a dark corner before parking. The driver and passenger waited for several minutes after Sarah and Baruti entered the restaurant before exiting their vehicle and going inside.

The Chinese couple presented themselves to the hostess. The man was dressed in a black polo shirt and slacks that appeared new. However, the hostess noticed that his shoes were brown, scuffed, and badly in need of polish. The woman, wearing a modest sundress, turned to examine the interior garden, and the hostess saw a price tag peeking above the back neckline of the dress. The customer whispered quietly to her companion.

Interesting, thought the hostess, but many people chose Caravela for a special night out.

The man requested seating on the far side of the garden where the only open table was about six feet from where Sarah and Baruti were sitting. The hostess took the couple to the requested table.

Sarah and Baruti were absorbed in each other and barely noticed the pair seated so close to them. If they had been paying attention, a Chinese couple in a

Portuguese restaurant in Gaborone, Botswana, might have seemed somewhat odd. But they were too busy talking about Victoria Falls.

"It would be a mortal sin for you to leave Botswana without seeing Victoria Falls. It's only forty-eight miles from our border," Baruti said with heart-felt pride and enthusiasm.

"Your enthusiasm is impossible to resist. Luc echoed the same sentiments, so I guess it's on my list," Sarah replied.

"We can catch a plane and be there in four hours. Let's go Saturday. We can come back Monday morning," he exuded.

"Whoa, slow down, my friend. I'm not sure what you have in mind."

Baruti understood immediately. "Not to worry. I'll book separate rooms at The Victoria Falls Hotel. I know the manager. He'll roll out the red carpet for a distinguished American VIP. You'll love it," he replied, recovering quickly.

"With the bidding delayed, I guess it won't hurt to take a little time for myself."

"Fantastic."

They continued to chat about the trip while they ate. They didn't linger over dessert and coffee so Baruti could get back to the hotel and make the reservations.

Neither of them noticed that the pair next to them rarely spoke, ordered only one appetizer between them, and drank just water. What they did do was listen attentively to the conversation next to them.

The Chinese couple left a few minutes after Baruti and Sarah, and returned to Chinatown.

CHAPTER 36

THE ZAMBESI RIVER IS the border between Zambia and Zimbabwe. One of the Seven Natural Wonders of the World is created at Victoria Falls where the river, spanning one thousand and seventy-eight meters, drops eleven hundred cubic meters of water per second one hundred and eight meters down onto solid rock. The impact sends clouds of mist four hundred meters into the air that's visible for miles upstream. The largest curtain of falling water in the world has a roar that creates vibrations that can be felt in one's chest.

Sarah had been mesmerized as their plane tracked the river from several miles above the falls. Lush green islands sat in the wide river that continued its lazy journey to the falls. She spied elephants along the shoreline, some with their trunks in the river. Hippos floated in the river from time to time, opening their enormous mouths. At Victoria Falls, the pilot circled it both clockwise and counterclockwise so the passengers on both sides of the plane had the chance to snap pictures.

Fifteen minutes after landing at Victoria Falls Airport on the Zimbabwe side of the river, their taxi passed through the gates of the iconic Victoria Falls Hotel. Manicured lawns and lush gardens filled with colorful flowers flanked the drive leading to the hotel with its white facade, broad porch, and red tile roof. Built in 1904, the building retained its Edwardian splendor.

Sarah felt they had stepped back in time when they were greeted by a doorman wearing a white jacket with braid and gold buttons, as well as a jaunty pith helmet. She could see the massive Victoria Falls Bridge across the broad lawn and the mist that rose from the falls a short distance behind the hotel.'

"Welcome to Mosi-oa-Tunya, the smoke that thunders," the smiling doorman said while two porters took possession of their carry-on bags. "We have been expecting you, Mr. Masisi, and we are honored to host you and your lovely lady."

As they entered the hotel, Sarah took Baruti's arm and whispered, "This is a very special treat, Mr. Masisi."

Baruti smiled. "We're off to a good start. Let's unpack and have a drink on the rear patio. There is a spectacular view of the bridge."

On the way to their rooms, they stopped at a photograph of the bridge under construction in 1905. The caption said: *The steel bridge was prefabricated in England; shipped to the port of Beira, Mozambique; and transported to the falls by rail. It spans 198 meters at the Second Gorge of the Zambesi River 128 meters below.*

Sarah's room continued the Edwardian theme of the hotel with traditional colors and beautiful wooden furniture. The white mosquito netting draped around the bed added romance to the elegant surroundings. She quickly unpacked and joined Baruti on Stanley's Terrace, from which they had a picture-perfect view of the massive bridge in one direction and the spray from Victoria Falls just across the lawn.

Baruti ordered a bottle of South African chenin blanc, which Sarah found delightfully dry, light, and zesty. They sampled a few of the pastries offered with the high tea being served.

Sarah felt herself surrendering to the wonder of Africa. She had been immersed in wild animals and survived the heart-stopping possibility of attack by a bloodthirsty lion whose roar still vibrated within her, all while pursuing acquisition of the world's most valuable diamond mines. Now the South Side orphan was sitting on the terrace of an iconic hotel next to Victoria Falls, one of the Seven Wonders of the World, with a handsome, intelligent, and successful African man who was obviously interested in her. She had no words for her feelings as she gazed at Baruti, framed in the mist of the falls behind him.

For dinner, they decided to pass on the elegant Livingstone Room and chose the casual Jungle Junction restaurant, where they looked out on the gorge of the falls and saw the ever- present spray rising in the air. Entertainment was provided by costumed dancers and a lively band of local musicians with an emphasis on drums. The colorful performance was exciting, loud, and primitive, stirring her blood. Sarah squeezed Baruti's hand, ready and eager for sex.

CHAPTER 37

SARAH'S SCENT FLOATED INTO Baruti's consciousness as he slowly awakened. Half-awake, he buried his face in the sheet, luxuriating in her essence. He sighed quietly, remembering the softness of her skin; her long, strong legs wrapped around him; the hunger of their lovemaking that had ended in sweet, loving tenderness.

He slowly rolled over and languidly reached for her. Nothing.

His eyes opened slowly. She was not there. Her side of the bed was cold.

"Sarah," he called softly. There was no answer.

He called again, a little louder. Still no answer.

He looked at the bathroom door, which stood open. There was no sound of running water. He rolled over, pivoting to get his feet on the floor. Shakily, Baruti got to his feet and yawned. On his bedside table was a napkin with the outline of Sarah's lips in red. Underneath, she had written, *Call me for breakfast.*

She had obviously gone back to her room. Baruti was disappointed, but assumed she had her reasons. It was a just after 7:00 a.m. He showered, shaved, and dressed, thinking about what to do on their only full day at the resort. They would tour Victoria Falls, of course, and then maybe a helicopter ride through the gorges. Or a cruise on the river above the falls. Or, if they wanted a rush, whitewater rafting below the falls. Maybe the zip line or bungee jumping. Well, he would pass on the bungee jumping.

He called Sarah's room. No answer. He waited a minute and tried again. Still no answer. He tried her mobile. Straight to voice mail. She was probably showering.

Baruti waited a few minutes and tried again. When there was no answer, he walked down the hall to her room and knocked. No response. A slight tightening in his chest foreboded something was not right.

Calm down.

Was she in the restaurant waiting for him? Of course. He was being silly. Baruti hurried downstairs and eagerly scanned the dining room.

She was not there. His breathing became uneven, and the muscles in his neck were tensing.

Think.

Could she have gone for a walk? That made no sense. She would have told him in her note, and she would have taken her phone.

Was she lying on the floor in her room needing help? Baruti rushed to the front desk and asked for a housekeeper to meet him at Sarah's room for a welfare check. He ran to her room, where the housekeeper was just opening Sarah's door. He held his breath as he entered. She was not there. He could see her computer on the dressing table and her clothes in an open closet. The housekeeper walked out from the bathroom and shook her head.

Where is Sarah?

He returned to the lobby and began asking the hotel staff if they had seen her. No one had since dinner last night. He went to his manager friend, who sent several staff members to search the hotel grounds. Baruti paced the lobby anxiously, hoping she would walk through the door. She didn't.

A half hour later, there was still no sign of Sarah. Baruti's breathing now came in short, sharp bursts.

When the manager called the local police, they suggested checking Victoria Falls. Baruti and two staff members raced through the walkways at the falls. No sign of Sarah.

It was now close to noon. Something was definitely wrong. He did not even have a picture of her. Wait, the hotel had taken her passport when she had checked in. Maybe they had kept a photocopy of her passport vitals page? He was in luck. He asked for multiple copies.

Baruti walked around the hotel showing her picture to guests without any luck. The manager delivered her picture to the police station and was told that they would alert their patrol officers to be on the lookout, but it was still too early to file a formal missing-persons report.

The Victoria Falls Hotel was in Zimbabwe, where he had no leverage with local authorities. Calling his father would be useless. He paced the lobby, looking constantly at the entrance, hoping she would walk in with a big smile. Finally, not knowing what else to do, Baruti called Luc Johannes in New York.

Johannes listened calmly to Baruti's recitation of Sarah's disappearance and what had been done to find her without any success. He had no proof that foul play was involved, so it would be another twenty-four hours before he could file a formal missing-persons report.

Johannes could feel Baruti's helplessness. He asked if Wang Jin had been located.

There was dead silence as Baruti processed the implications of Johannes's question. He swallowed and answered, "No, Mr. Johannes, he's still missing. Do you think he might have taken Sarah?"

It was Johannes's turn for a moment of silence. Then he started to think aloud.

"She was with you until midnight and was gone by this morning. There is no reason for her to be wandering around Victoria Falls in the dead of night, so she was taken from the hotel between midnight and five in the morning under cover of darkness. Someone wanted her specifically and came into the hotel to get her. You said there was no sign of a struggle in her room, so they probably grabbed her on the way to her room after she left you about midnight. Wang Jin could not have done this by himself. There must be others involved."

Baruti wanted to scream. Johannes had avoided asking where they had been at midnight or why he had not walked her back to her room. Whoever had taken her must have been following them. They would have known he and Sarah had been in his room and had gotten lucky when she had walked out into the hall. Otherwise, they would have broken into Baruti's room. If she had stayed, they might have been able to have fought them off, or maybe Baruti would be lying in a pool of blood.

Johannes continued. "An organized-crime kidnapping for money is possible, but Victoria Falls is not Mexico, so I'll rule that out for the time being. She doesn't know anyone in Africa that would have a grudge against her except Wang Jin. So the question is, why would he kidnap her?"

"Maybe he thinks he can use her to get back in the bidding for Debswana or that you will withdraw from the bidding to save her?" Baruti suggested uncertainly. Tears began to leak from his eyes. "What if he just wants to hurt her?"

"Baruti, you must stay calm. I'm coming to Victoria Falls and should be there within twenty-four hours. While I'm in the air, I want you to call your father and have him get the Botswana border police on the lookout."

"Mr. Johannes, Zambia is just across the bridge. The Botswana border is less than fifty miles from here. There has been more than enough time to cross the border into either of those countries. They may still be in Zimbabwe, or they could have slipped across the Namibia border, which is a short distance from here. These borders don't stop criminals. They could have taken her anywhere," Baruti said, his voice cracking.

"You must hold it together. You are no good to anyone if you get emotional. Concentrate on getting the word out. Push the local police. I've got to charter a plane. You get ahold of your father and stay strong," Johannes said.

While he desperately wanted to be wrong, Johannes was sure that Wang Jin had kidnapped Sarah. According to her, he was doing drugs and seemed unstable. He had a lot of prestige and probably money invested in the Debswana deal. Losing face and being kicked out of Botswana might have sent him over the edge. There was no way he could return to the Debswana bidding. His motive had to be either kidnapping for ransom or simple revenge. If it was the latter, Sarah was probably already dead. If she was alive, Johannes was going to find her no matter what it took. If she was dead, Wang Jin would join her.

Johannes called a private jet charter service across the Hudson River in Teterboro, New Jersey, that specialized in long-range business travel. He chose a Gulfstream G650ER that could be wheels up in three hours and arrive in Victoria Falls in about eighteen hours.

Johannes quickly packed a couple of business outfits and casual safari clothes. Then he packed a Browning Lightweight '81 rifle, a Mossberg 590A1 tactical shotgun, and his favorite GLOCK 19, together with several boxes of ammunition for each. Flying privately, he was not worried about airport security.

He hoped that by the time he got to Victoria Falls there would be a ransom demand. To pull off a ransom, Wang Jin would have to furnish proof of life. That meant keeping her alive.

Johannes was familiar with the International Hostage Negotiation Institute and had even attended a course in advanced hostage negotiation strategies for businessmen at Harvard University. If the situation required negotiation, he would do so. But with a loose cannon like Wang Jin, rational negotiations were unlikely.

When he was in the air, Johannes called Aiden Bekker and asked him to come to Victoria Falls ready to go hunting for the most dangerous animals of all: human beings.

CHAPTER 38

AS AIDEN BEKKER LISTENED to his old friend tell him what had happened to Sarah, a change came over him. His eyes narrowed. The lines in his face deepened, hardening his features. It had been his usual expression during the Rhodesian Bush War of the 1970s, where Bekker had been a member of the Selous Scouts. At seventeen, he had left the family ranch in Botswana in search of adventure, which he had found in what was then called Rhodesia. He had left a boy and returned a hardened fighter.

The Selous Scouts were one of the finest counterinsurgency units in military history. They traversed cultural and racial barriers using pseudo guerilla tactics to wreak havoc and destruction on their Soviet- and Chinese-backed enemies.

Back on the ranch, poachers were a constant problem. The skills he came home with kept the problem manageable. But there was more than one poacher who entered the Bekker ranch in search of trophy animals or cattle and remained there under the ground.

As an Army LRRP in Vietnam, Johannes had survived the crucible of guerilla warfare and became a seasoned guerilla fighter. Given similar military experiences, they had a bond built on trust and mutual respect.

Bekker and Johannes represented the finest fighters of their generation. Despite being in their late sixties, they were in good physical condition and were experts with their favorite firearms. When he had reached out for help, Johannes had chosen well.

An hour after ending the call with Johannes, Bekker was on the road for the eight-hour drive to Victoria Falls in his modified Toyota Land Cruiser. The vehicle was equipped for any eventuality one might encounter on his vast ranch, supplemented by a Weatherby Mark V .460 Magnum big-game hunting rifle and a Ruger Super Redhawk handgun.

Bekker had been brought up to respect women who, in the Afrikaner community, worked and, when necessary, fought alongside their men. The idea that Sarah had been kidnapped outraged him. He had eight hours to think about the kidnappers. The why of the kidnapping was for Johannes to ponder. Bekker was going to assess who would help Wang Jin do such a thing, which would inform him where they would have taken her.

CHAPTER 39

AFTER CALLING HIS 14K triad contact, Wang Jin stuffed casual clothes in his backpack and slipped unseen out of the hotel service entrance while the two government agents sat in the lobby looking at their iPhones. Two blocks from the hotel, a nondescript Toyota sedan picked him up and delivered him to the Golden Dragon restaurant in Chinatown.

With his backpack over his shoulder, he walked into the Golden Dragon, where he was greeted by the aroma of oyster sauce, green onion, garlic, and ginger being cooked over an open flame. The restaurant's generic ambiance consisted of linoleum floors and laminated tables highlighted by neon signs for Chinese beer and posters of Chinese movies stars. A few customers were scattered around the interior.

A harried-looking waiter in a stained white coat motioned for Wang Jin, who followed him through a multicolored beaded curtain down a narrow corridor past the restrooms to a metal door. The waiter knocked three times, pausing briefly between each knock. A young Chinese man of average size holding a large-caliber pistol opened the door.

Wang Jin stepped into the room. The young man closed and locked the door, staying behind Wang Jin.

Seated at a metal desk facing the door, wearing a loud Hawaiian shirt, was another Chinese man whose black hair was streaked with gray. His shirt was the only color in a room with a cement floor and three bare walls. An old sofa, two chairs in front of the desk, and metal filing cabinets were the only furnishings. Four monitors on the wall to the left of the desk showed the exterior of the restaurant and outside the office door. The man behind the desk did not stand.

"I am Chin Bambang. You may sit." He gestured toward one of the old straight-backed wooden chairs in front of his desk. The young man remained standing behind Wang Jin.

Wang Jin was not used to being treated with such disrespect and started to remind this common criminal with whom he was dealing. He abruptly changed his mind. He needed this man who did not need him, so he swallowed his pride and sat, placing his backpack at his feet.

Chin silently scrutinized Wang Jin's face long enough to make Wang Jin uncomfortable. Then he asked, "Do you have a cell phone or computer with you?"

Wang Jin nodded.

"Take them out and hand them to Mr. Song. He will remove the batteries and destroy them."

"But…" Wang Jin began.

"Quiet, fool. They can track your electronic signal. It's a wonder that the police are not barging through the front door as we speak."

Wang Jin realized that he should have removed the batteries at the hotel. Perhaps with a little less coke in his system, it would have occurred to him. He handed his computer and phone to Mr. Song, who disappeared through another beaded curtain.

"I understand that you have been ordered to leave Botswana because you were caught bribing the Minister of Mines. You refused to accept your freedom and are now hiding from the authorities here in Chinatown."

Wang Jin had not told him why he had wanted to see him and wondered how the man could have this information.

"You blend in here, so it's the logical place for you to hide. But it is small enough that the police can go door to door looking for you. They will be greeted with silence, but the police can learn many things from body language and will not hesitate to search wherever they want. No warrant is necessary. It is dangerous to be around you, Mr. Wang. What do you want from 14K?"

"Simply put, Mr. Chin, I want to recover the money I lost in this Debswana mess, and I want revenge against two people who have caused me to lose face."

"How do you propose to accomplish your objective?"

"With your help, I want to kidnap two people and hold them for ransom."

"Who?"

"Sarah Taylor-Jones, a US businesswoman, and Baruti Masisi."

"You want to kidnap the son of the president of Botswana?" Chin was incredulous. "Have you lost your mind? Do you have any idea what that would set in motion?"

Wang Jin had come up with the idea right after he had snorted the coke in his hotel room. It had seemed like a good idea at the time. But Chin had a point. The Botswana authorities may not care too much about an American woman, but the son of their president was a different order of magnitude.

"Yes. I see what you mean. The woman's company has money, so I don't need Masisi. But I would like to beat the hell out of him."

"Listen to me very carefully, Mr. Wang. 14K has very profitable operations here and in South Africa. We stay under the radar. Forget about Masisi. It is a nonstarter. In fact, I will not involve any of my people in kidnapping an American."

Wang Jin started to speak, but Chin held up his hand to silence him. "What I will do is put surveillance on the American woman until we have her pattern of movement."

Wang Jin held his breath. He could not pull this off by himself.

"Our triad has a mutually beneficial, long-standing relationship on matters of mutual interest with a South African gang that calls themselves Hard Livings. They have a steady supply of men who are released from prison with no money, no job, and no prospects. For enough money, these kind of men will do anything. I will put you in touch with Rashied Strangle, the gang leader, once we have the woman's pattern. Our service is complimentary this time, but Strangle will want to be well paid in advance."

"Thank you, but how do I know I can trust these people? They may just take my money and tell me to piss off."

"Look, Mr. Wang. The 14K triad is connecting you with them. We do a lot of business in South Africa, and we work regularly together. Once you make your deal, you will pay me, and I will send them half the money then and the other half when they perform whatever you agree upon. Our relationship is worth far more than whatever deal you put together with them."

Wang Jin nodded, liking what he was hearing.

Chin continued. "Now I want you to listen to me very, very carefully, Mr. Son of the CCP chairman. Trust works both ways in these arrangements. By putting you in touch with Strangle the triad is vouching for you. If you don't live up to your promises, there will be no excuses or explanations. We don't care who you are or where you try to hide. The triad will find you, and your death will be extremely unpleasant before your body disappears. Do you understand?"

"Perfectly," Wang Jin replied.

"We are working with you because of your father's position. At some point in the future, a representative of 14K will ask you for a favor, which you will grant without question. Do you understand?"

"Sure, no problem. Can you put someone on the woman right away?"

"It will be done. Mr. Song will take you to a safe house that is not in Chinatown where you may call South Africa undetected. Goodbye."

Chin did not stand. Mr. Song appeared and escorted Wang Jin through the curtain into a garage where another nondescript Toyota sedan sat waiting.

CHAPTER 40

IN ZHONGNANHAI, A ONE-TIME imperial garden in Beijing adjacent to the Forbidden City, Wang Chen paced back and forth across his large office.

Outside, the smog was so thick that highways and school playgrounds were closed. Most of the few pedestrians on the street wore masks and goggles to protect them from the pollution. People would most certainly blame him for the smog and everything else that was wrong in their miserable little lives.

When his soft knock was ignored, Wang's assistant opened the door slowly and quietly, assessed his boss's mood, and quickly retreated. The man had been in a horrendous mood since he had gotten the news about his son's latest mishap, and the chairman's current expression told him things were getting worse.

Wang was under intense political pressure and could not afford to have his son create an international incident. The Chinese Communist Party had two main factions: The Shanghai Group were mostly costal- and business-oriented; The Chinese Communist Youth League were mostly from the interior and supported agrarian interests. Wang, a member of the Shanghai Group, had become chairman under a power-sharing agreement with the CCYL. According to the agreement, at the next party conference, he was to relinquish his post to a CCYL representative. Wang had no intention of stepping down and had been working since he had become chairman to change the laws so that they would allow him to remain in power.

As part of his plan, he had been pressuring other members of the Shanghai Group to support the changes necessary to keep him in office. When Alibaba Group chairman Jack Ma had balked at supporting the changes Wang wanted, government regulators had descended upon Alibaba, and what had been Asia's largest corporation had lost 60 percent of its $860 billion market value almost overnight. Ma had disappeared for a while, but now, like a phoenix rising from the ashes, he was back and working against Wang.

Wang had every reason to believe that if Wang Jin created an international incident that reflected poorly on China, the CCYL would hang his son around his neck to discredit him. The loss of face for China would be immense. It was possible that all he had worked for would be destroyed.

Wang Jin was off the grid. He had ignored Botswana's order to leave the country and was a fugitive. Now the Chinese embassy was reporting that an American businesswoman who worked for Consolidated Diamonds, one of his son's rivals in the Debswana auction, had been kidnapped. Sources in the Zimbabwe, Zambia, and Botswana police departments reported that Wang Jin was being discussed as a possible person of interest in their investigation. If true, it would not be long before Interpol got involved.

The chairman's back was against the wall. He unconsciously glanced at the huge painting of the Great Wall of China behind his desk. He had to find Wang Jin, erase whatever problems he had created, and bring him home where he could be managed.

He jerked open his office door and barked at his assistant to get the minister of State Security on the phone. The Ministry of State Security was responsible for counterintelligence, foreign intelligence, and political security—in other words, it was the secret police.

Wang's directive to the minister was brief and to the point: Dispatch his best team of MSS operatives to Botswana immediately. Their orders were to undertake covert action to find Wang Jin and return him to Beijing. If he was involved in the kidnapping, they were to erase all evidence that could connect his son to it—including the victim.

Masisi sat in his office in Gaborone, looking at Wang Jin's recent phone records. His last call before the phone had gone offline was to a number in Chinatown that belonged to Chin Bambang, who his police believed was the local head of China's 14K triad. Chin had probably told Wang Jin to get rid of his phone. No doubt they were now using burners.

Masisi had to decide how to deal with Chin. He allowed him to operate in Gaborone because it kept a certain amount of order in the Chinese community without the government having to hassle Chinese citizens and incur the displeasure of China. Before his decision to ban Eastern Enterprises from the auction, Masisi had done everything possible to keep China happy. The Belt and Road projects were helping Botswana, but like most things in life, they had come with a cost. If China pulled those projects because the chairman's son could not steal Botswana's diamonds, so be it. His country would carry on and choose a different path to achieve its goals.

He could bring Chin into the police station for formal questioning, but Masisi was quite sure that Chin would not cooperate with the police. An informal interview at his restaurant would most likely bring the usual silence. Masisi was not averse to harsh interrogation techniques in a ticking-time bomb scenario but, as much as he liked Sarah, her kidnapping was not a matter of national security. He needed to think.

Pressure. He needed to apply pressure to Chin. How?

Why, of course—make Chin an offer he could not refuse.

Here in Gaborone, Chin was a big fish in a small pond, where he lived quite well. Back in China, he would be just another goldfish in a very large pond of sharks. Masisi would threaten to deport Chin if he did not cooperate.

Masisi gave the two agents who had allowed Wang Jin to escape an opportunity to redeem themselves. He sent them to question Chin. If he did not cooperate, their instructions were to immediately take him to the airport and put him on the first plane out of Botswana. The Embassy of the People's Republic of China would be notified, sealing Chin's fate.

The agents were back in under three hours. Chin's story, which he told quickly once he knew the government was serious about deporting him, was that he had refused to help Wang Jin, but he did give him the phone number for a member of the Hard Livings gang in Cape Town.

The story seemed believable to the agents and Masisi. It would have been stupid to use Chinese for the kidnapping; they were too visible. Wang Jin needed Black criminals, and Hard Livings had a history of working with the triads in South Africa. Surely some of their members were familiar with the Victoria Falls area.

Now that Masisi had the information, what to do with it?

CHAPTER 41

BEKKER MET JOHANNES AT Victoria Falls Airport. Once they were in Bekker's Toyota for the short drive to The Victoria Falls Hotel, he laid out the magnitude of the problem they faced.

"Luc, we've got our work cut out for us. We are in the four corners of Africa. Seventy-five kilometers west of here, Zimbabwe, Zambia, Botswana, and Namibia converge. The kidnappers had plenty of time to cross into any of them—four separate countries with four separate law enforcement organizations. Hwange National Park is in Zimbabwe and less than a hundred and twenty kilometers from here. Chobe National Park is in Botswana and only a hundred kilometers away. These parks total about ten thousand square miles and are connected by forestry or private safari areas. There are no fences. Then there is Zambesi National Park just across the bridge in Zambia."

Johannes inhaled slowly and exhaled. "Christ almighty, Aiden. Where do we start? We've got to narrow down the search area."

"Let's meet with Baruti and see what he can tell us."

Baruti met them in the hotel lobby and gave Johannes an enthusiastic man hug. When he reached for Bekker, the Afrikaner put out his hand to hold him off and then shook hands. Bekker was not into man-hugs.

"I reserved the private dining room for an hour. I've got some very interesting news," Baruti said, his tone reserving judgment on the nature of the information.

A waiter brought them water and closed the door.

"I got off the phone with my dad an hour ago. The last call Wang Jin made on his phone was to a Chinese gangster named Chin Bambang in Gaborone's Chinatown. Dad sent some agents to question him with instructions to immediately deport him if he didn't cooperate. It seems Chin would rather help us than return to China. Anyway, he said he refused to help Wang Jin, who wanted to kidnap Sarah and me. He claims to have persuaded Wang Jin to leave me alone because of my father, but Chin did give him the phone number for a Hard Livings shot-caller in Cape Town."

"What…" Johannes said, obviously taken by surprise.

Baruti continued. "The Hard Livings are one of the most dangerous gangs in Cape Town and often work with Chinese triads. Apparently, their members are in and out of prison so often that there's always a fresh batch of criminals leaving jail who are desperate for money. Chin said he had no further contact with Wang Jin. Dad and the men who questioned Chin think he's most likely telling the truth while minimizing whatever help he gave Wang Jin."

Johannes shook his head slowly and asked, "How did Wang Jin and these South African gangsters know you and Sarah would be here at Victoria Falls?"

Baruti's eyes dropped in embarrassment.

"I don't know for sure, but a couple of days before we left, Sarah and I were in a restaurant talking about coming up here this weekend. I didn't think anything of it at the time, but a Chinese couple was sitting next to us and could have overheard our conversation. They could have been spies for Wang Jin or Chin."

"Bingo," Bekker said. "All Wang Jin had to do was call the hotel and confirm you were staying here."

Baruti's face collapsed as his eyes grew moist. "I should have known better, been suspicious instead of…"

"Enjoying the company of a fun, beautiful woman and planning a holiday?" Johannes filled in. "Don't beat yourself up. There was no reason for you to be suspicious."

The men were silent for a while, each lost in his own thoughts.

"We've got to narrow down the area where they could have taken her," Johannes said.

A hotel staff member knocked and announced that there was a message for Baruti at the front desk. He jumped up and hurried out of the room.

Five minutes later, Baruti, crestfallen, returned. He was holding a Polaroid picture of Sarah, who appeared alive but heavily sedated, with a sheet of paper that said, *Wire $5 million US consulting fee to account number 98560345 at the First Bank of Rarotonga no later than 5 p.m. Cook Island Time on August 31 to secure the release of Sarah Taylor-Jones. If you fail to pay, she will be well used before being sold or fed to lions. Which fate is worse?*

"Thank God she's still alive," Bekker said.

"We have kidnap insurance for the five million. I'll get in touch with the insurance company," Johannes replied.

Obviously relieved, Johannes and Bekker stood. Baruti remained seated, not sharing in the relief.

"Alive, maybe. That's good, but kidnapped by gangsters who may have just gotten out of prison? Sarah is so beautiful. What if they hurt her?"

"Baruti, we can get Sarah back. Just focus on that. We'll meet back here in an hour and figure out how to proceed," Johannes said.

Johannes was not as upbeat as he wanted to sound. There was no way to contact the kidnappers, no way to negotiate, no mention of an exchange, no way to know if she was still alive. All one could do was pay and pray.

Back in the conference room, the mood was glum. The insurance company had declined coverage, pointing to a policy rider that excluded Africa from their kidnapping policy.

Johannes had called Peter Hess, chairman of Consolidated's board of directors, and asked for authorization to pay the $5 million. It was a short conversation.

"Luc, you have a demand for five million dollars. You don't know if Sarah is alive. You have no way to contact the kidnappers and demand proof of life. You have no assurance that if she *is* still alive, her captors will release her. You're in Zimbabwe, for God's sake. Why should they release Sarah? I like her, but the odds are we'll never see her again. I have a fiduciary duty to our stockholders, and I can't authorize paying that kind of money on a prayer she's OK and will be released. It hurts me, but I can't do it."

While Johannes was worth more than the ransom demand, his assets were not liquid. It would take quite some time to come up with $5 million. Bekker's wealth came from a family trust. The trustee was a Dutch bank that was notoriously tight-fisted since its fee was based on the trust's asset value. Baruti had less than $5,000 in his checking account.

"A Cook Islands bank won't tell us anything. We have no way to contact the kidnappers. No way to negotiate. No way to pay. We must find Sarah before the deadline," Johannes said.

Bekker was standing with his hands on the back of a chair. He said, "I have been thinking about how to go about our search. Very few people live in the national parks and the contiguous areas. Two groups constantly patrol those parks: park rangers and safari guides. I know a lot of them, and the ones I know will know the others. I'll put the word out to be on the lookout for city boys with a woman who look out of place and a Chinese man who's not on safari. If they move or go somewhere to get supplies, someone will see them."

"Great idea," Johannes said. "How about asking these people for ideas about where Wang Jin might hide Sarah? We could have an informal search party in the thousands."

The glum mood had evaporated. They were formulating a plan, moving forward. With a little luck, Sarah might be located quickly.

Baruti's cell phone vibrated on the table. He looked at the caller ID. "It's Dad." He listened for a full minute before saying, "OK, I'll pass it on," in a voice barely above a whisper. Something was clearly wrong.

"Dad says that an hour ago, a private plane from China landed in Gaborone with four passengers who claimed to be diplomats. They had the proper paperwork, but Dad says his people are positive they are Chinese secret police who have come to find Wang Jin."

"That's not surprising. He's the son of the chairman of the CCP," Bekker said.

"Dad says it's significant that the Chinese aren't relying on their embassy personnel to search for Wang Jin. If he's captured with Sarah and some South African gangsters, the publicity blowback on Wang Chen would be horrendous. He has enemies in China that would like to use his son to destroy him."

"And we care about that why?" Bekker asked.

Johannes answered for Baruti. "The secret police deal with political problems. Right now, there's no proof that Wang Jin kidnapped Sarah. If Sarah and the gangsters disappear and he returns to China, the problem goes away. Chinese secret police exist to make political problems disappear."

Baruti nodded in agreement.

"Shit," Bekker said. "I'll get on the phone to my people and tell them to watch for Chinese goons also. They'll be easy to spot."

CHAPTER
42

SARAH SLIPPED QUIETLY OUT of Baruti's hotel room floating on a cloud, completely distracted and lost in thought.

The sex had been wonderful, but more than that, she cared for this man a lot. For her, the relationship was accelerating like a runaway train. She needed to slow it down to protect herself until she really knew Baruti. Until she was sure she wasn't simply being caught up in the romance of an African affair with handsome man, one that was flaring brightly but would die when the real world intruded on this dream. She had left him a note to call her for breakfast. Keep him guessing. Give her a little space. It had seemed like a good idea at the time.

Lost in her thoughts, Sarah did not see the three rough-looking men who came around the hallway corner behind her just after she had turned toward her room down the hall.

The three men had a picture of Sarah and were on the way to her hotel room. They recovered quickly from the surprise of finding her in the hallway. The biggest one moved quickly toward Sarah with the others close behind.

Thinking of Baruti, she didn't hear the footsteps until the big man was a step behind her. She made a half turn, but it was too late. A massive forearm wrapped around her neck, choking off her air supply and squeezing her carotid artery.

She could not yell. She tried to stomp on her attacker's foot but missed. She collapsed her knees, trying to throw him off-balance, but he held her up. A few seconds later, she was unconscious. Another man immediately injected her with ketamine.

Sometime later, she returned to the edge of consciousness and had the sensation of being jostled around in a vehicle on a bumpy road. Someone grabbed her arm, and an injection followed. Quickly, the curtain of blackness dropped.

Blackness began to fade again. Sarah was lying on her back. Her first sensation was stifling heat mixed with the smell of dirt and sour human sweat. She did not feel restrained. The fuzziness in her head began to clear, and she cracked her eyes open. She was lying on bare earth atop a stinking sleeping bag.

As her vision cleared, there was enough light to survey her surroundings. A tin roof covered the top of a single room of about twelve feet by fifteen feet made from wooden planks. Light came from gaps between the planks. Plywood covered what she thought were two windows. There was one door, closed.

A spider crawled across Sarah's face. She frantically brushed it away and struggled to sit up as her head exploded in pain. Closing her eyes, her hands went to her temples, pressing hard, trying to contain the discomfort. After a few moments, she forced her eyes open. Of course, she had been drugged.

Sarah rolled onto her hands and knees, wanting to cry out as her head throbbed mercilessly.

The muthafuckas.

She let her anger wash over her, gathered her strength, and took a deep breath as she tried to stand. She collapsed and wanted to cry but refused. She marshaled her anger again.

The muthafuckas will pay for this.

She pushed up, made it to her feet, and staggered toward a supporting beam, which she grabbed. Sarah stood holding the smooth beam.

What happened? Where in the hell am I?

She started to call out and thought better of it. *Think.*

The first rule of self-defense was situational awareness. She moved unsteadily to the door and put one hand on the wall for support, reaching for the handle with the other.

No! Look first.

Sarah peered through a small gap in the siding next to the door. She seemed to be on a small hill above a semiarid landscape, nothing but brush, trees, grass, and rocks for as far as she could see.

Using the wall for support, she moved to the next wall. Thick brush outside. Nothing to see there. Third wall: an old van covered by camouflage netting with two small pup tents pitched nearby. Last wall: a huge pile of boulders. Nothing to see. Where were her captors?

Back at the door, she pulled on the handle. It gave one-quarter inch. That was it. Locked. She could see a new stainless-steel hasp secured by a padlock through the gap where the door met the frame.

Think, girl. Find a way out.

An urge to pee hit her. In a corner was a five-gallon bucket with a loose top. Her chamber pot? Why not? Sarah pushed down her slacks and, for the first time, realized that her panties were still in place. No sexual assault. Yet. She pulled them down and emptied her bladder in the bucket.

Her mouth was dry and tasted as if a troop of baboons had overnighted there. She needed water.

Call out? Bang on the door? Not yet.

Sarah spent the next minutes systematically examining each plank of the structure for weakness. She noticed a few fresh nails, but most depressing were two strips of sturdy tree branches nailed to the siding parallel with the ground, which made it highly unlikely that one could kick a piece of siding loose. The metal roof was hot to the touch, and without something to stand on, she could not test it for weakness.

Call out or wait? Wait and think.
Who did this? Why? What do they want?

Fifteen minutes from The Victoria Falls Hotel, Wang Jin was comfortably ensconced in the luxurious Stanley & Livingstone Boutique Hotel at the Victoria Falls Private Game Reserve, having used a false English passport under the name Bruce Lee. Here in Zimbabwe, he had no reason to be worried about the Botswana authorities, but he wanted to keep a low profile because he was sure his father would know what had happened with Eastern Enterprises and would be trying to contact him.

The old man might even send people from the embassy to look for him. He also did not want to accidentally run into Baruti.

For $50,000 US, which Wang Jin had handed to Chin Bambang, Strangle, the Hard Livings shot-caller, had sent three men to join Wang Jin in Victoria Falls. All of them had grown up in the area. The leader of the group had been a park ranger in Hwange National Park for several years. All of them had gone to South Africa looking for work that they could not find and ended up joining the gang to survive. They rendezvoused with Wang Jin on a deserted dirt road ten miles from the falls and put their plan together.

The local gangsters knew several Victoria Falls Hotel employees and, for a few US dollars, secured a pass key to the guest rooms, Sarah's and Baruti's room numbers, and an unlocked service door. At two in the morning, the three gangsters entered the hotel through the unlocked entrance while Wang Jin, wearing a balaclava mask, waited in the van. If Sarah was in her room, they would take her there. If she was in Baruti's room, they were to take her and severely beat Baruti.

Wang Jin's head was on a swivel while his fingers tapped a nervous rhythm on the steering wheel. They were most vulnerable here. If there was a loud struggle capturing Sarah or if someone saw them carry a woman out of the hotel and raised an alarm, escape would be difficult. The black men could fade into the night, but a Chinese man—that would be different. He had thought long and hard about exposing himself like this, but he wanted to be sure they got the right woman. He wanted to ensure he got a usable proof-of-life picture and, most of all, he wanted to experience her comeuppance firsthand.

The plan was to silence and immobilize Sarah with minimum noise. She would be injected with ketamine, whose anesthetic effect would take about five minutes to kick in. During that time, the men would bring her to the van, where Wang Jin would take a proof-of-life picture while she was obviously alive.

Wang Jin could barely contain his excitement as one of the gangsters opened the service door and Sarah appeared supported between the other two. He could see that the effect of the anesthetic had already set in. She seemed awake but no longer ambulatory.

They shoved her roughly through the van's side doors. Wang Jin was ready. The men held her head for the camera. Sarah's eyes were open but unfocused. Wang Jin took several photos, the cumulative effect of which showed she was alive but under the influence of something.

He pulled away from the hotel and drove to the airport parking lot where he had left his car. As he drove, Wang Jin's penis throbbed against his pants, expressing his sexual pleasure at the humiliation of Ms. Sarah Taylor-Jones, one dumb cunt who should never have messed with him. Now all he needed was the money.

The gangsters continued to their hideout in an isolated and abandoned park ranger cabin in Hwange National Park. Hwange held one of the greatest concentrations of game in all of Africa and was noted for its lions, which preyed upon elephant calves and young elephants. No one went in this area unescorted. The trip to the hideout was only a little over one hundred kilometers, and they arrived before daylight.

The pictures and note were delivered to The Victoria Falls Hotel by a young boy whom one of the gangsters had recruited for $1 US.

Wang Jin returned to his hotel. His experience with kidnapping was derived from television. He wanted to avoid negotiations that would draw him out and delay resolution. Hence, a take-it-or-leave-it offer.

If Baruti, who he was sure had access to money from the government or Consolidated Diamonds, paid the ransom, Wang Jin had no intention of releasing Sarah. He would sexually humiliate her for as long as he pleased before turning her over to the gangsters. Then he would hire a driver to take him to Angola, about a thousand kilometers from the falls, where he would be out of the danger zone and could easily book a flight to Hong Kong.

If the ransom was not paid, Sarah would suffer the same fate.

His concern was what to do with her while he waited for the ransom. The gangsters had her alone in the middle of nowhere. They were men. She was a beautiful woman. They had control over her. Did he care what happened to her in the meantime? Yes.

Wang Jin didn't know what was going to happen before the ransom was paid or it wasn't. As much as he hated Sarah, he needed to keep his options open. He might want to make another ransom demand that would require proof of life. That meant keeping her unharmed for the time being. Something else might happen that would require him to prove she was alive and unharmed.

In the final analysis, as much as he wanted the bitch to pay for the way she had treated him, this was about the money. He needed it. He would keep his options open for as long as possible. That was why he had told the gangsters that he would directly pay them $10,000 US if they kept Sarah secure and unharmed until the ransom issue was resolved. Africa was full of women they could abuse. They did not have any opportunities to have that kind of money laid in their hands.

CHAPTER
43

JOHANNES, BEKKER, AND BARUTI had turned the Victoria Falls Hotel conference room into their search headquarters. A large map of Zimbabwe, Zambia, Namibia, and Botswana was taped to a large whiteboard.

Bekker reported that he had gotten the word out to his contacts, who promised to pass it on. The willingness to help among the guides and park rangers was overwhelmingly positive, and Bekker was sure that if the kidnappers moved, someone would spot them. In fact, they were likely to be more visible than they would be in a sizable city where they could blend in with other people.

Baruti's cell phone vibrated on the table. He picked it up. "It's Dad."

"If it's about Sarah, put the call on speaker so you don't have to repeat things," Johannes said.

Baruti nodded, listened for a moment, and pushed the Speaker button. "Dad, you're on speaker with Mr. Johannes and Mr. Bekker."

"Hello, gentlemen. Aiden, it's been a long time. I would love to swap lies, but I don't think there's any time to lose.

"I put surveillance on the Chinese operatives and have a report to share. They went directly to the Chinese embassy for about an hour. Then all four went to Chinatown and visited Chin Bambang's restaurant. They were there for about thirty minutes. We assume they were talking to Chin because they immediately returned to the airport. Two of the operatives left on the Chinese plane with a flight plan to Cape Town. The other two chartered a small plane for a flight to Victoria Falls. We don't have eyes on them any longer."

There was silence in the room as the men considered the implications of this information. Johannes spoke first.

"Chin must have told them about Wang Jin and the Hard Livings gang. Whoever runs that gang would have no reason to talk to the Chinese secret police over the phone. I assume the two men on the way to Cape Town are going to gather information about the gangsters who are helping Wang Jin."

Bekker interjected, "Since Wang Jin knew in advance that Baruti and Sarah would be in Victoria Falls, he probably requested that the Hard Livings send him men familiar with the area. Lord knows there are plenty of those who went to South Africa looking for work."

Baruti joined in. "Wang Jin doesn't know the area, so to hide Sarah, he would have to rely on the knowledge of whoever the Hard Livings sent."

Bekker jumped up and approached the map with a black marker. "Right, so their options to hide Sarah are going to be limited by their knowledge of the Victoria Falls area. I don't think they would have kept moving her after daylight, so our search area is within a circle with about a hundred-mile radius." He drew a circle on the map around Victoria Falls.

Masisi said, "The Chinese are going to Cape Town to identify the goons sent to help Wang Jin. If they know who they are and learn something about them and their families, it may give them clues as to where Sarah is being held."

"Mok, do you know if the Chinese operatives are armed?" Bekker asked.

"I don't but they're traveling as diplomats, so they could have brought weapons in a diplomatic pouch, or they could have picked up guns at the embassy. Since they're diplomats flying private, there is no security check at the airport. Given the nature of what they are up to, I think you should assume they're armed and willing to use their weapons."

"I agree," Johannes said. "Thanks for the update, Mok. We'll keep you informed."

Baruti disconnected the call. "Now what?"

"The Chinese have a good idea. If they can identify the gangsters who are helping Wang Jin, it could lead to their families and local associates who may be in touch with them or provide leads. We don't have time to go to Cape Town, and those gangsters wouldn't talk to us anyway," Johannes said.

"Why would the gangsters talk to the Chinese?" Baruti asked.

"The oldest reason in the world…money," Bekker replied.

"The Chinese in Cape Town will surely contact the two who came here. I think we should put surveillance on the ones coming here," Johannes said.

"I could do that," Baruti said. "They won't pay any attention to another black man in this town."

Johannes and Bekker nodded. "I'll talk to local guides at the nearby safari camps about where they could hide Sarah within that circle," Bekker said, pointing at the map on the wall.

"OK. Good," Johannes replied. "I'll contact the US Embassy in Harare and ask them to put pressure on the local police to get off their ass and find Sarah, a high-profile missing American businesswoman. Relations between the United States and Zimbabwe aren't very good right now, but if it's pitched that kidnapping of foreigners at Victoria Falls is bad for tourism, it might light a fire under the government to push the cops into action."

Baruti and Bekker left. Johannes looked at his watch, grimaced, and picked up his phone.

CHAPTER 44

SARAH HEARD SOMEONE MOVING AROUND.

"Asshole chink better pay us. That is one fine piece of ass in there."

Hearing the comment, Sarah moved quietly to the wall nearest the old van.

"Shut up, Foxtrot. Ten grand to lay off her until the ransom is paid. That's more money than you earned in the last ten years."

Sarah put her eye to a gap in the siding and saw two black men arguing. One was average height and rail thin. The other was about the same height but wide as a bulldozer. The men were standing at the back of the van, drinking beer. A third man appeared from the far side of the van. He was taller that the others, maybe six feet, with a muscular build that was evident in a dirty, olive-green wife-beater T-shirt and green army pants. He swaggered over to the skinny one and grabbed a handful of his shirt.

"I want that money, Foxtrot. You so much as touch that woman, and I'll gut your ass and leave you for the hyenas."

Foxtrot bowed his head in submission. "Yeah, sure, Dingo. I was just sayin'."

Dingo slapped him. "Keep your mouth shut."

Foxtrot slinked out of Sarah's line of sight.

That was something. Kidnapped. The only bastard who would do that was Wang Jin. He was going to pay them to leave her alone…at least until the ransom arrived.

Weakness was settling in. Her head continued to pound like a ten-pound hammer hitting an anvil. She needed water, food, and a plan to get out of here. Wherever here was. She would act weak and exhausted while she built her strength and figured out how to escape.

She did not want these awful people to know she had overheard their conversation, so she waited for several minutes before pounding on the door and shouting, "Hello, is anyone out there? Please, I need water and something to eat."

"Bull, get her some water." It was Dingo's voice. The wide man was Bull. Three captors: Dingo, Bull, and Foxtrot. Not their real names. What a trio.

A few minutes later, the door opened, and Bull threw two bottles of water on the floor.

Sarah scrambled after the bottles like they contained the nectar of life. Which they did. "Food! What about some food?" she yelled.

"Shut up, bitch. You'll eat when we do."

Sarah sat against the wall nearest the van, listening for any further conversation from the men as she slowly worked her way through the first bottle of water. They weren't wearing masks. That did not bode well for her. Maybe they didn't know she could see them. Maybe they thought she would succumb to the American stereotype that all black men looked alike. Maybe they were stupid, and her identifying them to the police hadn't occurred to them. Maybe they were going to kill her, or…No, not that…No. Never. She would kill herself before she would let them sell her.

A solitary tear leaked from Sarah's left eye. She angrily wiped it away. She was going to escape. There was no other choice. The only question was how and when.

What to do when she was free? Find someone to help her, of course.

In the middle of Africa? In the middle of nowhere?

For the first time in her life, she cursed her attractiveness, regretted her tall, slim figure. If she had been ugly, short, and fat, she would not be the subject of these criminals' sexual fantasies. But she could run faster and longer than they could. She was in better physical condition. If she could just get away, they would never catch her in that old van in the virtually roadless wilderness of this rough country.

The sun was high in the sky when Foxtrot shouted from the door, "Get away from the door! Against the far wall if you want something to eat."

Sarah saw a flash of him as he opened the door and put a metal bowl and plastic spoon on the floor and quickly closed the door.

She picked up the bowl, which was warm to the touch. The contents looked like dog food. She took a very small bite. Freeze-dried stew made edible with hot water. It tasted like wet cardboard, but it would keep her alive.

As she hungrily ate the stew, Sarah thought about how she could get these goons to let her outside. If she could get out, she could run. They wouldn't shoot her; it would cost them $10,000. Then she looked down at her feet. Running shoes that she had worn to dinner. Thank God the dinner had been casual. What if she had been wearing flats or, even worse, heels? Thank God again that they hadn't taken her shoes. These guys were amateurs when it came to kidnapping, but then, she was an amateur when it came to escaping from kidnappers.

She took the last bite of stew and washed it down with a swallow from the second bottle of water.

How do I get them to let me out of here?

CHAPTER 45

BEFORE BARUTI LEFT THE Victoria Falls Hotel, Bekker and Johannes handed him a small duffel bag. Inside were several items they thought might be needed: binoculars, a GLOCK handgun with an extra magazine, a prepaid cell phone, an electronic tracking device and receiver, and two bottles of water. Baruti made it to the airport just as the MSS operatives' plane touched down.

The Chinese rented a Toyota sedan, and Baruti followed them to the Victoria Falls Safari Lodge, where they both went inside.

He took a big risk by pulling up next to their car, getting out, and sticking the magnetic tracker inside the rear bumper. As he turned away from their car, he heard Chinese being spoken behind him. Baruti's heart missed a beat. Had they seen him?

He gambled that they would see just another black man in a country of black people and wouldn't pay any attention to him. Taking a deep breath, he walked past them toward the hotel lobby. They ignored him, and he breathed a deep sigh of relief.

Baruti kept walking into the lobby and approached the reception desk, where the desk clerk greeted him with a big smile.

"Tell me, brother, out of curiosity, what were those Chinese guys doing here?" Baruti asked.

The desk clerk shrugged. "They wanted to know if we had a Chinese man, early thirties, staying here. I said no and they left."

"Thanks, brother."

Baruti returned to his car and followed them with the tracker to another hotel, where they went inside. Less than a minute later, they returned to their car.

He called Johannes and told him what was going on.

"They must have some reason to think Wang Jin is still in Victoria Falls," Johannes said. "I can't imagine that they're holding Sarah in a local hotel. I think the Hard Livings goons have her somewhere else and Wang Jin stayed in town to be in communication with his bank. They might get lucky, so keep following them."

CHAPTER 46

FIFTEEN MINUTES FROM VICTORIA Falls and just inside the Victoria Falls Private Game Reserve, Wang Jin sat on the balcony of his luxury bungalow at the Stanley & Livingstone Boutique Hotel, enjoying lunch with a glass of fine South African sauvignon blanc. A tower of giraffes walked past, moving first both legs on one side and then both legs on the other. Something spooked them, and they ran away, swinging their front legs and rear legs in unison.

He had given Baruti seventy-two hours to pay the ransom and no way to contact him to negotiate a different deal or ask for another proof of life. It was a big ask for him to pay without more assurance that Sarah would be released unharmed. Maybe he should have played it differently, let him bargain, make some demands and so forth…No. All that would do was give them clues as to her whereabouts and draw things out. His plan had been to strike quickly, make a nonnegotiable demand, and be done with this while the others were still off-balance.

He was increasingly worried about his father's reaction to the Eastern Enterprises failure. Because he hadn't answered his father's calls and emails, Wang Chen would be worried and would probably have State Security locate him by his electronic signature. When he found out Wang Jin was offline, things would escalate quickly. While the old man was gruff with him, he knew that his father loved him unconditionally. He would move heaven and earth to be sure his only son was safe. He should have contacted Wang Chen before he had gone off the grid. Told him not to worry. It was possible the old fool was doing something that would interfere with his plans.

He poured another glass of wine and noticed a group of impalas drifting past. He saw the long grass behind the last impala move and picked up a pair of hotel binoculars from the table. Not one but two cheetahs were creeping along behind the impalas. He noted there was a breeze keeping the cheetahs' scent from reaching their prey.

Wang Jin had been told that a cheetah's top speed is around seventy miles an hour for a relatively short distance. An impala can reach fifty miles per hour but sustain it for a much longer distance than a cheetah. The cheetahs would have to time their attack perfectly, or they would run out of speed before they could overtake the impalas. How close could they get?

The cheetahs leaped forward in a blur of motion. The impalas took off a fraction of a second later in a cloud of dust. Ten seconds later, the cheetahs had not quite reached the last impala and gave up. The cheetahs had missed a meal, and the last impala lived for another day.

Life and death in Africa depended on preparation and timing, whether animal or human.

He had to know what, if anything, his father was up to. If he called Wang Chen, he would have to listen to a tirade about how it was Wang Jin's fault that the Debswana deal had blown up, causing China to lose face. He would lecture him about his failures and order him home immediately. He could not defy a direct order, so he would not contact his father.

Wang Jin put down the binoculars, picked up one of his burner phones, and called Tommy. The conversation was short, with Tommy seeming to enjoy telling him his father had sent four secret police after him with orders to bring him home immediately and clean up his mess. The most recent report from the secret police stated they had been in touch with the 14K triad in Gaborone and the Hard Livings gang in Cape Town. They had reported that Wang Jin had engineered the kidnapping of the American businesswoman and was holding her for ransom or sexual pleasure. The Chinese secret police were on their way to Victoria Falls to follow up on the leads they had developed. According to Tommy, these men were under immense pressure to find Wang Jin and put an end to what could be a catastrophe for China and, more importantly, the chairman.

Wang Jin poured a third glass of wine. Tasted it and spit it out. He knew how the secret police worked. He would be forced onto a private plane and flown directly to Beijing. The three goons and Sarah would disappear.

The secret police would assume he was in Victoria Falls to monitor the kidnapping and would begin their search here. He had registered under a false name, but they would assume that. If he were them, he would search every hotel in the area for a Chinaman traveling alone and check him out.

He had to elude the secret police until the ransom deadline. The ransom would be paid or not. He would return home in triumph or disgrace. He would not be forced home like an errant dog before his plan had a chance to succeed. The best place to hide was also the worst: with the Hard Livings goons.

He hurriedly checked out of the Stanley & Livingstone Boutique Hotel and headed for the highway to Hwange National Park. Dingo had given him the GPS coordinates for the abandoned ranger cabin where they were holding Sarah.

―――

Baruti wondered where the Chinese were going as they drove out of Victoria Falls toward the airport. About ten minutes out of town, they turned down a long gravel road where there was a sign indicating it was the way to the Stanley & Livingstone Boutique Hotel. When they reached the hotel, they turned off the road and pulled up to a guard gate. Baruti stopped on the lightly traveled road and backed up, leaving just enough room to observe the gate.

They spoke to the guard, who picked up a telephone—probably calling the front desk—and said something. When they backed up and began turning around, Baruti could see that the men were in animated conversation. One of them pounded the dashboard.

Baruti was caught off guard by the maneuver and had no choice but to immediately drive forward, passing the gate and the Chinese as they pulled back on the road. He held his breath, hoping they wouldn't recognize his car from the last hotel. They continued their animated conversation and paid no attention to Baruti's car.

He breathed a sigh of relief, wiping the sweat off his forehead with the back of his hand. When they were out of sight in his rearview mirror, he took his time turning around, drove back to the guard gate, and pulled up to the barrier. The guard approached with a welcoming smile.

"Welcome to the Stanley & Livingstone Boutique Hotel. Do you have a reservation?"

"No. A friend of mine is staying here. A Chinese man in his mid-thirties with a thin mustache."

"That's Mr. Lee. He checked out a couple of hours ago. Popular fellow. Two Chinese men were just here also looking for him. Is there a problem?"

"No, not at all. We must have crossed our signals about where to meet. Sorry to bother you."

Baruti pulled back onto the road and started after the Chinese.

The tracker's red dot led him to The Three Monkeys bar and restaurant on the outskirts of Victoria Falls. The Chinese were sitting at an outside table where he was able to observe them as they ate. An hour later, one of the operatives got phone call. Talked for a minute, took a notebook and a pen from his pocket, and made some notes. They hurriedly paid the bill and rushed to their car.

Their next stop was a crowded village a few miles outside Victoria Falls. They stopped at a thatched-roof hut, and Baruti pulled under a tree down the street. A short time later, the operatives came out with one of them talking on his cell phone. When they were out of sight, Baruti went to the door of the hut.

"Hello, anyone home?" he called.

A stooped old woman leaning on a walking stick shuffled to the door. "What do you want?" she asked suspiciously.

"Those Chinese are bad men sent here to hurt a friend of mine. I must stop them. What did you tell them?"

"Nothing," the old woman spat out. "Go away."

An undernourished teenager pushed aside a dirty sheet separating the room from another and walked toward Baruti, smirking. "I know, but it will cost you."

The old woman spat in disgust and hobbled into the other room.

Baruti pulled out a US twenty-dollar bill and showed it to the teenager, who eyed it hungrily. He reached for the bill, but Baruti put his hand with the bill in his pocket. "Tell me everything first."

"Money first. Talk after," the teenager said with a smirk that indicated he had the upper hand.

Baruti's expression went from neutral to outrage in a flash. He didn't have time for this bullshit. His hands flashed out, and he grabbed the teenager by his dirty T-shirt, pulling him close. "Tell me and you get the money. Otherwise, I will beat it out of you."

The teenager's bravado evaporated as he looked at Baruti's face. "OK, OK. Let me go."

Baruti released his shirt.

"They're looking for my brother and can't find him. They paid me, and I told them he used to be a Hwange Park Ranger and he might be at an abandoned ranger cabin where we used to go camping. I told them how to find it."

"Where is it?"

"Twenty dollars more," the teenager said tentatively, looking away from Baruti.

He had to know the Chinese weren't looking for his brother to discuss the weather. He had sold out his blood for a few dollars. Would he tell Baruti the truth or send him on a wild goose chase?

"OK," Baruti said, pulling out another twenty and holding the bills in his hand where the teenager could see them. "But understand, young man: if you don't tell me the truth, I will come back here, and you will be very, very unhappy."

To Baruti's surprise, the teenager went to a table in the corner and wrote down GPS coordinates. He handed the paper to Baruti. "There's no other way to find the cabin unless you know the roads."

Baruti handed him the money, started to leave, then stopped. "Why did you tell them where your brother might be?"

"I hate the Chinese, but we need the money more. Besides, if my brother is there, he'll see them coming from far enough away to escape easily, and they'll never find him. Maybe they'll get lost, and the lions will get them."

Baruti nodded and left.

Back in the Toyota, he saw the red dot heading toward the airport. While continuing to follow them, he called the airport to inquire if any flights were arriving from Cape Town that day. There was a private plane due to arrive at five that evening.

CHAPTER 47

WHILE HE WAS DRIVING, Wang Jin's remaining cell phone vibrated. The only person with that number was Dingo. It couldn't be good news. Wang Jin answered gruffly. "Yes?"

Dingo was equally abrupt. "My mother just called. Two Chinese goons were at her house asking about you and me. She told them nothing, but they paid my little brother, and he told them where I might be. I'm going to move the cargo to site number two. You have the GPS coordinates?"

"Yes, but…"

"No buts. We're out of here. Your countrymen aren't coming here to pay their respects. Our separate fees are now ten thousand each. Agreed?"

That wasn't the deal, but at this point, Wang Jin had no choice. "OK."

"We'll meet you at site number two. Have our money with you." Dingo disconnected the call before Wang Jin could speak.

He only had $20,000 left. He had promised the goons $10,000 to leave Sarah alone and figured he might need the remaining $10,000 to pay his way home. Using a credit card was out of the question. If the ransom wasn't paid, he didn't have another $20,000 for the gangsters. Even if the ransom was paid, turning some of it to cash for use in Africa wouldn't be easy. The money would have to be wired somewhere. These goons weren't complete idiots. They would insist on accompanying him to the bank. What would stop them from demanding even more from him? How would he say no to a gun at his head?

Wang Jin could feel that things were beginning to spin out of control.

Baruti found the Chinese car at a sporting goods store. Counting on all blacks looking alike to the Chinese, he went inside and saw them piling more outdoor clothing on the counter than was necessary for two men. They were getting four men outfitted for the bush.

He called Johannes.

"The Chinese just missed Wang Jin at the Stanley & Livingstone. They got a call and went to a village outside town looking for a guy whose family lives there. He must be one of the kidnappers. They got GPS coordinates for an abandoned ranger cabin in Hwange. I also got the coordinates from the guy's younger brother. Now they're at a sporting goods store in Victoria Falls, getting outfitted for the bush. My guess is that they're going to wait for their buddies who are coming in at five. If we start now, we could get there a few hours before them."

"OK, I'll get a hold of Bekker, and we'll get geared up. Come on back to the hotel, and we'll hit the road."

CHAPTER 48

SARAH SAT AGAINST THE back wall of the cabin and took a small sip of water while analyzing her situation.

She was being held for ransom. These three goons were being paid extra to leave her alone until it was paid. That implied that once the money was received, these animals were free to abuse her to their hearts' content.

The kidnappers weren't wearing masks. It was obvious that Wang Jin had no intention of letting her go even if he got the ransom. She was going to end up dead—or worse. Until the ransom payment was resolved, they couldn't hurt her too badly and would surely not intentionally kill her. Once the ransom was paid, or refused, there would be no chance to escape, so she had to make her move as soon as possible.

Sarah didn't know where she was, but it was reasonable to believe that the kidnappers had wanted to get her to this cabin without being seen, which meant traveling in darkness. Logically, she was within a five- or six-hour drive of Victoria Falls. Since they had kidnapped her in Zimbabwe, the smart move would have been to take her to bordering Zambia. To get to Zambia from the hotel, they would have to cross the bridge and go through customs. They wouldn't take that risk in the middle of the night when the border guards had nothing else to do but check vehicles.

Taking her to Botswana would be dangerous since Wang Jin was a fugitive there and Baruti's father could flood the area with troops and police. So her best guess was that they were still in Zimbabwe, a country that didn't have very good relations with the United States. There was no traffic noise, no sense of a city. Baruti had told her about how forest and game preserves connected Hwange National Park in Zimbabwe and Chobe National Park in Botswana. She was most likely being held somewhere in Hwange National Park.

If she could get away from the goons and elude them long enough, she was likely to come across a safari guide or park ranger. She took another small sip of water. There had to be water out there for the animals. A water hole—or, better yet, a river. The water might make her sick, but it would keep her alive.

She looked at her feet. Thank God they hadn't gone to the fancy restaurant. She was wearing ripstop safari pants and a sleeveless beige top with her running shoes. The weather would be cold at night and in the morning. Not freezing, just uncomfortable. She could do this. She had to.

Loud voices came from outside. Sarah stood, crossed the cabin, and peered through a gap in the siding. The goons were packing their gear, obviously getting ready to move. If she let them tie her up, it was all over.

Foxtrot walked toward the cabin. It was now or never.

"Get against the far wall!" Foxtrot shouted as he reached the door.

She did. He checked where she was, then looked down and began unlocking the door.

Sarah moved quickly next to the door opposite the hinges. As Foxtrot pushed the door into the room and stepped inside, Sarah, taking advantage of his forward momentum, grabbed the back of his shirt and belt, and threw him into the room, where he tripped and fell. Then she was out the door.

She turned away from where the other two men were loading the van and began running. Sarah was across the small, flat area, moving at full speed and down the short hill before Foxtrot shouted the alarm.

In a matter of seconds, she was on the flat grassland heading toward a tree line flanking a dry riverbed about a quarter mile away. She could hear the men shouting.

She ran full speed through tall, brown grass, wincing as it scratched her arms. Thank God she had on long pants, or the sharp edges of the grass would be slicing her legs to pieces. She risked a glance over her shoulder. Bull was lumbering after her.

At that moment, she tripped over something and went flying forward. Her innate athleticism kicked in, and she automatically tucked her shoulder and rolled through the fall. Then she leaped to her feet and continued, not risking another look back.

Sarah lengthened her stride and eased her pace, picking her way through the rough terrain. If necessary, she could do twenty-six miles like this. The roar of the van engine was coming after her. The tree line and the dry riverbed were now one hundred yards away.

Sarah picked up her pace. She had to get across the riverbed, which should stop pursuit by the van. If not, they would just cut her off and tackle her. The realization of what lay in store for her if they caught her spurred her on.

The roar of the engine was bearing down on her. Intermingled with the sound was the noise of the van getting slammed about on the rough ground. Sarah made it to the tree line.

The van wasn't four-wheel drive, and the sand in the fifty-yard-wide riverbed looked deep. As she approached, she was surprised to find it was sunk into the landscape. Sarah leaped off the riverbank and dropped three feet down into the sand. She slogged across.

As she climbed up the bank on the other side, the van shot off the bank behind her and slammed into the riverbed. The vehicle moved a few feet before its rear wheels began to spin, digging themselves deeper into the soft sand.

The van was stuck.

Sarah alternated trotting with brisk walking as she headed toward a brush-covered ridgeline about a mile away. None of the men pursued her. She scrambled up the rock-strewn ridge and ended up bent over, hands on her knees, breathing heavily.

From the ridge, Sarah could see all three men digging in the sand around the vehicle. She selected a spot where she could keep an eye on them as she caught her breath and decided which way to go.

Not far from the van, Sarah saw an elephant enter the riverbed and began pawing the sand to make a hole. This went on for a full minute before the elephant put its trunk in the hole, apparently sucked in water, and moved its trunk into its mouth. She was thirsty. She would have to find water soon.

Sarah climbed to the top of the ridge. From where she stood, the ridge gradually sloped downward into a huge, grassy plain that seemed flat from the top of the ridge. The plain was dotted with various kinds of antelopes, elephants, zebras, and a few wildebeests. Under other circumstances, she would have marveled at the beauty of the scene. Across the plain, maybe two miles away, it stopped at the edge of a treed area. It was well past noon, and her shadow was off her right side. That made the treed area to the north, which was the right direction toward Victoria Falls.

She didn't see any evidence of dirt roads or tracks in the grassy plain, so the men would have a hard time driving their van out there. They were probably still digging it out. Once they did that, they would have to follow her on foot, which would be difficult, given her lead. Nevertheless, she would hurry to the tree line and figure out how to find water and help from there. Sarah picked her way down the ridge and began walking at a fast pace across the plain.

Her plan was to stay far away from any elephants and hope the big cats were all sleeping in the warmth of the afternoon. If she came across a big cat, the one thing she would not do is run and become prey. Sweat began to roll down her back and bead on her forehead. From exertion or nerves, she did not know.

CHAPTER 49

JOHANNES AND BEKKER CARRIED duffel bags with their rifles, ammunition, and other equipment to Bekker's Toyota. Their pistols were holstered on their belts, with extra ammunition in belt pouches. Baruti pulled up beside them and transferred his equipment to Bekker's vehicle.

On their way out of town, they stopped at a petrol station, where they loaded up on extra five-gallon cans of fuel, water, energy drinks, and protein bars. It was after 2 p.m. when they headed to Hwange National Park. As they drove, Bekker called a friend who guided in Hwange and discussed where they were heading.

An hour later, they were on Botswana's M9 roadway twenty miles from a formal entrance to the park when Bekker said, "Help me watch for a half-buried tire on the left, and turn in there. Jokko said it's a way into the park to avoid the entrance. Locals use it to avoid park fees, so it's probably the road the kidnappers used. We won't be more than ten miles from the abandoned cabin, but it will be rough going." He handed his mobile device to Johannes, who opened Google Earth, then its search bar, where he entered the GPS coordinates the teenager had given Baruti.

A short time later, the tire appeared, and they turned onto a rough dirt track. They bounced up and down and side to side in deep sand and deeply rutted dirt for forty-five minutes before Johannes held up his hand.

"The GPS says we're close. We can't just drive in there," he said.

"Right. Here's my idea," Bekker replied. "We turn this vehicle around to be ready for a quick exit. Baruti stays here ready to drive us out in a hurry. Luc, you and I move off this track into the bush and work our way together toward the cabin. Jokko said it sits in the open on a small hill about a quarter mile above a dry riverbed. Once we have it in sight, we can evaluate what we want to do."

Johannes was quiet, evaluating the plan. Then he looked at his watch. "The Chinese plane is due in about now. We must assume they're geared up and ready to go. We don't know how they plan to get to the cabin, but they may come up this track. If they do, we have a little over an hour before they could arrive."

The three men sat, silently considering their options. Johannes was the first to speak. "There was a faint sidetrack about a half a mile back. If Baruti doesn't hear from us in forty-five minutes, he should go back to that track and pull into it far enough to be out of sight. If the Chinese come up this track, they won't waste time getting to the cabin. Are you OK with that, Baruti?"

"Luc, I may be a city boy, but I spent my share of time in the bush growing up. I'll be fine."

Bekker took camouflage face paint from the equipment box and painted Johannes's face and then his own. Then they each painted their hands. Next, they removed their rifles from the duffel bags.

Bekker handed each of them a bottle of water. Bekker and Johannes drank deeply and put their water bottles in the Land Cruiser. Without another word, they slipped into the bush with Bekker, the wilderness guide and tracker, leading the way. He had become the de facto leader without any formal discussion. Baruti turned the vehicle around and stood behind it, listening and scanning the bush.

Ten minutes later, Bekker and Johannes reached the edge of an open area from which they could see the cabin on a small hill off to their right a quarter of a mile away. The dry riverbed was off to their left.

Bekker took binoculars from his backpack and surveyed the hilltop. "I don't see anything moving or out of place up there. Let's stay in the bush, circle to the right, and come up the hill behind the boulders. Then we can split up and circle around to the cabin," he whispered.

Johannes nodded and moved off.

It was eerily quiet as they moved up the hill and stopped behind the huge boulders. The men looked at each other and moved off in opposite directions, circling the small hilltop. Five minutes later, they stood facing each other in front of the cabin. They were alone.

"Luc, stay here and keep your eyes open while I look around."

Bekker started inside the cabin and then moved outward in increasing circles. A few minutes later, he returned.

"Someone was here for sure. There was a camp set up over there." He pointed. "There's an old sleeping bag in the cabin with a lot of fresh footprints. Come with me."

Bekker went to the cabin door and pointed to footprints leading away from the door and to the edge of the hill.

"There are four sets of footprints and one set of vehicle tracks on this hill. These are smaller than the others. See how long the interval is between prints? If this was Sarah, she came out the door running."

They followed the prints to the edge of the hilltop, where they were joined by a large set.

"Here comes someone following her. Why don't you get Baruti while I start following these tracks?"

A short time later, the Toyota nosed out of the bush and headed toward Bekker, who was halfway to the riverbed. He waved them over.

"They are chasing her with the van. She may be fast, but she can't outrun a vehicle."

The trail of prints continued to the riverbank, where it was instantly obvious that the van driver hadn't realized there was a three-foot drop-off into the deep sand of the riverbed. Piles of sand next to fresh holes showed that the van had been stuck, dug out, and moved down the riverbed until it was able to climb up the bank and out of the riverbed on the same side it had entered.

Bekker stood on the bank and studied the scene. "Wait here."

He crossed the riverbed and climbed out, studying the ground. He walked off to the north a bit, turned around, and returned to Johannes and Baruti.

"The good news is that no one followed her as she headed north. My Toyota will cross the riverbed with no problem, so we can follow her. For sure Sarah doesn't know where she's going. We don't either, except she seems to be heading north. The problem is that the Chinese will be here shortly and can follow us. Also, we don't know where the kidnappers have gone. One of them knows the park, and they may be heading to cut her off. To top it all off, we don't know where Wang Jin is."

"We have to go after Sarah," Baruti blurted without hesitation. "Chinese be damned, what about lions, elephants, hippos? My God, we must find her. Once we have her safe, we can worry about the fucking Chinese."

Bekker and Johannes looked at each another and nodded.

"I'll get the Toyota across the riverbed and then walk the trail," Bekker said.

He entered the riverbed where the van had come out and crossed through the deep sand without any problems. He turned the driving over to Baruti and then instructed, "Luc, you keep looking around for the Chinese or anyone else."

CHAPTER 50

WANG JIN STOPPED AT the main gate to Hwange National Park and picked up a road map of the park. On the way back to his rental car, he paused when he saw a sign for the Hwange Safari Lodge. He could be comfortable at the lodge and avoid the gangsters in case the ransom wasn't paid, but if the secret police came here looking for him, he would be easy to find. While he was contemplating which of two bad choices to make, his cell phone buzzed. It was Dingo.

"The bitch got away from us. She jumped that moron Foxtrot and ran away. We went after her in the van, but she runs like the wind. Anyway, the van got stuck, and by the time we dug it out, she was out of sight."

Sputtering with anger, Wang Jin started, "How could you—"

Dingo interrupted. "Just listen. She took off north but has no idea where she is or where she's going. I spent two years patrolling this part of the park. I'll find her. We're going to circle around to get in front of her and work our way back. If the lions don't get her, we'll have her by noon tomorrow and will bring her to cabin number two."

The incompetent fools! He wanted to scream at Dingo, but that wouldn't help things. He probably didn't need the bitch anyway.

"OK, but that means she'll spend the night in the bush. Is she likely to survive?"

"If she's lucky and does not do anything stupid, her chances are better than even," Dingo said.

"Maybe she'll be smart enough to climb a tree," Wang Jin said half-seriously.

"Lions can climb trees. Leopards drag their kills into them to keep other predators from stealing their food. What she really needs is luck," Dingo answered.

Wang Jin sighed. "All right. I'll wait for your call."

The gangsters didn't know he was in Hwange. They would only come to camp number two if they found Sarah, so he would be safe there for the time being from both the gangsters and the secret police. He looked at his watch. The ransom deadline was getting closer.

Wang Jin pulled away from the gate on the way to cabin number two.

Fifteen minutes later, an enclosed Toyota SUV pulled through the Hwange National Park gate. Inside were the four Chinese operatives and a black man. The Chinese had exchanged their vehicle and paid an exorbitant amount to hire a guide who was familiar with the park.

The guide put the GPS coordinates of the abandoned ranger cabin into Google Maps, and they were off on a smooth dirt road. Ten miles later, they turned off onto a dirt track that veered into the thick shrubs and trees of the bush.

Three miles down the track, the guide halted the vehicle and told the Chinese that the abandoned cabin was just around the bend and up a short hill. When the Chinese opened backpacks and removed pistols, the guide's eyes got big.

"Hey, now wait a minute. I didn't sign on for this."

The man sitting next to him stuck the barrel of a Norinco NP27 semiautomatic pistol under his chin and said in perfect English, "You signed on for what we tell you to do."

The guide was forced out of the SUV and handcuffed to a door handle. His cell phone was taken and placed in one of the men's backpacks. The four Chinese removed Norinco CQ-A rifles from a duffel bag and, using hand signals, moved off down the dirt track.

When they got to the edge of the clearing, the men, again using hand signals, separated and quickly approached the hill from the four points of the compass, rifles at the ready. No one was there, and they looked around in disgust.

One of them returned to the SUV, unlocked the guide, and drove them to the base of the hill, where the men held a conversation in Chinese.

"You're a tracker. Look around and tell us what you see," the English-speaking Chinese said.

The guide could feel the tension among the Chinese, who had turned from generous employers to murderous captors. They did not have to speak; the guide had no doubt his life was on the line. He took a deep breath, nodded, and headed up the hill. A short time later, he came back down to a point a short distance from the Chinese and waved them over.

"The older sign and prints say four people made camp up there with a vehicle and small tents. One stayed in the cabin and left from there running. The running footprints were either from a small man or a woman wearing running shoes. The vehicle came off the hill here, following the runner.

"The fresher footprints say three people came later and covered the area. They followed the vehicle tracks down the hill to this point. From here, they all went that way," the guide reported, gesturing toward the tree line and dry riverbed in the distance.

The Chinese conversed rapidly before the English-speaking man said, "Follow the tracks."

The guide started off, following the tracks toward the riverbed. The English-speaking Chinese man followed him closely while two men separated on either side of the track and kept their heads on a swivel, watching for surprises, whether from animals or humans. They stopped at the riverbed and waited for the guide, who walked in widening circles studying the mess of overlapping tracks and tire prints. Then he returned.

"A vehicle chased the runner into the riverbed and got stuck. The three men with the vehicle dug it out and went back that way." He pointed toward the cabin. "Another heavy vehicle crossed the riverbed over there." He pointed again. "And the driver and two men on foot followed the runner's tracks to the north."

There was a rapid-fire conversation among the foursome in their native language while the guide stood by, beating himself up for having been seduced by their money.

CHAPTER

51

AS SARAH WADED THROUGH dry, waist-high khaki-colored grass, she wiped sweat from her forehead with her fingertips and flipped it away. The grassy plain might have looked like a midwestern wheat field, but it wasn't. She had tiny cuts and slices on her arms and hands to prove it.

The distant line of dark-brown leaved trees and shrubs was interspersed with occasional gold and green, reminding her of late fall in Central Park. She wasn't in Central Park. The tree line that had not seemed that far away when she started didn't seem to be getting any closer. As she continued walking under the cloudless light-blue sky, the pale-yellow orb of sun off to her left began its descent toward the horizon.

Sarah stayed as far away from the elephants as possible while maintaining what she thought was a northerly direction. The antelopes, or whatever the horned animals were, moved away as she approached, as did the zebras and wildebeests, who were out in force. The predators were probably resting during the heat of the day and would begin looking for their next meal when the sun got closer to the horizon.

Sarah unconsciously quickened her pace. She needed to get out of the open and find water before dark.

Bekker followed Sarah's tracks to the bottom of the ridgeline and studied it while he waited for the Toyota to come alongside him. When it arrived, he walked over and spoke to Johannes and Baruti.

"We can't drive up there. My guess is that she went over the ridge and kept going. If she stays north, she'll eventually cut a track and eventually a dirt road with some regular traffic."

"Fantastic," Baruti enthused.

"It's a mixed blessing," Bekker replied, placing a calming hand on Baruti's arm. "At least one of the kidnappers is familiar with this part of the park. My guess is that they returned to the main park road system and are circling around to the north to get in front of her. Then they'll work back south looking for her. Maybe not, but that would be the smart play, and it's never wise to underestimate your enemy."

Johannes looked at the sun and his watch. "If we can't catch up with Sarah, it's beginning to look like all of us will have to spend the night in the bush."

Bekker nodded. "The animals won't bother us if we're in the vehicle, but Sarah…well, we just have to hope and pray she's lucky."

"Maybe she'll climb a tree," Baruti offered.

"Lions and leopards can climb trees, but if she got up in one with a walking stick to poke at the cat, it might work unless the cat's starving."

"OK, OK," Johannes interjected. "We're burning daylight. If we can't drive up the ridge, can we go around it?"

"I don't know," Bekker said, looking along the ridgeline, which did not get any lower. "If we try it, we may lose Sarah's trail."

"We could split up. Mr. Johannes and I could try to drive around, and you could follow the trail. Otherwise, our choice is to leave the vehicle here or drive back to the main road and try to get ahead of Sarah where the gangsters are probably waiting."

After a quiet moment considering their options, Johannes broke the silence. "If we try to drive around together, we may lose Sarah's trail. If we split up and can't get around or meet up on the other side, Aiden may be left to face the three gangsters and perhaps Wang Jin, or you and I could end up facing them."

Bekker looked at the ridge. "If we go on foot and find Sarah, we'll have to return here to get the Toyota. Otherwise, there's too much of a chance of running into the gangsters."

Baruti turned and looked behind them. "And what about the Chinese secret police? They're back there somewhere. We left a clear trail to follow. If we proceed on foot, we'll be between the gangsters and the Chinese. If we find Sarah and try to return here, we're likely to walk into the Chinese."

"OK," Johannes said, "we're between them. There's nothing we can do about that. Our priority is to find Sarah as soon as possible. Once we have her, we can decide what to do."

"If we have a choice," Bekker warned.

"I say we leave the Toyota here and follow her on foot," Johannes said.

"Luc, with respect, I'm out and about on the ranch all the time. Baruti is young. You're a senior citizen and work in an office. Are you fit enough for this?" Bekker asked quietly.

Johannes started to answer, and Bekker interrupted him, speaking quietly. "We're starting a search and recovery mission. We can expect to find Sarah exhausted, thirsty, and hungry. We may have to carry her to safety. We're going to have to avoid or engage two armed groups that won't hesitate to kill us. If you slow us down, the mission, the whole team, is at risk."

Bekker's eyes bored into Johannes's own. Baruti stood with his mouth slightly open, stunned at the reality of Bekker's statement.

Johannes maintained eye contact and was silent for a moment before answering.

"Aiden, I run three days a week and lift some weights, but you're right. I think I'm in good shape for a sixty-eight-year-old, but that may not be enough. As you said, we're dealing with three armed gangsters and Wang Jin on one side and four skilled Chinese operatives on the other. The bottom line is you need my gun. Let's get our gear out of the Toyota and get started."

Bekker nodded without hesitation. Matter settled.

The men filled their backpacks with water and the rest of their gear. Baruti handed the keys to Bekker, and they started up the ridge in single file: Bekker on point, Baruti in the middle, and Johannes walking drag, keeping an eye out behind them. As they moved out, a sense of déjà vu came over Bekker and Johannes.

CHAPTER 52

WANG JIN PULLED INTO a clearing on top of a long ridgeline overlooking another dry riverbed bordered by thick trees and shrubs. When the wet season began in November, these riverbeds would overflow, their banks turning brown leaves and grass to green.

He parked behind the dilapidated cabin against the bush line and inspected the structure. One of the door hinges hung loose, so he had to drag the door open. Inside, he had to fight through cobwebs. One of the tin panels that made up the roof was lying on the floor, which was covered with animal droppings of some kind. There was no furniture, no stove, and no fireplace. He backed out, wiping his face. He wasn't going to stay in there. He would sleep in the car.

He had stolen blankets, pillows, and towels from the hotel, along with all the snacks, water, and soft drinks in the minibar. Best of all, he had taken the complimentary half-pint bottles of gin, vodka, and whiskey. That would hold him over until the ransom deadline.

He checked his satellite phone. He had service. Now he needed to think about the extra money that the gangsters had demanded. To help him think clearly, he did a line of coke off the hood of his rental SUV.

His arrangement with the Hard Livings gang had called for him to pay $50,000 to the 14K triad as an escrow agent of sorts. Half was to be delivered to the gang to get the men moving and the remainder once the ransom was paid or declined. The deal wasn't that complicated. What had gone wrong?

Wang Jin didn't trust gangsters, who had just gotten out of prison, to leave Sarah alone until the ransom was resolved. He should have made that part of the original deal, but he hadn't thought about it at the time. If he was going to stick with his original demand, it didn't matter what happened to Sarah. But if Baruti didn't pay, Wang Jin wanted the option to make another demand, and for that, he would need to show she was alive and reasonably healthy. Baruti would be more likely to pay if he thought Sarah was unharmed. He also wanted the option of being able to threaten to send Baruti pieces of his lover.

It had been a mistake to offer these criminals $10,000 off the books, so to speak, to leave Sarah alone. He should have gone back to Strangle and renegotiated the deal, sending the gang the $10,000. That would have solved the problem in a businesslike way. It was the off-the-books money that had given these three criminals the idea that they could demand more for themselves. Wang Jin opened the vodka bottle and took a healthy swallow.

The fact that third parties might come after the kidnappers had been obvious from the outset of the deal. That was not a new development. These goons had breached the deal made by Strangle when they had demanded additional under-the-table funds. Now that they had no fear of demanding more from him, what was the limit? What if they put a gun to his head?

Wang Jin didn't have the extra money the goons were demanding and wouldn't have access to the ransom if it was paid without a wire transfer to a suitable bank. For the first time in his life, there was a good-size chink in Wang Jin's narcissistic arrogance. He was in over his head. He knew nothing about gangsters. These men weren't afraid of or intimidated by him. Why shouldn't they hold a gun to his head and force him to give them the ransom? With the money, they could kiss the Hard Livings gang goodbye and go wherever they wanted.

He had no choice. He got out his satellite phone and nervously called Strangle.

Wang Jin played it straight and told him the truth. He was careful not to complain or say anything about the gangsters except that they were demanding money that wasn't part of the deal. Strangle listened but said nothing except for Wang Jin to have Dingo call him.

Wang Jin thought Strangle would demand the $10,000 from the men and tell them there would be no more money from Wang Jin. He wouldn't have believed it before, but it looked like he was going to be saved by an informal code of honor among African gangsters. To celebrate and help him relax, he did another line of coke and chased it with a pull from the vodka bottle.

For the millionth time, he asked himself, *Will Baruti pay the ransom?*

If he did, Wang Jin was in fat city. He could return to Hong Kong with full pockets and deny everything. Releasing Sarah had never been part of his plan. Regardless of whether he was paid, she couldn't be allowed to speak to the African police, and she had to pay dearly for disrespecting him. He would abuse her sexually until she begged for death. When he was finished with her, whatever was left would be given to the gangsters with only one condition: she could not leave the bush alive.

The gangsters had returned to the main park road and were following it in a loop that went east and then north. Using GPS coordinates, Dingo planned to reach a point on the main road directly north of the cabin from which Sarah had escaped, which he figured was about twenty miles away. Assuming she kept moving north, she would cross a large, grassy plain and enter an area of rugged hills that were thick with bush vegetation. The hills did not permit any east-west vehicle tracks. There was only one lightly traveled north-south track. If she stayed off the ridges, the terrain would lead her to the track. It was human nature that she would follow it.

It was late afternoon when the gangsters reached the junction of the main road and the faint vehicle track coming from the south. Since there was no way Sarah could reach them before dark, they pulled off the main road onto the vehicle track and followed it for a short distance, where they would spend the night in their van.

In the morning, Dingo planned to have Foxtrot and Bull move into the bush along the track, where they would set up listening posts on opposite sides of the track. He would patrol the park road. When Sarah passed one of them, they would contact one another with their handheld radios and fall in behind her. He would head south, and they would have her trapped.

It was a red-orange twilight when the Chinese operatives and their guide saw Bekker's Toyota in the distance. They stopped and, after a brief conversation, three of the Chinese spread out and worked their way through the bush toward the vehicle. Finding no one there, they signaled the fourth man, who drove up with the guide.

The footprints going up the ridge told them the story. Three men were following the woman.

The Chinese were shouldering their backpacks and getting ready to continue following the tracks when their guide spoke up.

"Hey, listen up. It's going to be full dark in a few minutes, and we'll be on foot in the bush. We cannot follow them in the dark. The lions and leopards will be out, and you may walk into a buffalo. It you stay here in the vehicles, the animals will leave you alone. We can get an early start and be more rested than spending the night on the ground."

The foursome conducted an animated conversation in Chinese, after which the English-speaking man said, "Good idea. We'll stay here."

CHAPTER 53

THE INSIDE OF SARAH'S mouth stuck to her teeth. Creating moisture by sucking on a couple of pebbles failed. Panic nibbled at the edge of her consciousness. Water. She had to have water.

As she hurried toward the tree line, Sarah felt like she was in a losing race with the sun, which seemed to be accelerating its inexorable fall to the horizon. Predators. Big cats. Her back tingled. She could feel them slowly stirring and leisurely stretching after an afternoon in the shade. It was almost time to begin their nightly quest for their next meal.

When she finally pushed out of the tall grass, she found a clearing that ran to the tree line. In the middle of the clearing was a good-size water hole where a half dozen elephants were using their trunks to suck up water to drink and spray themselves with water and mud.

Sarah slipped back into the grass and kept a low profile as she moved in a big arc to the tree line. Once there, she stayed hidden from the water hole and watched the young elephants play in the water, slapping it around with their trunks. In another context, this would have been fun to watch, but now, she waited impatiently for the elephants to leave.

Water. There it was, right in front of her. Sarah was beyond caring if it was safe to drink. The city girl wanted nothing more than to run to the water, cup her hands, scoop water into her mouth, and dump it on top of her head. The damn elephants showed no sign of leaving. Worse, she could see horned animals drifting toward the water hole. Bekker had showed her the differences among kudus, sables, elands, and several other horned animals, but it had been too much too fast to remember without repetition.

The sun continued its relentless march to the horizon as Sarah idly picked apart a vine that was hanging from the tree next to her. When she felt moisture with her fingers, she greedily stripped bark off the vine and sucked on the exposed fiber. Moisture. She pulled more of the vine loose, stripped off the bark, and continued to suck on the exposed fiber. It wasn't water, but the moisture provided some relief to her parched mouth and cracked lips.

While she did this, the elephants wandered away and were replaced by a dozen horned animals about the size of American cow elks. She remembered that sables were the ones with an almost black pelt with white streaks on their faces. Their pelts glowed in the golden light of the setting sun while they stood next to the now copper-colored water hole. Despite her weakened condition, Sarah marveled at the beauty of the scene.

Suddenly there was an explosion of movement. Two cheetahs burst from the grass. In less than a heartbeat, the sables took off, but the cheetahs leaped onto one of them and brought it to the ground. One cheetah had its mouth on the sable's throat, and the other held it down. They weren't tearing out the sable's throat but strangling it. The sable struggled for a short while. Then its movements became terminal jerks as it died.

The quick and the dead in the African bush. The cheetahs began to drag the sable toward the tree line about one hundred yards from where Sarah stood frozen with the shock from how quickly it had happened.

The grass exploded again, releasing a pack of hyenas that roared toward the cheetahs making high-pitched staccato sounds, intent on taking their kill. The cheetahs wisely retreated into the tree line to hunt for another meal. The hyenas tore into the sable, and in an instant, Sarah could see their bloody muzzles as the hyenas came up for air.

The water hole was a killing ground. It would soon be dark; she couldn't stay here any longer. She would have to find water in the thick bush. Sarah looked toward the setting sun, put it on her left, and moved off into the bush.

As she walked through the lengthening shadows, the terrain began to rise on both sides of her, creating a sandy path where walking was easier. As near as she could tell, it was running north. The unmistakable roar of a lion shattered the bush, bringing Sarah to a halt.

Should she climb to higher ground? No. If she was going to find water, it would be down here, not up there. She had to find water before anything else. There was nothing she could do about the lion, so she continued to trudge along the sandy base below the ridgelines.

The image of the elephant pawing a hole in the dry riverbed flashed before her eyes. She found a low spot, dropped to her knees, and began digging with her hands like a wild woman. Six inches down—nothing.

She grabbed a rock with a sharp edge and pounded the bottom of the hole, loosening the sand. She continued scooping. The color of the sand became darker. She kept digging, tearing at the sand with her fingers. The sand got darker. She felt moisture. She grabbed the sharp rock and pounded the sand viciously. A little water seeped into the hole. Sarah tore at the sand like her life depended on it, which it did.

Gradually, water began to seep into the hole. Then enough appeared that she could cup her hands and drink. She got two mouthfuls before she fell back on the sand and laughed giddily. She, Sarah Taylor-Jones from the South Side of Chicago, a bona fide city girl who was lost in the African bush, had dug a hole in the sand and found water. She was going to live. Sarah drank two more mouthfuls, spit out some sand, and leaned against a huge boulder.

Thick shadows shrouded the wash. It was time to do something. Sarah stood and picked up a branch that could be used as a walking stick. She decided to find a suitable tree to climb and would use the branch to poke anything that tried to join her.

Bekker led the group up the ridge, over, and down to the grassland, where he stopped, studying the sky.

"Gentlemen, we have a decision to make. You can see Sarah headed into the grass here. It looks several miles to that tree line. We can't make it before dark. Walking through the grass at night will attract the wrong kind of company. That's particularly true if we use a flashlight to follow the trail. I don't want to, but I think we should move back up the ridge and set up camp under that overhang."

Baruti began to object. "But Sarah is out there alone—"

Johannes interrupted. "Think with your head, not your heart, young man. You can't help Sarah if we lose her trail or have an unpleasant encounter with a wild animal."

Baruti nodded resignedly. "At least we can make a fire and keep warm."

"No," Bekker said. "Lions are attracted to campfires. Generally, they don't want anything to do with humans unless they feel threatened, are hunting, or are protecting their young, but on many occasions, I've seen them walk into a camp with a campfire and look around. Hyenas won't bother humans unless they smell blood. Then all bets are off. We'll be better off with a dry camp under that overhang back there, taking turns keeping watch."

The men climbed back up the ridge and settled in under the overhang. As the twilight deepened the blackness of the shadows below the ridge, a quarter moon crept over the eastern horizon, followed by a high-pitched chirping sound below them but not too far in the distance. In a moment, it was answered from some distance away.

"What is that?" Baruti asked.

"Wild dogs calling one another," Bekker answered from the darkness. "There aren't many of them left these days. Farmers have been killing them off, but now people are waking up and trying to save them. A lot of what they get blamed for is done by leopards and cheetahs. There is a good-size pack in this park."

"I've never seen one," Johannes said. "What do they look like?"

"About the size of an undernourished American coyote. Large, bat-like ears. Medium brownish with black spots and a bushy tail that always has a white tip. Each one is marked differently, like zebras."

"Do we have to worry about them tonight?" Baruti asked as the chirps moved away from the ridge.

"No. Like any sensible animal, they avoid humans," Bekker replied. "Now get some sleep."

CHAPTER 54

A FALLING SENSATION JERKED Sarah awake. Thank God, she wasn't falling, but sitting on a thick tree branch with her back against the trunk and legs dangling off the sides. She had taken her pants off and tied her torso to the trunk. With her belt, she had secured her left arm to another branch. For hours, she had heard no telling what moving around below the tree, but she had had no visitors. At some point, she must have drifted off and gotten some sleep. It was now past dawn, and the early light told her which direction was east. Sarah untied herself, climbed down, and put on her pants and belt.

She had survived a night in the bush. Bekker had told her that predators were still at work in the early-morning hours, but she was afraid to stay put lest the gangsters that might be following her catch up. First things first.

She retraced her steps back down the wash to her personal water hole, which still had some water in it. She used her hands to make the hole deeper and a little bigger. Her reward was enough water to drink and splash on her face. After checking the rising sun, she headed north along the wash.

Sarah walked over a small rise in the wash, and not ten feet away was one of nature's ugliest creatures. The warthog looked like a wild pig that was covered in sparse hair with a large, elongated face and distinctive tusks at the corners of its mouth. Sarah stopped walking and breathing at the same time. Before she could react, the warthog, as surprised as Sarah, scurried off into the bush. She resumed breathing and moved forward cautiously.

Her plan was to keep moving north, hoping to come upon a road where she could find help. Moving through the wash wasn't too hard, and it continued to head north. From time to time, she stopped to look behind her and listen. Between the gangsters and wild animals, she was surrounded by danger, but she would survive.

As she walked along the wash, Sarah told herself that girls—no, women—from the South Side of Chicago knew how to survive. Some gangsters with guns were after her? Big deal. Guns and gangsters had been part of everyday life on the South Side. She was alone in the bush with no idea where she was? No problem. She had found water. She had survived the night. She was tired and a little hungry maybe, but fit and moving well. She would find help soon. She repeated this mantra as she moved along the wash.

Johannes, who had taken the last shift, woke Bekker and Baruti. The men gathered their gear and ate protein bars. When they were ready to move out, he spoke.

"Aiden, I've been studying that little strip of bush we have to walk through to get to the grass. It looks like there are some smaller trees with springy branches that could be bent almost to the ground—"

Bekker interrupted. "Set a trap for our friends?"

"I still remember how to do it."

"Let's get to work."

The men moved down the ridge and began their work. They walked on the path that Sarah had originally made through the bush and made sure their footprints were clearly visible. Johannes cut off a foot-long piece of a tree branch and sharpened the end. They attached the sharpened stake to a tree branch that they could tie down and would spring up at chest height. The final step was to bend it back and attach a trip wire about four inches off the ground across the path. In the shadows created by the bush, the trip wire was almost impossible to see.

Baruti stood by amazed that these senior citizens were so proficient at setting a trap that could kill someone. He didn't say anything but wondered where and how they had learned to do this. He watched as Johannes cut and sharpened a half dozen more stakes, which he put in his pack.

As they moved off into the grass with Bekker on point, he said, "Luc, you must have been hell on wheels back in the day."

Johannes responded with a wry smile, "I learned about traps the hard way from the best ... Vietcong."

Johannes said nothing more. Bekker respected the silence. He had memories of his own.

CHAPTER
55

AFTER BEING TOLD TO sleep outside the vehicles, the guide put on his fleece jacket and a wool watch cap, and slept under Bekker's lifted Toyota. The Chinese were still grumbling to one another when he drifted off to sleep wondering whether the money they had promised him was worth gambling that these evil men would not kill him.

He was startled awake by the memory of the Chinese goon shoving the pistol under his chin. A thin gray line on the eastern horizon presaged the coming dawn as the guide rolled out from under the Toyota and stretched. The assholes hadn't even offered him a blanket.

He studied the sleeping Chinese, who were spread out two to a vehicle while he fondled the handle of the four-inch sheath knife on his belt. He could easily cut the throats of two of them, but there was too good a chance that the others would awake before he could reach the other vehicle. These men were trained killers. He had been in his share of fights as a younger man but had no particular fighting skills. The risk was too great. Failure would mean death. His decision finalized. The choice between a big payday balanced against the loss of his life was easy.

The guide quietly picked up his backpack and added two bottles of water and several protein bars before looking at the satellite phone sitting on the fender of the Chinese SUV. It was the only one they had brought with them and their only means of communication with the outside world. The guide added it to his backpack. Now he didn't have to worry about them calling someone to catch him. He slipped into the shadows and disappeared.

As the band of gray in the eastern sky expanded, he began to retrace their path at a trot. If they came after him in their vehicle, he wanted as much of a start as possible. It would be no problem for him to hide if they followed. If they pushed forward on their own, the bush would take care of them. After a mile, the guide stopped and destroyed the satellite phone with a large rock before burying it.

A band of orange was pushing its way into the gray-blue sky when the English-speaking man awoke. He shook his companion and yelled at the guide to get a fire started. He was greeted by grumbling from the other vehicle, but he didn't hear the guide moving about. The disrespectful black idiot needed a good beating to learn his place.

He jumped down and looked for the guide, whom he could not find. It finally occurred to him that the guide was gone. The miserable black *gweilo* had left them alone in the bush. The rest of the men gathered together, and they all began talking at once in frantic Chinese.

The guide was right. These men were experienced killers, but they weren't soldiers. They had police training and were good at terrorizing innocent civilians. They had been sent on this mission with no notice, no preparation, and limited instructions to bring Wang Jin home and clean up any mess he may have gotten himself into. They didn't know Africa, and neither did the people who had sent them. The unspoken assumption by all involved had been that they would be working in an urban environment where they would have diplomatic immunity, help from local Chinese, and could terrorize enough people to find Wang Jin. It had seemed simple enough at the beginning, but then they had to enter the vast emptiness of the bush. They had had enough sense to hire a guide but not enough sense to tie him up at night. It had never entered their minds that he would just leave them in the middle of the emptiness.

Looking for the guide was out of the question. It would be too easy for him to hide. Then they realized that he had stolen their only satellite telephone. They had no means of communicating with the ministry. There was simply no way they could explain how they had allowed themselves to be put in this position. Their choice was to push on or return to Victoria Falls and start over.

The English-speaker was the leader. It was painfully obvious that they had made a huge mistake in letting the guide escape and steal the phone. If they told their superiors that they had wasted time or perhaps failed in their mission because of their own mistakes…well, that would not end well.

After explaining this to his companions, they decided the only choice was to push on. The trail was easy to follow. After all, they were Chinese, the master race; in good shape; and would move quickly. They would probably catch up with the people they were following in a few hours. The men hoisted their backpacks and started up the ridgeline, following the obvious tracks left by the others. Once they crested the ridge, they moved down the far side quickly and started out at a trot.

The man in the lead was shorter than an average American. When he hit the trip wire, the branch whipped up from the ground and drove the sharp stake into his neck and through this larynx, severing his spinal cord and emerging from the back of his neck. The next man in line couldn't stop himself from running into his companion in a kind of embrace. The blood-soaked stake just missed his eye and gouged his cheek.

He stepped back, holding his cheek with blood oozing through his fingers. The tree branch held the dead man upright, blood gushing from his neck.

The remaining Chinese looked at one another, speechless. They were used to inflicting terror, not receiving it.

As they finished bandaging the injured man, they heard high-pitched staccato sounds coming from the west. They didn't know that a pack of hyenas had smelled the blood and were fast approaching, but they did realize that they needed to get away from their dead comrade. They broke into a lope following the tracks and left him standing impaled on the branch. The idea of burying him never entered their minds.

Dingo and his men made a small fire next to the van to warm themselves, heat water for coffee, and eat freeze-dried pouches of breakfast. The freeze-dried food wasn't very good, but it would keep them moving. Squatting while eating, they discussed their plan.

Dingo knew the terrain well and was sure it would force Sarah to follow the only track out there, which ran to the north where they were waiting. They would take her to cabin number two, where Wang Jin would be waiting with their money. The ransom was due by the end of the day, at which point they would have earned an extra $10,000 each for leaving Sarah alone and having some Chinese dickheads look for them.

"Why don't we take all of the money from the chink and leave him in the bush?" Foxtrot asked.

Dingo, chewing the last bite of his meal, stood and shook his head slowly. "He's not stupid enough to bring the ransom money out here. It will be in a bank halfway around the world in China. He'll show up at camp with only what he owes us. You can be sure of that."

"What if he doesn't bring the money?" Bull asked. "Strangle doesn't know about the extra money, so he can't make the triad pay us."

"We'll take care of the woman and take the chink to a bank where he can get the money from his daddy," Dingo blustered to hide the fact that he hadn't thought about Wang Jin reneging on the extra money. "Let's get you two set up. That woman was in good shape. She could get this far north later this morning."

CHAPTER 56

BEIJING WAS BLANKETED IN thick smog. There was nothing to see from the windows of Wang Chen's office. He had just finished an hour-long meeting with his closest associates in the Chinese Communist Party. The message they had carried was not good.

People were blaming him for COVID-19 and the lockdowns that were making people crazy. They blamed him for the polluted smog from the coal-fired factories that blanketed the city every time the wind blew from the northeast. The Chinese Communist Youth League faction had come to realize that Wang had no intention of relinquishing power as he had promised. They intended to challenge his attempt to extend his rule at the party convention. His grip on the party was slipping, and then there was his only son, Wang Jin.

It had been twenty-four hours since he had heard from the men he had sent after his errant son. The news of Sarah Taylor-Jones' kidnapping was gaining traction in the American and British press. The Office of State Information was getting inquiries about Eastern Enterprises's abandonment of the Debswana auction and her disappearance. If the press tied Wang Jin to the kidnapping, his political enemies would demand his resignation to protect the honor of China.

He yelled for his assistant, and the thirty-something man appeared in his doorway seconds later.

"What is the latest from the men we sent to Botswana to bring Wang Jin home?"

Over the years, the assistant had become adept at reading the chairman's tone of voice. His voice was normally tense when discussing his son. Now the assistant had the feeling he was close to losing his temper.

"Sir, there is nothing new. In their last report, they believed Wang Jin was behind the kidnapping of the American woman. They were leaving Victoria Falls to follow a lead that should take them to the men who are helping Wang Jin. They should be holding the woman. The men you sent will eliminate that problem. If Wang Jin is not there, they will continue to search for him."

"That report is twenty-four hours old. What in the hell is happening? This is unacceptable."

The assistant replied cautiously, "I called our Botswana embassy while you were in your meeting. They were not in the reporting loop and have no idea where our operatives are. The minister has no further information."

"Get the minister on the telephone for me. He ought to be able to call the men and get a situation report."

The minister reported that they had lost contact with his men. Their satellite phone was no longer emitting a signal, but he did have the GPS coordinates of its last location in the middle of Hwange National Park.

Ninety minutes later, a private jet lifted off from the Luanda International Airport in Angola with four Chinese People's Liberation Army special forces operators who were in that country protecting Chinese mining operations from insurgents. Their destination was Victoria Falls, Zimbabwe. These operators were among China's best. They had weapons, the GPS coordinates for the deserted cabin, and the last know location of the satellite phone that the secret police contingent was using.

CHAPTER 57

THE SUN WAS HIGH in the bright-blue sky, creating a sauna-like dry heat that turned the tall grass brittle and golden as Bekker followed Sarah's trail. Baruti followed him, with Johannes's head on a swivel watching behind and to the sides of their line of march. The ground sloped downward and then straightened out when Johannes called a halt.

"This is a perfect spot," Johannes said. Bekker nodded in agreement.

Johannes dropped his backpack and rummaged inside, removing the five sharpened stakes he had made earlier that morning.

Bekker eased out of his backpack and unhooked a small entrenching tool from the side of the pack. Using it initially as a pick and then a shovel, he dug a rectangular hole across the trail, where it leveled out from the slight downward slope. While he dug, Johannes cut a pointed end on each of the sharpened stakes.

Baruti watched for a moment and then said, "Guys, I need to relieve myself... badly."

"Do it," Johannes said as he worked on the stakes.

The hole was almost two feet deep when Bekker stopped and smoothed out the bottom. Johannes used the shovel to securely pound the sharp end of the stakes into the ground, leaving about six inches exposed. Then he used his knife to resharpen the exposed ends of the stakes.

"Baruti, use a leaf and bring me a handful of your shit," Johannes said, catching his breath after bending over the hole in an awkward position to sharpen the stakes.

The other man returned a moment later, and Johannes said, "Rub it all over those stakes."

Baruti understood immediately, dropped to his knees, and began applying the excrement.

Bekker wove some ferns and grass into a mat and placed it over the hole, covering it with a thin layer of dirt before blending it into the trail.

The men stood together for a moment and admired their handiwork.

"This should even the odds a bit, and even if it doesn't work, it's bound to get inside their heads and slow them down," Johannes said.

They hustled down the trail. A short time later, they emerged from the grass and found the water hole Sarah had passed the previous evening. Bekker spent some time following Sarah's trail around the water hole to the tree line. Johannes and Baruti were examining the sable's carcass when Bekker waved them over.

"Come over here…She stood here for a while. Look at this vine. The poor woman was sucking on it for moisture while looking at the water hole. From the looks of things, elephants and sables were here. She needed water badly and there it was, but she couldn't get any. I imagine she hustled out of here when that sable was attacked."

Johannes nodded sadly. Baruti teared up and started to say something, but his voice broke, and he retreated into silence.

The men entered the tree line and continued their pursuit of Sarah. Sometime later, they came upon the little water hole in the wash, which still had some water in it.

Bekker smiled broadly. "She found water. This is one smart lady. Look at the footprints arriving here. She dug the hole and moved on but came back and left again. She must have spent the night near here and came back for water this morning."

The three men were all smiles. Sarah had made it through the night. They would find her soon. The little water hole had filled them with hope, and they moved off quickly.

Next, they came upon the tree where Sarah had spent the night.

Bekker studied the tracks and said, "If she was careful, she didn't leave here at first light; still too many predators prowling around. If she waited for some solid daylight, she's about two hours ahead of us. Let's get moving."

The wash Sarah was following led into a small clearing in the bush that had been made by vehicles turning around. Across the clearing, she saw the vehicle track that continued northward. Finally, a sign of civilization. The track wasn't fresh, but it wasn't overgrown either. It had to lead to a bigger road—and help.

As she moved down the vehicle track, Sarah had a burst of emotional energy. She was going to make it.

CHAPTER
58

THE CHINESE SECRET POLICE were in good physical condition, which enabled them to move quickly, following the obvious trail through the grass. As they became used to the footing, they quickened their pace to a slow jog.

Their English-speaking leader urged the man in front to pick up the pace. "We can take a water break when we hit the tree line and have some shade."

The man in the lead took two strides down the little slope and planted his left foot firmly on the ground at the bottom. His foot disappeared into the hole that Bekker had dug. His body weight and downward momentum helped a sharpened stake slide easily through the thin sole of his cheap shoe; then through his foot, depositing excrement; and out the top, leaving his foot impaled on the stake. His momentum kept his upper body moving forward and down, putting immense pressure on his fibula bone, which snapped, creating a compound fracture with the upper part of the broken bone piercing the skin. Blood began to flow from the man's foot and where the bone had broken his skin while he screamed in pain.

The man following him, who was two strides behind, avoided running into the downed man by leaping to the right and landing on his right foot. His left foot would have landed in the pit with a second disaster. He looked on with horror as his comrade continued screaming.

The two uninjured men were momentarily frozen. Then they sprang into action, lifting their injured comrade upright. They could see his impaled foot in the hole. They had a choice: They could pull on his broken leg to jerk his foot off the stake, undoubtedly increasing the pain and making the break worse, or they could try to loosen the stake at the bottom of the pit and lift his leg out of the hole with the stake imbedded in his foot.

One held the injured man upright, and the English-speaking man dropped flat on the ground and reached inside the hole. The stake was immobile. He got up and found a rock that fit in his hand. Back on the ground, he pounded the stake amid the shrieks from his comrade. After four vicious strikes, the stake loosened, and he was able to pull it out of the ground.

Surrounded by the tall grass, they laid the injured man on the trail. His high-pitched shrieks were subsiding, being replaced by a sustained howl of agony.

Their predicament was obvious. They had a small first aid kit, but it was not equipped to handle injuries of this magnitude. They didn't know what was in front of them, but if they retraced their route carrying their comrade, they would have to spend another night in the bush before they could get to the vehicle. They had no morphine. The noise and the smell of blood were sure to attract predators. Even if they survived the night, their mission would be a failure. They would have failed the chairman of the Chinese Communist Party. Things would not end well for them.

The two uninjured men did not say anything further. They just looked at one another and nodded. The English-speaking man removed his pistol from the holster on his belt and shot his injured comrade twice in the forehead.

This death had sealed their fate. They could not quit. The mission was paramount.

The remaining men started off with the one in the lead moving carefully with his eyes on the trail. The English-speaking man put his head on a swivel. There would be no more jogging.

Dingo gave his men instructions. He could not be sure whether Sarah would just walk up the vehicle track, but he was confident she would stay near it in case a vehicle came along. Foxtrot and Bull were to separate on either side of the track about a half mile down and stay well off to the side in case she came their way. He would stay a quarter mile down and just off to the side. They would wait and watch for Sarah, keeping in contact with their handheld radios.

His last instruction was emphatic: "Keep quiet. Whisper on the radio only when necessary. If she thinks we're in front of her, she'll turn around and go back.

We can't let that happen." Then his mouth twisted in a cruel slash. "Tonight, we'll be rolling in money and banging that bitch until she begs for mercy."

Foxtrot and Bull nodded with flat, dead eyes before moving off into the bush. Dingo parked the van on the other side of the main road and moved down the vehicle track, where he set up to wait.

Foxtrot moved slowly through the bush. He was a city boy and would not have agreed to this job if he had known he would be walking around alone in the bush. This was a national park. It was full of wild animals.

After a half hour, he thought he was staying the right distance from the vehicle track when he came to a deep wash. He climbed down into it and looked to his left. Standing there was a hyena that started to move toward him.

Panicked, Foxtrot scrambled up the bank and ran into the bush. He fell several times in getting away from the hyena that he was sure was going to eat him. Finally, out of breath, he stopped and held on to a tree, gasping while sweat dripped down his dirt-smeared face. When his breathing returned to normal, he looked around and was no longer sure which direction led to the vehicle track. He reached for his radio. It was gone. He had dropped it somewhere in his mad dash to escape the vicious hyena.

Back at the wash, the hyena was gone, but lying in the sand was Foxtrot's radio. A big male baboon wandering along the wash picked it up, looked at it, and scrambled along with his prize.

CHAPTER 59

THE REGULAR NOISES OF the bush were shattered by two rapid gunshots. Bekker stopped and waited for Baruti and Johannes to catch up.

Johannes spoke first. "Pistol, not a rifle. And certainly not a big-game rifle. Not far away."

"Good news and bad news, I think," Bekker offered. "Good news, the pit caught one of them, and I'm betting his companions, the merciless bastards, shot him. Bad news, they're getting close to us. We're going to have to do something."

"But Sarah—" Baruti said before Johannes interrupted him.

"We have no choice. We can't let them catch up with us and control the encounter. Especially after we find Sarah, when we'll be moving slowly. We must control the engagement. We pick the time and place here in the bush, and soon."

"Luc, I think Baruti means to say that if we stop, Sarah pulls farther away from us and closer to the gangsters that are probably waiting somewhere up ahead. Assuming the traps worked, there are only two of them; at most, three. I'll hold back and set an ambush for them. You two keep moving after Sarah. I'll double-time to catch up with you."

"I think I should stay. You two can move faster in tracking Sarah," Johannes said.

"Valid point. But Luc, I know the bush, I'm in better shape than you, and I can catch up quicker to help with Sarah and the gangsters. Once we have her, we'll have to move as quickly as possible. We can't wait around for you to catch up."

Johannes was quiet for a moment. He knew Bekker was right.

"All right, kill them quick. Do you need anything from us?"

"Just your backside moving down the trail."

Johannes led and Baruti followed as they moved quickly down the track. Bekker followed them slowly, looking for a place to ambush the Chinese. The location would dictate the tactics. The simplest plan would let them walk past him so he could step out and shoot the one in the rear in the back of the head. As he fell, Bekker would shoot the other man or men. A few other ideas passed quickly through his mind, but the old Selous Scout was a firm believer in applying Occam's razor: the simplest method was least likely to fail.

He couldn't find any trees or bushes that would be good to hide behind or climb. He worked with what he had, quickly weaving big palm fronds, long grasses, and thin branches into a primitive ghillie-type blanket. His plan was to lie beside the track in a shallow depression covered by the blanket. When the Chinese passed, he would rise to one knee and shoot the closest man and then the others. If there were three, he would have to be fast, but it was doable. Simple, but Bekker had learned many brutal lessons about how the best-laid plans could fall apart in an instant. If they saw him on the ground through his camouflage, he was a dead man if they were carrying their rifles in the ready position or had a pistol in their hand, or if the first man he shot fell in a way that blocked his shot at the next man, he would be in trouble.

Bekker finished weaving the blanket and examined his Redhawk handgun, carefully wiping it clean and checking the loads. His Weatherby Mark V .460 Magnum rifle would be lying next to him, and his razor-sharp hunting knife was close at hand on his belt. He got as comfortable as possible under his improvised blanket and waited.

Fifteen minutes later, he could hear the Chinese coming down the track. As they walked, two men were talking to each other in what he assumed was Chinese. Amateur hour. Professionals would move without talking.

They stopped talking before reaching Bekker, and he knew they might have seen him.

One set of footsteps passed by. Thousand one. Thousand two. Thousand three.

The second set passed. Thousand one.

Bekker moved up to one knee, but the last Chinese sensed his movement and spun toward him, pistol in hand but at shoulder height. His shot went over Bekker's head.

Bekker shot him in the face, immediately rolled once to his right, and stopped with his Ruger trained on the second man.

The lead Chinese had also spun around at his partner's movement, but for a split second, his partner blocked his view. As the man fell, Bekker and the other Chinese fired at the same time. However, the Chinese fired where Bekker had been. Bekker shot him in the heart.

The secret policeman crumpled. He was dead before he hit the ground.

Realizing that they might have to come back this way, Bekker dragged each of the men off into the bush and hustled after Johannes and Baruti.

―――

The remorseless sun beat down on Sarah. She was in desperate need of water, but there was no more sand where she could dig for it. Her face, neck, and arms were covered with bug bites and grime. Her shirt, soaked with sweat, stuck to her body. Her feet hurt and were beginning to blister. Slivers of pain radiated up her arms from her filthy, shredded fingernails. Scratches from the bush grass itched.

Bugs flitted around her head, but she was too weak to wave them away. Hot, thirsty, hungry, and exhausted, she fantasized about Victoria Falls and its endless supply of water. The temptation to sit in the shade and rest was becoming increasingly difficult to ignore. But if she did, she would probably fall asleep and become some animal's next meal. The thought of the kidnappers that had propelled her in the beginning had faded. The issue now was basic survival.

―――

Bull had a clear view of the track from a spot on a slight rise about a hundred yards away. He stood next to a tree and blended into it. If Dingo was right, Sarah would come along between him and Foxtrot, hopefully following the track.

―――

Sarah trudged along the track, trying to look around and keep her mind engaged, but it was taking all her concentration to put one foot in front of the other. If a lion appeared before her, she would not run because she wouldn't be able to summon the energy. How much farther could it be? She had to get to a road, and soon.

Just keep putting one foot in front of the other. Girl, you can do it. You are tough. You are woman. One foot in front of the other. That's it, girl. One foot, then the other.

Bull saw her appear from behind a stand of trees as she walked on the track and quietly keyed his handheld radio. "She's here walking on the track as we hoped," he whispered.

"Good, let her pass and fall in behind her. Don't get too close. When I see her, I'll tell you to close in," Dingo said.

There was silence from Foxtrot.

CHAPTER 60

Dingo's voice came through the handheld radio. "I see her. Move in slowly. When she gets here, I'll grab her, but be ready to help."

"Roger," Bull softly replied. There was no acknowledgement from Foxtrot, but Dingo didn't need one.

Dingo was standing behind a thick bush when Sarah trudged past. He stepped out quietly behind her, unnoticed by the bleary-eyed woman. He bent over and grabbed her back leg below the knee and lifted. Sarah hit the ground face first, stunned.

Dingo put his knee on her buttocks, wrenched her arms behind her, and used a short piece of rope to tie her hands. Once her hands were tied, he jerked her upright. Hitting the ground had knocked the wind out of Sarah, and she could not stand, much less walk.

Bull ran up and grabbed one of her arms. Dingo took the other, and they tried to walk her two hundred yards to the dirt road. The men dragged her a short way and then quit. It was too hard.

"I'll get the van," Dingo said before trotting toward the road.

He was back in a few minutes, and they dumped Sarah into the van through the side door. Bull climbed in after her and gagged her with a bandana before looping her legs together with a length of rope. The hostage secured, Bull climbed out and shut the door.

"Where the hell is Foxtrot?" Dingo asked.

"No idea," Bull replied.

Dingo keyed the handheld radio and tried to raise Foxtrot. Several miles away, the baboon, frightened by the noise, dropped Foxtrot's radio and ran.

Dingo looked at his watch. "We'll give him five more minutes, and then he'll have to find his own way back to camp. The ransom is due by five. Six more hours until payday."

Bull, looking down the trail for Foxtrot, asked, "What if they don't pay it?"

"That's the chink's problem. He owes us regardless," Dingo replied, also watching back down the trail.

At the cabin, Wang Jin paced back and forth from his vehicle to the cabin, alternately looking at his watch and where the vehicle track emerged from the bush. There was no shade on this small ridge, which had been selected for its view of the surrounding area. He thought about sitting in his SUV to escape the glaring sun, but he was too nervous to sit still. From time to time, he wiped the sweat off his forehead. His shirt was black with sweat. He could smell himself. That had never happened before. Every half hour since he had woken up, he had used his phone to check his bank account at the First Bank of Rarotonga. No money yet.

What if Baruti did not pay?

Had $20,000 in cash. Ten for the gangsters and ten to get home. What if these men didn't listen to their boss and demanded $10,000 each? What could he do? No—what would *they* do once they searched him?

That was it. He needed to hide his get-home money. Where?

He wrapped $10,000 in a plastic bag and duct-taped it to the frame of his SUV behind the rear bumper. Then he walked to the front of his vehicle, dropped a line of coke on the hood, and snorted it.

Payment of the ransom did not change what he had in store for Sarah. He was going to fuck her every way he could think of until he was disgusted by her crying and begging for mercy. Then he would turn her over to the gangsters. When they were all sated, they would cut her throat and leave her for the lions. Better yet, he would tell them to break her legs and arms, smear her with her own blood, and leave her for whatever animal got there first. That would be a suitable payback.

Dingo looked at his watch.

"We don't have time to look for the idiot. He'll have to find his own way back to camp."

Dingo and Bull climbed into the van and drove away.

CHAPTER 61

JOHANNES AND BARUTI WERE making good time following the track when Johannes stopped abruptly and signaled Baruti to move to the side of the trail.

Not far ahead, Foxtrot pushed through tree branches onto the trail. He looked left, giving them time to step out of his line of sight. The man looked back down the trail but didn't see them. Then he moved off in the other direction.

Baruti whispered, "Is that one of the kidnappers?"

Johannes shrugged and whispered back, "Maybe. Probably. There's no other reason for a lone man to be out here on foot. Whoever it is, he's between us and Sarah."

They heard footfalls behind them and spun around. It was Bekker, approaching at a jog. He gave them a thumbs-up. Johannes signaled for him to be quiet.

When Bekker arrived, Johannes quickly explained about the man moving down the track away from them.

"I think you're right," Bekker said. "He must be one of the kidnappers. We need to take him prisoner and find out whether they've recaptured her."

"The kidnappers don't know we're out here," Johannes said. "We're a couple of white tourists who got lost hiking. We catch up to him and ask for directions. When we're close enough, we can take him. Baruti, you hang back out of sight, but be ready to move up and help us if things go wrong. He's most likely armed."

They hurried after Foxtrot, who didn't hear them coming until they were about twenty yards away. Foxtrot stopped and turned around with a smile on his face like he was expecting someone. Johannes and Bekker separated to the sides of the trail, and Johannes raised his hand in greeting as they kept moving forward.

Foxtrot's smile vanished when he realized they weren't his fellow gangsters, and he clumsily reached for the pistol in the cargo pocket of his pants. Bekker slipped his rifle off his shoulder and butt-stroked the side of his head with enough force to knock him down but not out.

As Foxtrot lay on the ground, dazed, Johannes reached into Foxtrot's pocket and took his pistol. Baruti trotted up and looked at the fallen man. "Nice work, gentlemen."

Bekker handed him his rifle and searched Foxtrot and his backpack, removing a hunting knife and a roll of duct tape. The men jerked Foxtrot to his feet, backed him into a tree, and bound his hands behind him and around the tree with duct tape. Another strip of tape went around his chest and a final strip just above his knees.

Foxtrot cursed and spit at his captors. Bekker casually backhanded him and said, "Shut up. I'll tell you when to speak."

Foxtrot, a prison-hardened criminal, was used to abuse. He spat blood and said, "Fuck you, whitey."

"You shouldn't hurt my feelings," said Bekker, who moved behind him while tearing off a strip of duct tape. He slipped the tape around Foxtrot's throat and pulled his neck against the tree, securing the tape with enough slack that he could swallow. Then he tore off another strip, wound it around Foxtrot's forehead, and secured it to the tree. Johannes and Baruti stood by silently.

Foxtrot sputtered, "My partners will cut your fucking throat."

Bekker looked at Johannes and Baruti. One question answered. This man was one of the kidnappers.

Bekker moved around in front of Foxtrot, roughly unbuckled his belt, and jerked Foxtrot's pants and underwear down to where the duct tape secured his knees to the tree. He unsheathed his hunting knife, which had a six-inch razor-sharp blade, and held it up so Foxtrot could see it. Then he used the flat edge of the knife to flip Foxtrot's penis.

The red-hot anger burning in Foxtrot's eyes disappeared when he felt the knife blade manipulating him. It was replaced by uncertainty.

Bekker stepped back, picked up a stick, and silently began sharpening one end to a long, thin point, holding it so Foxtrot could watch. Foxtrot's eyes widened as he began to comprehend what Bekker was planning.

Bekker held the stick up in front of Foxtrot's eyes and tested the point with his index finger. Satisfied, he nodded to himself. Then he spoke.

"I want you to realize that you are going to tell me what I want to know. The only question is how damaged you're going to be before you do." He shifted his tone from menacing to that of a doctor describing the risks of a medical procedure. "In the interests of full disclosure, I must inform you that this procedure entails a substantial risk of permanent damage to your penis, and we've had some men die from it. Not too many, but a few. You can accept the risks that come with the procedure, or you can obviate the need for it. The choice is yours."

Bekker held the stick close to Foxtrot's eyes and retested the sharpness. When he spoke, the menace had returned to his voice. "Back in the day, I spent some time with Somali warriors. You know their reputation. They did not like to waste a lot of time with interrogation, so they developed some very effective techniques. Tell me, what is your manhood worth?"

Fear began to creep into Foxtrot's eyes.

"Castrating you is a simple procedure. Painful, but simple. You recover from it in due course, but it's irreversible. Or I could hold your dick and shove this stick up the opening. That would be excruciatingly painful, and you would probably beg for castration to end the pain. If those procedures don't make you want to tell me, we can move to your eyes. They pop out rather easily."

Urine began to dribble from Foxtrot's penis onto his underwear and pants.

"I see I have your attention. You also need to know that I am a man of my word. I do not particularly enjoy maiming another human being. In fact, I don't enjoy it at all, but one must do what one must do. If you cooperate fully with us, I assure you that you will not be maimed or physically abused. When our mission is complete, we will let you go. Think of it like the immunity from prosecution you receive if you help the state punish fellow wrongdoers. I don't know the men you are with, but I suspect they would take this deal in less than a heartbeat.

"Before we start, I want you to say that you understand that whatever happens to you is a result of the choice you make. Do you understand?"

"Y-y-yes," Foxtrot stuttered.

"What is your name?"

"Call me Foxtrot."

"Did you help kidnap Sarah Taylor-Jones?"

"Yes."

"How many men are with you?"

"Two others and the chink who hired us."

"Very good. Did any of you hurt Sarah?"

"No. Honest. The chink is paying us not to hurt her."

Bekker paused and looked toward Baruti and Johannes. Relief showed on both men's faces.

"Have the others found her?"

"Honest to God, I don't know. I got turned around in the bush and lost my radio. We were waiting for her to come up this track. I don't know what happened. Honest."

"Where were you going to take her?"

"A different place. There are some more chinks looking for us."

"Where is the new place?"

"In the bush. I can take you there."

Bekker walked over to the others, and they moved away so Foxtrot could not hear their conversation.

"What do you think?" Bekker asked.

"The odds are they've retaken her. This track must lead to a more traveled road where we can get help," Johannes replied.

Bekker cut Foxtrot loose while Johannes held his gun on the man. After Foxtrot pulled up his pants, Bekker used duct tape to retape his hands behind him and secure his legs with three feet of tape between his ankles.

The group moved down the track toward the dirt road.

CHAPTER 62

THE SUN WAS HIGH in the sky when they found where Sarah had been captured. The footprints, smeared ground, tire tracks, and some blood told the story. She had been walking on the track when someone had stepped out of the bush behind her and followed. A short time later, another person had stepped out of the bush behind her and knocked her to the ground, where she had left a trace of blood, perhaps from her nose. A set of footprints on either side of drag marks told them that Sarah had been unable to walk. One of the men had retrieved a vehicle. They had loaded her into it and driven away.

The men pushed on, lost in their own thoughts. Shortly, the bush thinned out, and they reached a well-maintained dirt road. They secured Foxtrot to a tree in the shade and moved out of his hearing.

Johannes looked at his watch. "Now we're going to be lucky or not. We need a vehicle to find Sarah. The ransom is due at five. If we don't find her before then… well…we had better find her before then."

Bekker's face was inscrutable. Baruti's eyes misted, and he looked absolutely miserable. Foxtrot had his head against the tree trunk and appeared to be sleeping in the midday heat.

The three men discussed that they didn't know where they were and whether it would make sense to split up and walk in both directions looking for help, or to start walking toward where Sarah was being held, or to stay put and hope a park ranger, not a vehicle full of tourists, came along.

An hour passed. The men were low on water, hot, dirty, and becoming increasingly frustrated.

"It's two fucking o'clock. I can't stand here any longer. Let's start walking toward Sarah. That way, if we get a ride, we'll be that much closer," complained Baruti, who kept pacing, unable to stand still.

"Our friend over there said it's about an hour drive to the camp where she's being held. That's too far to walk by five o'clock," Bekker replied.

"Baruti does have a point," Johannes said. "Sarah is to the east. If we start walking and a ranger comes from that direction, we'll have saved time. If we walk east and the ranger comes from the west, we won't have saved any time. So I think we should start walking to the east as long as we stay on this good road. If we have to go off into the bush, which we will at some point, it will make finding a ranger much less likely."

Bekker nodded. "OK. Roust him and let's get started. Cut the tape on his legs so he can move faster."

An hour later, the men were trudging along the dirt road, hot, sweaty, and under siege from insects. Foxtrot, who had been out of prison for less than a month, was in the worst physical condition and was beginning to slow them down. Bekker and Johannes had been watching him for a while and sharing concerned looks.

Baruti shouted, "Look! Dust coming our way! Please God, let it be help."

"OK," Johannes said. "We need to look less threatening, or whoever this is may not stop. Aiden, take Foxtrot off the road. Don't hide, but maybe the driver will focus on Baruti and me."

Johannes handed Bekker his rifle and stood with Baruti in the middle of the road as the dust cloud came closer and closer.

"Please God, let this be a park ranger, please," said Baruti, who mumbled a prayer in Tswana, his native language.

"Baruti, you talk to the driver," Johannes directed.

A white Toyota pickup truck appeared, followed by a dust cloud. Baruti waved his arms, and the vehicle came to a stop. A single park ranger was inside the small vehicle, which had a two-person bench seat with an open bed. Lettering on the side of the truck proclaimed it was part of the Scorpion Anti-Poaching Unit of Hwange National Park.

It took Baruti several minutes to explain the situation to the ranger, who seemed reluctant to get involved until Baruti told him that he was the son of the president of Botswana, Johannes was the CEO of Consolidated Diamonds, and

Bekker was a former safari guide and Botswana rancher. The clincher was when Foxtrot very reluctantly admitted that he was from South Africa and had helped kidnap Sarah.

"Look, guys, I will call for backup. But it will take an hour for anyone to get here, and by the time we get to wherever your woman is, it will be well past five," the ranger said.

"Don't you have a helicopter?" Johannes asked.

The ranger smiled ruefully. "No. This is Zimbabwe. Only the army has helicopters, and they are all in Harare to protect the government."

"Do you know where this abandoned cabin that Foxtrot is talking about is located?" Johannes asked.

"If it's the one I'm thinking about, it's about an hour from here."

"All right," Bekker said, addressing the ranger. "That settles it. You and Baruti are in the front. The rest of us will ride in the truck bed. You can keep the backup team apprised of our route. I imagine they have the cabin on their map. Let's get going."

"Listen, mister, I have an old rifle with four bullets. I'm not going to take on armed gangsters. I have a wife and three young children."

"Understood," Bekker replied. "We have the necessary weapons. You just get us near the cabin, and we'll deal with them. You'll stay well out of the way with our friend Foxtrot until backup arrives."

The ranger was quiet understanding that while he might be out of the immediate line of fire, once the shooting began, all bets were off. Bekker's body language told Johannes that he was getting ready take the truck away from the ranger.

"If you get us close to that cabin, I'll pay you five thousand dollars," Johannes said, knowing that at best, this ranger's salary was $300 or $400 a month.

"OK. Let's get going," the ranger agreed.

Baruti sat in the cab with the ranger. Bekker and Johannes sat in the truck bed with their backs to the cab. Foxtrot sat in front of them.

CHAPTER
63

A WET BLANKET OF smog continued to smother Beijing. The few people walking about wore hi-tech masks, and many also wore eye goggles. To say people were in a foul mood was a vast understatement.

Wang Chen was not immune from the general malaise that had beset the people of the Chinese capital, but his foul mood was primarily caused by Wang Jin, who remained off the grid. After reporting that Wang Jin had engineered the kidnapping of American businesswoman Sarah Taylor-Jones, the men he had sent to find his wayward son had gone radio silent. The situation was intolerable and getting worse by the minute.

Next week was the National Congress of the Chinese Communist Party, which was held every five years in Beijing's Great Hall of the People. According to his original agreement with the Chinese Communist Youth League, he was to relinquish power to their nominee. Nevertheless, he had been working for three years to cultivate the right party members to lead a "spontaneous" movement at the conference to extend his rule. Now, thanks to Wang Jin, his carefully laid plans were in jeopardy.

The Guardian, a British newspaper with a substantial online following in the United States, had published a lead story about Botswana's sale of its interest in the Debswana Mining Company. Starting in the third paragraph, the article had run with how Wang Jin had formed an offshore company to bid for the interest and how Eastern Enterprises had bribed Minister Obdura Leballo, planted a false news story about tariffs on De Beers diamonds, and influenced major banks to withdraw financing from the Consolidated Diamonds bid. It had also played up how Eastern Enterprises had been forced out of the bidding.

These statements were true, as Wang knew, but if he could find his errant son and bring him home, Wang Jin could give interviews to state media and blame everything on overzealous lawyers. It wouldn't be comfortable, but he could handle it. It was the potential fallout from the last two paragraphs of the article that had sent him to DEFCON 3.

After being ordered out of Botswana, Wang Jin evaded Botswana security officers and disappeared. Shortly thereafter, Sarah Taylor-Jones, the CFO of Consolidated Diamonds, was kidnapped from The Victoria Falls Hotel. According to independent sources, the primary person of interest in the kidnapping is Wang Jin. The alleged motive is revenge and/or a ransom demand to recover a lost investment in Eastern Enterprises.

Wang Jin could not be reached for comment, and the press officer for Wang Chen did not return calls for comment prior to press time.

Facebook, Twitter, Instagram, Gmail, and other websites were blocked from the internet in China. Wang immediately added *The Guardian* website to the list, along with any others that had picked up the story, but the article had been up for six hours before he had been informed. Blocking those websites had helped, but he knew that mainland Chinese could access them by using a virtual private network or the Tor Browser. Once something like this gained traction, it was hard to stop. Still, if he could slow dissemination of the information until after the conference, his position would be secure.

Wang issued an executive order that the story not to be reported in China. He also required twenty highly placed Chinese national security officials to sign a document stating that the allegations about Wang Jin had all the hallmarks of an American disinformation campaign designed to interfere with the party conference. Failure to adhere to his order would be considered insurrection and obstruction of the conference, with a term of up to twenty years in prison.

If he could just get Wang Jin back home to deny everything, he could make it through the conference. Maybe.

His special ops troops were due to land in Victoria Falls that evening. They had orders to do whatever was necessary to bring Wang Jin home and clean up his mess.

There was a tentative knock on his door. It was his assistant with unsettling news. The chairman of the Central Committee of the Chinese Communist Party and three of its other officers wanted to meet with Wang that evening.

CHAPTER 64

WANG JIN HEARD A vehicle approaching the rear of the cabin through the bush. For the millionth time since entering Hwange, he wished he had a gun. All he had for protection was a six-inch hunting knife he had purchased on the way to the park. He had just enough time to drop a generous line of coke on the hood of his SUV and snort it before picking up the knife and standing behind the vehicle.

When Dingo nosed the van out of the bush and up the small hill to the cabin, Wang Jin dropped the knife on the front seat of the SUV and walked out to greet the gangsters with mixed emotions. They must have found Sarah, or they would not be there.

Dingo stepped out of the van and, with a blank face, said, "Good, you're here. We found her."

Wang Jin forced a big smile. "Wonderful. Great work."

The side door of the van opened. Bull stepped down, dragging Sarah behind him, and unceremoniously dropped her on the ground. The woman's eyes were closed, and she looked barely alive. Her hair resembled a nest for field mice. Dirt, sweat, and blood leaked from cuts on her cheek and her nose, covering her face. Her shirt and pants were filthy. Wang Jin wrinkled his nose at the smell of sour sweat and body odor floating around her.

"Water," Sarah croaked through cracked and split lips in a barely audible whisper.

"Give her some water," Wang Jin said to no one in particular.

"Do it yourself, Mr. Big Shot," snapped Dingo. "This is one trouble-making bitch."

Bull kicked Sarah half-heartedly in the stomach. "She doesn't look so hot now. Come on, Dingo, the beer in our cooler is still cold."

Dingo and Bull opened the back of the van and pulled out two beers. They did not offer one to Wang Jin, who cut the ropes binding Sarah's hands and feet before getting a bottle of water out of his SUV. He opened it and held it out to Sarah, who was lying flat on the ground. She was too weak to lift her arm.

Wang Jin propped her up against his SUV and held the water bottle for her to drink. For every drop that made it down her throat, two drops spilled down her chin. In an uncharacteristic gesture of humanity, he soaked a bandana with water and wiped dirt off her lips. Then he put the bandana around the back of her neck and put the bottle next to her hand.

Dingo and Bull walked over to Wang Jin with their beers. "Payday, Mr. Big Shot," Dingo said menacingly.

"Your shot-caller wants to talk to you," Wang Jin replied smugly, getting his phone out of the SUV. "I'll dial the number for you."

Dingo and Bull looked at each other. This was unexpected. Both were Zimbabweans who had gone to South Africa looking for work. When they could not find any, a friend from home had introduced them to the Hard Livings gang, which had offered a way to make some money. Six months later, they were sent to prison for two years for assaulting an Indian shopkeeper who had refused to pay protection. They had been out of prison for less than a month when Strangle, knowing they were familiar with the Victoria Falls area, had sent them to help Wang Jin. They had only joined the gang for the money and had not been with Hard Livings long enough to absorb its culture.

Dingo's conversation with Strangle was short and very one-sided. As Wang Jin listened, Dingo's expression changed from curiosity to anger. He said yes several times before shaking his head in disgust and handing the phone to Wang Jin.

Strangle told Wang Jin to give Dingo the $10,000 for leaving Sarah alone, which he would deliver to the gang. Wang Jin did not have to give them any more money. Wang Jin disconnected the call with a self-satisfied smirk.

Dingo and Bull walked away from him and engaged in an animated conversation. It was clear that they were angry. He heard Bull exclaim, "You mean we're only going to get a few hundred for this job? That's bullshit!"

"Agreed," Dingo said quietly. "I've got an idea. Why don't you pull sentry duty while I talk to this chink? If I can't get more money out of him, I'll call you over, and you threaten to beat the hell out of him before shooting him in the knee to cripple him."

Bull nodded, pulled the handgun out of his belt, and began to walk along the edge of the hill. Dingo walked over to Wang Jin and made a show of looking at his watch.

"The boss said you owe us thirty thousand: ten for the woman and ten each for the chinks that are on our tail. He cut you a break because Foxtrot isn't here."

"That's not what he said," Wang Jin countered.

"Are you calling me a liar?" Dingo snarled, stepping very close to Wang Jin with his fists clenched.

By the time the ranger truck pulled off the dirt road onto a little-used vehicle track, Johannes, Bekker, and Foxtrot were covered with dust. The sun was sliding down the western sky, virtually blinding the men. Bekker pulled the brim of his floppy bush hat low, as did Johannes with his MalaMala Game Reserve ball cap. Sweat oozed down their faces, creating tracks in the dust and grease paint that they had not had the time or place to wash off. Water was for drinking, washing an afterthought. They had used their backpacks to cover their sidearms and kept the working mechanisms of their rifles under their legs.

They got out of the truck, perfunctorily dusted themselves off, and examined the track, which showed fresh tire prints.

"The cabin I know about is about a mile down this track on a small hill overlooking the river and a vast grass plain," the ranger said.

Bekker went to Foxtrot, who was still in the truck bed, and asked, "Is this the way to the cabin?"

Foxtrot managed to stand up and look down the track. "Yes." Then he sat down and looked at his hands.

Bekker walked silently down the track, studying the tire prints. The others stood watching him. His body language said he had completed his examination, and he walked back to them.

"There are tire prints for two vehicles. One set is fresh, not more than a few hours old. The other is older, maybe from yesterday."

"So we have to contend with the two gangsters we know about and however many were in the other vehicle," Johannes said.

Bekker nodded. "Looks that way."

"Maybe the other vehicle is Wang Jin," Baruti suggested.

"Or some more Chinese goons," Bekker snapped. "Shit." He put his hand on Baruti's shoulder. "I'm sorry. Riding in the bed of this truck has not helped my disposition. Odds are you are right, but assumptions in this business can get you killed."

"Don't worry about it, Aiden."

Johannes tried to drink from his water bottle, but it was empty. Fortunately, the ranger had a big water cooler in the truck. The men drank water, filled their bottles, and loaded back up in the truck.

As the vehicle bounced down the track, they were treated to a rough version of the African massage. Eventually, the truck nosed off the track into the bush and stopped.

Baruti and the ranger got out of the cab while Johannes and Bekker climbed stiffly from the truck bed. Foxtrot moved against the truck cab and watched the men.

Nodding at the ranger, Baruti said, "He says the cabin is about a quarter mile ahead. This approach is from the rear."

Bekker looked at Johannes, tacitly ceding command to him. Johannes pointed at the ranger and said, "You and Baruti stay here with Foxtrot and keep in touch with the incoming backup."

Baruti looked angrily at Johannes and spoke vehemently. "I'm coming with you. I got her into this, and I want to help get her out."

"You don't even have a gun," Johannes said dismissively.

Baruti's eyes narrowed, and he pointed at Johannes. "Cut the bullshit. I have Foxtrot's pistol, and the ranger will loan me his rifle. This isn't about having a gun; it's about my father. You're protecting me because of him. I haven't been a child that needs protecting for a long time."

Johannes did not relent. "We can't leave him here unarmed with the prisoner."

The ranger spoke up. "We can tie his legs and arms again with that duct tape. He won't be going anywhere. Backup will be here after a while, and I have this." He walked to the truck and pulled an eighteen-inch-long machete from under the seat.

Bekker dropped the tailgate and began to disassemble his pistol. "Looks like you've been outvoted, Luc. Baruti could be helpful covering the advance on our objective."

Johannes nodded and joined Bekker at the tailgate to clean their weapons. When they were done, Johannes cleaned Foxtrot's GLOCK and the ranger's rifle before handing them to Baruti.

"The GLOCK has seventeen rounds, no safety. There is a round in the chamber. Just point and shoot. The rifle's magazine is loaded with six rounds, and there's one round in the chamber. It's bolt action, so you'll have to work the bolt after each shot. Questions?"

"No." Baruti took the pistol and shoved it behind his belt in the front of his pants, then took the rifle.

The men, led by Bekker, moved silently down the track in single file ten feet apart; Bekker in the left track, Baruti in the center, and Johannes in the right.

CHAPTER 65

THE SUN WAS DROPPING relentlessly toward the western horizon as Bekker, Johannes, and Baruti came to a point where trees gave way to sparse bushes and grass. Baruti looked at this watch. It was almost 5 p.m. They could see the cabin on a small ridgeline about one hundred yards away, sited with a perfect view of the river and the vast grassland that sprawled out in front of it. A reasonably well-used vehicle track ran alongside the river. A van and an SUV were parked against boulders on the left side of the cabin from where they were standing. They could see a big man walking around in a manner that indicated he was watching for anyone who might approach his position.

Bekker removed small binoculars from his backpack and surveyed the area around the cabin. He spoke as he continued to watch.

"The big guy is holding a sidearm. Looks like he's watching for intruders. I don't see anyone else." When he moved the binoculars to the vehicles, he did a double take. "It looks like someone is leaning against the SUV with their arm tied to the door handle. I can't tell if it's a man or woman from here, but odds are that it's Sarah."

Two men appeared from the front of the cabin and walked toward the SUV.

"From their body language, those two are arguing," Bekker whispered. He handed the binoculars to Johannes.

"Definitely arguing," Johannes said. "It may be Wang Jin and the other kidnapper. It's almost the ransom deadline, and they may be arguing about what to do with Sarah."

"All right," Bekker said. "How do you want to approach?"

Wang Jin turned and walked toward his SUV with Dingo following him. At first, he thought he would call Strangle again but realized that would be a waste of time. The man had already told Dingo what to do. Either Dingo was telling the truth or ignoring him. But Dingo hadn't told Strangle that Foxtrot was no longer with them, so he couldn't have said to cut Wang Jin a break because of Foxtrot's absence. Wang Jin was sure that Dingo and Bull were freelancing and he was at their mercy. They were not leaving him any choice.

As he walked, Wang Jin looked at his watch again. It was a few minutes before 5 p.m. "Just hold on. Let me see if the ransom has been paid."

"Listen, Mr. Big Shot, it doesn't matter whether it's been paid. You owe us thirty thousand dollars, and we want it now."

Wang Jin kept walking.

After securing Sarah to his vehicle, Wang Jin had snorted another line of coke to give him powdered courage to deal with the gangsters. Now the effects of the drug were solving his problems. He had become confident that he could handle these two. He was Chinese, and they were subhuman creatures unworthy of his respect.

When they got to the SUV, Dingo grabbed Wang Jin's arm, spun him around, and stepped very close to the Chinese scion, stinking of sweat and testosterone. Still holding Wang Jin's arm, he snarled angrily with breath smelling of rotten garbage, "Listen to me, you chink asshole: if you don't pay up, you're not leaving here."

"OK, OK, just let me see if the ransom has been paid," Wang Jin snapped, jerking his arm loose. He opened the SUV's door, took out his phone, and dialed his bank. It was 5 p.m. The ransom had not been paid.

Dingo was standing very close to Wang Jin, who broke into a happy smile, and lied. "They paid the ransom! It's payday!"

Wang Jin turned, shielding the SVU's interior from Dingo, and put the phone on the car seat. He picked up his six-inch hunting knife, turned back to Dingo, and drove the knife into his stomach. Then he pulled it out and wildly slashed at

Dingo's throat as he fell. By chance, he hit the carotid artery, which sprayed blood on Wang Jin and the SUV as Dingo fell silently to the ground.

Wang Jin looked for Bull but could not see him. He was probably on the other side of the cabin. Wang Jin calmly reached down and took Dingo's sidearm before quickly rifling through his pockets and removing the keys to the van, an extra clip for the GLOCK, and a few crumpled South African rand.

Johannes stopped looking through the binoculars and turned to Bekker and Baruti. "We'll circle to the right and use the boulders to shield our approach. When we get to the boulders, we can decide how to take them, depending on where they are. Our primary goal is to protect Sarah and get her away from them. If we have to kill all of them, then so be it. Baruti will cover us from here."

While Johannes was talking, Baruti had his eyes on the SUV. Suddenly he grabbed the binoculars out of Johannes's hand and focused on the SUV.

"Something's happened up there. Wang Jin and the other guy were standing on the far side of the SUV. Now I can only see Wang Jin. Oh my God, now he's cutting Sarah loose and shoving her into the back seat."

Johannes and Bekker turned to watch also.

"Jesus Christ. He's getting in the SUV. The bastard is going to run for it with Sarah."

They could see the SUV lurch forward and spin its tires, trying to take off. In a second, it was roaring off the hill toward the river.

Bull ran around the cabin and then stopped, looking where the SUV had been parked. Then he started firing wildly at the vehicle, which was quickly out of range. Bull turned and ran back to where the SUV had been parked.

"I can't see from here, but it looks like Wang Jin hurt or killed whoever he was arguing with," Bekker said. "Spread out and move up the hill quickly. Try to take that man alive, but don't take any chances. He's still holding a gun. If he starts to raise it, shoot him," he urged.

The three men started up the hill at a jog, separating from one other by about twenty yards.

CHAPTER 66

EVEN WITH HIS COKE induced-feeling of invincibility, Wang Jin involuntarily winced at the sound of gunshots behind him. One bullet hit the driver-side rear panel with a thump that could be heard over the screaming engine. Others missed.

The SUV bounced in and out of ruts, ran over small bushes, and hit good-size rocks as Wang Jin roared toward the river. When he got to the riverside track, he jerked the wheel to the right and accelerated to the east, which took them deeper into Hwange National Park.

Sarah had been awake but incapable of resisting when Wang Jin had cut her wrist loose from the door handle and shoved her inside the SUV. She felt like she was on an out-of-control amusement park ride as the vehicle plunged downhill toward the river. To stay in the back seat, she put one foot and a hand against the front seat. The SUV's violent jostling propelled several bottles of water from the rear cargo area onto the floor, where she grabbed two of them and wedged the bottles behind her into the seat back.

Bull was kneeling beside Dingo when the three men crested the hill and slowed to a walk. Bekker was closest when Bull stood up shaking his head, eyes fixed on the body. He apparently did not hear them approaching.

"Drop the gun!" Johannes shouted, visibly startling Bull.

Bull whirled around, eyes wide. He raised his pistol toward Johannes, and Bekker shot him in the center of his chest. The .454 round from his Redhawk pistol drove Bull's body backward. When he landed, his pistol discharged into the ground.

Johannes stepped on his wrist and kicked the gun out of his hand. Then he knelt and put a finger on Bull's carotid artery. "He's dead," he said without emotion.

Bekker picked up the gun and ejected another round from the chamber. "Guess he wasn't out of ammo," he said, ironically breaking the tension.

"Now that you've saved my life, by Chinese custom, you are responsible for me forever," Johannes cracked with a smile.

"You aren't Chinese, and neither am I," Bekker retorted.

Baruti slammed the van door. "No keys in here." He moved to Dingo and went through his pockets. Nothing.

Bekker found a full magazine in Bull's pocket and replaced the empty one, then added the pistol to his backpack. They were now carrying a mini-arsenal of weaponry, but there were no keys for the van.

"I'll follow the SUV on foot while you guys get the ranger's truck," Baruti offered.

Bekker was the first to reply. "Don't waste your energy that way. Let's hustle back and get the truck."

The three men took off at a jog down the hill and disappeared into the bush.

As the cabin fell farther behind, Wang Jin slowed the manic pace that was brutalizing the SUV, which hadn't been designed as an off-road vehicle. As the coke started wearing off, he remembered that he had taken the keys to the van, so unless Bull had another set, he would not be following him. He tried to remember why he had brought Sarah with him. It had seemed like a good idea at the time. He could make another ransom demand or use her as a bargaining chip or something to sell or trade. Darkness was descending, and the thought that he had no idea where he was or where he was going started to creep into his addled brain.

Still lying on the back seat, Sarah surreptitiously sipped water. As her dehydration eased, she began to feel some strength creep back into her body. She was very weak but had been in excellent physical condition before her ordeal had begun.

She decided to keep quiet, rest, and gather her strength. If she timed things right and had a little luck, she could bash Wang Jin in the head and take the vehicle.

Wang Jin began to slow down and make some effort to avoid the potholes and depressions in the vehicle track.

CHAPTER 67

WHEN JOHANNES AND THE others got to the ranger truck, they found that backup had arrived: two more rangers in a park police SUV. The taller of the new arrivals wore a green uniform with epaulets on the shoulders and multiple gold hash marks on the sleeve of his short-sleeve shirt. Around his waist was an expensive belt/holster rig. On his head was a peaked military-style cap with an emblem on the crown and gold braid on the brim. Bekker immediately recognized an Idi Amin wannabe. His index finger was poking the air before the ranger's face. The other newcomer was unarmed and most likely the driver for this senior officer.

When the ranger noticed their arrival and glanced their way, the officer whirled and faced them with his hands on his hips, sneering. What he saw were two white foreigners and a black man, heavily armed, faces and hands covered with camouflage grease paint and grime, wearing filthy clothes. All three had rifles slung on their shoulders. The two white men's sidearms where holstered, and the black man's was stuck behind his belt in easy reach.

The officer was momentarily silent and then turned to both his rangers. "These men are carrying illegal firearms. Disarm them, and put the weapons in the back of my vehicle," he snapped.

Johannes stepped forward and calmly raised his hand. "Officer."

"Commander," the officer snapped again.

"All right, Commander. I don't think you understand what's happening here. We're in pursuit of the kidnappers of an American businesswoman. I'm sure you've heard about it in the news."

The Commander looked at Johannes with utter contempt, motioning his rangers forward. "There will be no conversation while you are illegally armed. You will surrender those weapons immediately, and we will return to my command post, where you may file a missing person's report."

"You don't understand. A Chinese criminal is getting away with her. We must get after him before it's full dark," Baruti pleaded.

"Shut up! Place your weapons on the ground in front of you…now!" the Commander shouted.

Bekker moved forward parallel with Johannes and said, "That is not happening, Mr. Commander. We will borrow the ranger's pickup. You and your men can take that kidnapper." He pointed to Foxtrot, who still sat in the truck bed. "The bodies of the other two kidnappers, who happen to be South African gangsters, are up at the cabin. You ought to gather them before dark. Then you can process them while we get after the Chinese criminal."

The Commander's face twisted with anger. He was used to being obeyed without question, and he was certainly not taking orders from a white foreigner, especially with an Afrikaners accent. "Take their weapons!" he shouted as he fumbled with the snap holding the cover over his sidearm.

Bekker took three quick steps toward the Commander while releasing his rifle from his right shoulder. In a blur of motion, he snapped the rifle barrel down and across the Commander's right wrist. The sound of the bones breaking was audible.

The Commander dropped to his knees, holding his broken wrist and howling in pain. Bekker reach down and took his sidearm from its holster.

The other two rangers were motionless, afraid to move. Bekker calmly released the clip from the sidearm and ejected a round from the chamber, putting both in the pocket of his cargo pants before turning to the driver. "Any more ammunition in there?" He gestured to the SUV.

The driver shook his head, stunned at what he had just witnessed.

Bekker handed the Commander's pistol to his driver. "I think we'll borrow his SUV. Keys, please." He held out is hand.

The driver handed him the keys, looking relived that the confrontation had passed.

"Luc, why don't you disable the radio in the pickup?" Bekker continued.

"What are we going to do with these guys?" Baruti asked while Johannes disabled the radio.

"Nothing. What they should do is pick up the bodies at the cabin and return to their base. We know that will take at least an hour. By then it will be dark. If they send someone after us, it will take another hour to return here, but we'll be two hours down the road. My guess is they won't send anyone until daylight."

Johannes got behind the wheel. Bekker rode shotgun, and Baruti took the back seat of the SUV. They left in pursuit of Wang Jin and Sarah.

CHAPTER 68

DARKNESS HAD SETTLED OVER Hwange National Park, where a full moon provided minimal visibility for humans. However, this was prime hunting time for predators whose vision was adapted for night hunting. Wherever the big cats hunted, they were soon followed by hyenas and jackals that dined on leftovers before the buzzards descended to pick the bones when daylight arrived.

Sarah continued to lie on the back seat, sipping water. She was increasingly uncomfortable, which she took as a positive development since before she had not felt anything. She thought about sitting up, but if she did, Wang Jin would probably tie her up, and that she did not want. She needed to gather more strength to fight for her life. She considered using her shoelaces to make a garrote. She could sit up quickly and loop the laces around his neck and pull, bracing her legs against the back of the front seat. Perfect if she had the strength to hold on. She wasn't sure, and she would not get a second chance. She would wait.

Wang Jin's coke high was long gone. His eyelids got heavier and heavier as he drove slower and slower to stay on the vehicle track that had left the river some time ago. How long ago, he could not remember. His eyes closed for a moment, and he was jarred awake when the SUV hit a three-foot boulder just off the side of the track. Sarah was thrown off the seat but managed to grab on to a seat belt strap and pull herself back up.

Wang Jin wanted nothing more than to sleep. Perhaps he should just pull over, tie Sarah's hands and feet, and get some sleep. Just a few hours would be enough.

No, he had to put more distance between him and whoever might be following him, if anyone. He could not think clearly. Coke would help him think.

Wang Jin got out of the SUV in the moonlight and dropped some coke on the warm hood, using a credit card to create a line. Snort. It was up his nose. He wrinkled and wiped his nose as he turned back to get in the SUV.

What was that in the distance? Just barely in sight were headlights coming his way. It was dark. No one should be moving about now. Wait, maybe it was a night drive from one of the safari camps? Maybe, but what if it was not? What if Bull had another set of keys? What if park rangers were searching for him? It could be anyone. It could even be the men his father had sent to find him. That would be a blessing, but he could not take the chance of waiting on that slim reed.

Wang Jin got back in the SUV, backed away from the boulder, and took off down the track, gradually picking up speed. About ten minutes later, headlights appeared in his rearview mirror. They were far away but getting closer. Wang Jin turned off his headlights and abruptly veered off the track into the grassland. He planned to get well away from the track and hoped the trailing vehicle didn't see where he had pulled off.

When the headlights they saw in the distance disappeared, Baruti said, "Come on, Luc, you must drive faster to catch up. They've already moved out of sight."

"Calm down," Johannes said. "You don't know that. If we saw their lights, they could see ours. It's more likely that he turned his off."

Bekker, moving his head intently from one side of the track to the other, said, "My guess is that he saw us, turned off the track to hide, and hopes we miss where he turned off. If we go any faster, I might miss it."

Wang Jin picked up speed across the grassland even though in the dim moonlight he could barely see where he was going. The SUV dropped over the edge of a shallow gully.

BAM!

The front end had buried itself in the opposite bank, leaving the rear wheels up in the air. Wang Jin's seat belt saved him from injury, but Sarah was thrown off her seat again and into the back of the front seat, ending up stunned on the floor.

Wang Jin levered himself out of the SUV and looked at it with disgust. This vehicle was not going anywhere. He heard Sarah groaning, roughly pulled her out, and let her settle on the ground. He looked back to the west, where the headlights were moving inexorably along the vehicle track.

He found the last two bottles of water, which he put in the cargo pockets of his pants before attaching the hunting knife to the right side of his belt and shoving Dingo's pistol behind his belt in the front of his pants. Ready to go, he jerked Sarah to her feet. Before she could react, Wang Jin quickly tied her hands in front of her with a long utility rope. Then he cut it, creating a four-foot leash.

"Come with me, bitch, and keep your mouth shut."

Sarah tried to resist. Wang Jin slapped her so hard that her head snapped to the side.

"Your choice: come with me and keep up, or I will cut you up and leave you to bleed out while the vultures pluck your eyes for breakfast."

Sarah stumbled along with him. Wang Jin located a faint animal track, which they followed in the dim moonlight.

Sarah had recovered from the shock of the accident but continued to artificially stumble, hoping to slow him down. She was confident he did not know where he was going and couldn't figure out why he was rushing into the unknown, unless maybe someone was following them and he wanted to hide. A glimmer of hope kindled in the back of her mind. Surely people were looking for her.

From time to time, he jerked on the rope, keeping it tight enough that she had no chance to reach down for a rock or stick. As they moved through the bush, the moon was well into its descent in the western sky.

The game trail bent around a clump of trees and bushes. At the edge of the moonlight, a massive male lion had his head buried in the entrails of a kudu. As they came to a stop, the lion lifted his head, showing a muzzle covered in blood. He gave an ear-splitting roar.

Wang Jin dropped the rope, jerked out his pistol, and fired a wild shot at the lion. Undeterred, the beast began to move toward them.

Wang Jin turned and ran in panic.

Sarah stood perfectly still.

The lion was a fifty-mile-an-hour blur as it passed Sarah. He hit Wang Jin at full speed, slamming him to the ground. In an instant, his massive jaws clamped around Wang Jin's throat, his enormous fangs buried deep in his flesh. Everything happened so fast and with such devastating finality that Wang Jin, scion of the chairman of the Chinese Communist Party, never made a sound.

As Sarah moved slowly back the way they had come, she distinctly heard bones cracking.

CHAPTER 69

"There!" Bekker exclaimed. "He turned off to the right."

Johannes slowed and eased into the grassland on top of Wang Jin's tracks. Bekker jumped out and examined the bent grass. "It's fresh. It's that son of a bitch."

"What about our lights?" Baruti asked. "He'll see us coming."

"True," Bekker replied, "but if we don't use them, I'll have to walk in front to keep us on his track, and that will slow us down. What do you think, Luc?"

"He could ambush us easily, but there are three of us and one of him. Not the best odds for him. He's not following a road, so he may not get far. Regardless, he'll hear our engine. Unless we want to walk, he'll know we're coming, and he could ambush us in the dark whether we're riding or walking. So, on balance, I favor assuming the risk and pushing ahead using our headlights."

"Best bad choice," Bekker agreed.

"I'm good with it," Baruti said.

The tension inside their SUV was palpable as the vehicle moved forward into the darkness.

Wang Jin's SUV, with its back wheels sticking up in the air, materialized out of the darkness. Johannes immediately doused the headlights and turned off the engine. Three doors opened simultaneously, and each man rolled out, using the doors for cover.

The only sound was the ticking of the SUV engine as it cooled. Bekker whispered through the vehicle to Johannes, "Cover me."

Johannes nodded and Bekker moved forward. It took him thirty seconds to assess the situation.

"Clear. No one's here," Bekker said as he walked back to them. "It's going to be hard to follow their trail in this light."

Baruti's mouth opened soundlessly as he pointed to the left of the ruined SUV.

A form had materialized out of the darkness. It was Sarah, trudging toward them, eyes down. She had not seen them yet. She raised her eyes, and for a moment, the scene froze as they all looked at one another.

Sarah was covered in grime and blood, her hair a rat's nest, her face and exposed skin scratched and filthy, her lips cracked, her left cheek swollen underneath an ugly bruise. The three heavily armed men matched her filthy appearance. Their exposed skin was covered in dirt and grime, the whites of their eyes peering out of grease-painted camouflage masks.

Sarah thought this must be a mirage. These creatures from a horror movie were actually the three most important men in her life: her boss and business mentor, the man who had taught her how to survive an encounter with a lion, and her lover. Tears of relief oozed from her eyes, leaving tracks on her grimy face. Her tongue was too swollen for her to speak. Her arms were too weak to lift.

She stumbled forward into the arms of the onrushing Baruti and held on as the tears became a torrent and mixed with Baruti's as he gently kissed her dirt-covered face.

Bekker and Johannes looked at each other with exhausted, misty eyes. Even the old warriors felt the emotional relief.

The men gave Sarah water and waited in patient silence for the exhausted woman to recover enough to speak. The gray line in the eastern sky grew wider, and soon, rays of reddish gold burst from the horizon, underlighting a string of fluffy clouds. Sitting against a large boulder with Baruti's arm protectively around her, Sarah was finally able to speak haltingly and with great effort.

"A…lion…Wang Jin. He…ran. The…lion got him."

"How far?" Johannes asked.

"Don't…know."

"That's all right. We can backtrack and find him," Bekker said.

Baruti snarled in response, "Let the buzzards clean his bones and scatter them across the bush."

"Not a bad idea," Johannes replied. "But I think we should return his body to the Chinese so there's no doubt how he died. They can't claim we murdered him if he was killed by a lion."

Baruti nodded reluctant assent.

"Let's load up and go find the body. Then we've got to get the hell out of this park, and out of Zimbabwe, before that Commander, or whatever he is, can find us," Bekker said, realizing that they were undoubtedly in trouble with the park rangers whose commander he had injured and upon whom the nuance of borrowing rather than stealing their vehicle would not register.

Driving slowly along the trail Sarah had left, it took almost a half hour before they saw buzzards circling. They knew the body had been found when they saw buzzards landing on something and quickly flying back into the air.

Two hyenas were tearing at the body with a few jackals awaiting their turn. The arrival of the SUV caused them to move away but within sight. Sarah was asleep with her head in Baruti's lap when Johannes pulled up alongside the corpse, which was almost unrecognizable. Wang Jin's head was barely attached, and his body cavity had been ripped open. The entrails were gone. Buzzards had pecked out his eyes, leaving cavities rimmed with dried blood.

Baruti strained to see without disturbing Sarah.

"Trust me, you don't want to see this. It will never leave you," Bekker said.

Baruti took the advice and relaxed, cradling Sarah.

Bekker got a tarp from the back of the SUV and spread it out on the ground next to the body. Then he and Johannes used their feet to roll it onto the tarp. They rolled up the tarp and lifted it into the back of the SUV.

As they started back with Johannes driving, Bekker said, "We'll never make it out of the park in this vehicle. By the time we get to an exit, the rangers will have had plenty of time to set up checkpoints. I know there are unofficial exits like the one we took to get in, but the rangers know where they are. If they pick us up, God knows what will happen to Sarah."

Baruti started to speak but changed his mind for fear of waking Sarah. Finally, Johannes broke the silence. "Maybe we could pull Wang Jin's SUV out of the gully and see if it still runs?"

Bekker nodded. "Can't hurt to try."

CHAPTER 70

THE SMOG CONTINUED TO hold Beijing in its grip, bringing early darkness. Streetlights and the light from building windows barely penetrated the haze of pollution as Wang Chen nervously paced his office waiting for the meeting requested by top party officials. The last word from his special ops team had been that they had landed in Victoria Falls and were underway to Hwange National Park using the GPS coordinates to the cabin the secret police had obtained. Any minute he could get a message that Wang Jin had been found and was on his way home.

His intercom buzzed. The party elite had arrived.

Wang looked quickly in his private bathroom mirror and straightened his tie. Closing that door, he buttoned his suit jacket and took a deep breath. His administrative assistant ushered in his four guests.

The chairman of Central Committee, Li Zhonghu, and two other men bowed slightly to Wang, who gave them a slight bow in return. Li immediately took charge and directed Wang to a chair at one end of the office conference table. He seated himself at the other end, and his three companions took seats on the sides.

Wang started to speak, but Li held up his hand.

"We, and much of China—indeed, the world—have read the *Guardian* article. I have personally checked the facts in the article through our embassy in Botswana. The statements about the diamond mine auction are confirmed, but whether your son has kidnapped the American woman remains unconfirmed. Your son's activities have brought shame upon China on the world stage. If he is in fact a criminal, the implications for our government are staggering." Li looked at his watch. "You have one minute to explain, so be succinct."

Wang's mind raced. There was no point in denying the known facts. But they did not yet know that Wang Jin had kidnapped the American. As in soccer, the best defense was offense. He sat forward, placing his forearms on the table, and began speaking forcefully and without hesitation.

"My son, as you surely know, is missing, so I have not been able to speak to him. However, I have spoken to the law firm representing him. They have taken full responsibility for how the auction was handled. According to them, Wang Jin had nothing to do with the alleged bribery and economic pressure on some banks. It was all their idea in an overzealous attempt to please the Bank of China.

"As for the missing American woman, I have sent a team to Africa to find Wang Jin and bring him home to explain whether he had any involvement in her disappearance. I expect to hear from them any minute that he's on his way back to China and that he knows nothing about what happened to her."

Li focused an icy stare on the chairman. "Are you telling us that this law firm is responsible for your son ignoring the order of the government of Botswana to leave the country, escaping from his hotel, and disappearing?"

Wang had not thought about how to respond about his son's disappearance because he had been so focused on getting him back to China, where he could create a plausible story to explain his actions. His mind spun like a tire in mud before an idea clicked. "Since I haven't spoken to him, I don't know what happened. There are some rumors floating around Botswana that local gangsters may have kidnapped him for ransom."

Li's disbelief was evident on his face, and the others looked at Wang in stony silence. He had no friends in this room.

"Is your son a drug addict?" Li snapped.

"What? Of course not! It's possible that he, like many of our youth, experimented with cocaine at a party or two with friends," Wang said defensively. "But he put that behind him," he said emphatically, slapping the table.

Li's eyes narrowed before he said, "Wouldn't you be better off blaming your son's bad behavior on his addiction to cocaine?"

"What?...That's absurd...no...Well, I can't be with him twenty-four seven... We'll have to ask him when he gets home."

"Understand this: if your son is arrested for kidnapping that woman, we cannot support you at the conference." Li and the other men stood together, and Wang hurried to his feet.

As soon as the door closed behind them, Wang stripped off his suit coat and loosened his tie. His shirt was soaked with sweat, and he could smell his own body odor. An improbable vision popped into his head: a bleeding shark being circled by his fellow sharks.

He began to slowly pace around his office, clearing his mind and breathing deeply. Then he moved into a slow series of tai chi exercises designed to relive stress.

CHAPTER 71

BEKKER AND JOHANNES FOUND a twenty-foot tow strap in the ranger's SUV and attached it to Wang Jin's SUV. Although their SUV's wheels spun a bit, by using first gear low range, they were able to pull the other one out of the ditch. Johannes got behind the wheel and turned the key. Nothing.

He pulled the hood release, and Bekker began to examine the engine. Soon he was smiling as he reattached a battery cable that had been jarred loose from the impact. A few turns of a wrench later, the vehicle started.

While they were bending the front fenders out of the tires' path of travel, Sarah awakened, and Baruti helped her into the resurrected SUV. Johannes and Bekker transferred their gear, and they headed back to the main vehicle track.

Bekker followed Johannes to the track in the ranger's SUV, where he used its radio to anonymously call in the location of that vehicle and hoped that would make the rangers focus on the SUV location and leave the checkpoints at the park's exits. If the rangers stayed put looking for the three men who had taken the vehicle, it was going to be a touchy and maybe a dangerous situation.

Sarah tried to speak a few times but couldn't summon the strength to finish a sentence. She was able to eat two protein bars and drink a bottle of water as they headed west for the park boundary and the Botswana border. The men wisely didn't pepper her with questions, and after a short while, she was again asleep with her head on Baruti's shoulder.

Bekker studied the park map and plotted a route to the northwestern boundary that avoided the abandoned cabin and where they had taken the SUV. They stayed off the main park roads but still passed several big Toyotas full of tourists. As each vehicle came into sight, Johannes and Bekker looked at each other and couldn't help but worry if it was a ranger vehicle. They hadn't discussed what they would do if a ranger confronted them.

Two hours later, they were a short distance from an unofficial exit on a narrow vehicle track that cut through thick bush. They came around a bend and almost collided with an oncoming vehicle. The vehicles came to a stop ten feet apart. There was no way for them to pass each other.

"Oh shit," Johannes whispered. "Four Chinese men. Who are they? What are they doing here?"

The driver of the other vehicle opened his door and climbed out, suspiciously looking at the two white men. His appearance answered the question: close-cropped hair, physically muscular, matching shirt and pants that looked like military issue. The sidearm he was wearing was certainly military issue. This was no tourist.

"Chinese military, probably looking for Wang Jin and the other Chinese we got rid of," Bekker said. "Be careful. Maybe we can bluff our way past them."

Johannes got out of the SUV without realizing his pistol was holstered on his belt. Simultaneously, Bekker opened his door and stood behind it with his hand on his Redhawk pistol. Sarah stirred, and Baruti picked up Foxtrot's pistol. It was too late to move her out of sight.

"Do you speak English?" Johannes asked, smiling as he approached the Chinese man.

He first spoke in Chinese, issuing what sounded like a command, then said, "Yes."

The other three doors of the vehicle opened, and Chinese men stepped out, mimicking Bekker's position by taking cover behind their doors. It was obvious to Johannes that the situation was deteriorating. Four against two, with Baruti protecting Sarah. This could end very badly.

"We can back up a ways and turn into the bush for you to get past," Johannes said in as friendly a manner as he could muster.

"Have you seen a Chinese man with three black men and a woman?" the Chinese soldier asked.

Johannes had to make a split-second decision that would likely determine whether they lived or died. There was no doubt these soldiers had been sent to find Wang Jin. He could let them see what the lion had done to Wang Jin and give them the body. The question was whether they had orders concerning Sarah. He could try to bullshit his way past these hardened soldiers, but that didn't seem likely. If he were in their shoes, he would search their vehicle and ask all kinds of unanswerable questions about Sarah.

"We have the body of a Chinese man who was killed by a lion in the bush. We're taking him to the police in Victoria Falls. I hope this isn't the man you're looking for."

"Show me," the soldier snapped.

Johannes led him to the back of the SUV and opened the hatch. "It will probably be easier to take the body out and unroll the tarp," Johannes suggested.

The solider shouted something in Chinese, and two of his men trotted over, lifted the tarp out of the SUV, and unrolled it on the ground. These men were battle-tested soldiers, and none of them looked away from the mangled body.

The leader studied the battered, eyeless face. He took out his cell phone and swiped to a picture, which he compared with the body. Then he took several pictures of Wang Jin's mangled carcass before giving a command in Chinese to his men. They rolled the body back into the tarp.

"We will take him with us back to China. Where did you find him?"

"A couple of hours from here. We've been camping for the last two weeks. At daylight this morning, we saw buzzards circling not far from our camp and went to see why. I expected to see an animal that a predator had gotten last night, but… well, you see what we found."

"Did you see a woman out there?"

"No. The only woman was our friend Jackie."

The soldier walked over to the SUV and looked in the back seat, where Sarah was now sitting up and sipping water.

"Is that Sarah Taylor-Jones?" the soldier asked.

"No. That's Jackie Smith. Look: the woman is black. Sarah Taylor-Jones sounds like the name of a white English woman."

The soldier nodded and stepped back. He focused on Johannes's filthy appearance and glanced in the back of the SUV, where there was no camping gear. He was about to say something when Bekker walked over.

"Listen, soldier, we both know who that is, and we know what he did. All the police in this part of Africa are looking for him. You found him. You successfully accomplished your mission. The fucker is dead. It's over. There is no mess to clean up. If you fool around here much longer, the park rangers will show up, take your guns, maybe arrest you, and surely take credit for finding the body. You will lose face and go home empty-handed. I suggest that you load the body, turn around, and we all get the hell out of here."

The soldier focused a steely-eyed glare on Bekker, who he sensed was another soldier giving him good advice. He could push things, but that would take time, and the man was right. If park rangers showed up, it would be a clusterfuck.

The Chinese loaded the body in the back of their SUV and backed into the bush until they were able to turn around. Johannes followed them, but far enough back to keep out of their dust cloud.

Thirty minutes later, they arrived at the unofficial exit from the park and found the track blocked by a ranger pickup truck and two armed rangers. The Chinese stopped, and one of the rangers approached the driver.

"This could go south really fast," Bekker said, unholstering his Redhawk.

Johannes and Baruti picked up their pistols. Sarah held Baruti's arm tightly.

At first, the ranger appeared to be angry. If he tried to search the Chinese vehicle, all hell would break loose. Then he nodded and smiled.

The driver handed the ranger a wad of bills and quickly turned toward Victoria Falls.

Johannes reached into his pocket and said, "Gentlemen, give me your cash."

When he reached the ranger, Johannes said nothing and handed him their money. The ranger pocketed the money, smiled, and waved them through. They followed the Chinese until they turned onto the road toward the Botswana border.

Baruti called his father, who arranged for a plane to meet them at a dirt airstrip just across the border. Bekker declined the flight to Gaborone, choosing to stay behind and make private arrangements to drive the SUV back to Victoria Falls and retrieve his Toyota from the park.

The small plane made a perfect landing on the dirt airstrip, turned and taxied back to where the four exhausted survivors were standing looking like survivors of the apocalypse.

Sarah hugged Bekker fiercely much to his embarrassment. Baruti insisted and Bekker submitted to a man-hug. Johannes and Bekker looked into each other's eyes and shook hands with a firm and familiar grip that did not need words. The job was over and done well.

Sarah had the last word as she climbed into the plane.

"You haven't seen the last of me Aiden Bekker."

CHAPTER 72

IT SEEMED TO THE Chinese Communist Party members gathered for the national congress that the thick blanket of smog over Beijing would never lift. These men were communists, but they were also politicians. They gossiped with the enthusiasm of attendees at Paris Fashion Week about Wang Chen's chances of being reelected chairman despite his agreement to cede power to a representative of the Chinese Communist Youth League. The Great Hall of the People was full of delegates milling about waiting for the opening ceremony.

Wang sat locked in his bedroom, head in his hands, overcome with grief. Just before dawn, he had gotten a call from the Chinese People's Liberation Army special operations commander. Wang Jin had been found mauled by a lion and partially eaten by the predators of the African bush. He had been unable to look at the picture of his dead son that had been forwarded to his phone. His administrative assistant had made the formal identification.

There was a knock on his door.

"Chairman Wang, you're scheduled to give opening remarks at the conference in two hours. Do you need anything?" his chief of security asked through the closed door.

Wang said no and headed into his bathroom to shower and get ready for his speech. It was written; all he had to do was read it from the teleprompter in a strong voice. He could do that.

Later, as he was knotting his tie and looking at himself in the mirror, it seemed that the bags under his eyes were twice as large as they had been yesterday. He told himself that he had to focus. His son's death was a tragedy for him, but no one else cared. Wang Jin was unmarried without children. His mother was dead, and his only friend had been spying on him for years. Trying to pump himself up, he thought that now that his son could not be arrested for kidnapping, the committee would continue to support him. In fact, Wang Jin's horrible death was likely to whip up sympathy for him that would help sway any reluctant conference delegates. Wang Jin's parting gift was avoiding the scandal of being arrested for kidnapping the businesswoman. Yes, something positive had come from his needless death. Wang's mind was in a fog of grief, but all he had to do was read a speech off the teleprompter, and he would continue as chairman of the Chinese Communist Party.

Two hours later, Wang strode powerfully to the podium in the vast hall, looked out over the hundreds of delegates, and began his speech. He spoke in the strong and commanding voice of the leader of the most populous country in the world.

Five minutes into his speech, he noticed some delegates rudely leaving the hall. Others were surreptitiously looking at their cell phones. He didn't know that they were looking at and listening to news reports from Botswana. The bulletin in *The Guardian* was typical.

Botswana authorities announced this morning that missing American businesswoman Sarah Taylor-Jones had been found in Zimbabwe's Hwange National Park, where she had allegedly been taken by three South African gangsters rumored to be working for Wang Jin, son of Wang Chen, chairman of the Chinese Communist Party. Ms. Taylor-Jones has been taken to Life Gaborone Private Hospital and is expected to make a full recovery.

The kidnappers were all killed during her rescue. According to reports, Wang Jin was mauled to death by a lion while attempting to escape the rescuers.

The rescue was led by Baruti Masisi, son of Botswana President Mokgweetsi Masisi. Baruti was joined by Luc Johannes—president/CEO of Ms. Taylor-Jones's employer, Consolidated Diamonds, PLC—and Aiden Bekker, a Botswana safari guide and cattleman…

Three men approached Wang from stage right. Two of them took him firmly by his arms and escorted him off the stage. The third announced a one-hour recess.

Bedlam erupted in the Great Hall of the People.

CHAPTER 73

A BRIGHT SUN IN a clear, cloudless sky poured light into Sarah's hospital room at Life Gaborone Private Hospital. The partially open widow was the gateway for fresh air that pushed normal hospital smells down the hallway.

Sarah, feeling clean and rested, sat up in bed with an IV for fluids attached to her left hand. Next to the bed in a chair facing her was Johannes, wearing a blue blazer, a crisp white shirt, and khaki trousers. Neatly barbered and shaved, he looked the epitome of a successful businessman. Sarah was due to be released from the hospital later that day.

They had been drinking coffee with Baruti and talking about the disappearance of Wang Chen from the National Congress of the Chinese Communist Party and what it might hold in store for China. They were about to move on to the Debswana auction when Johannes's phone vibrated in his pocket. He looked at the screen.

"Excuse me, I have to take this," he said, moving out into the hall and closing the door. He was back five minutes later with a puzzled look on his face.

"It was Peter Hess; he's called a board meeting in New York the day after tomorrow. I'll have to get a flight back tonight."

"That's strange," Sarah said. "Do you want me to go with you?"

"No. You should stay here, finish recovering, and prepare our revised bid for Debswana. There's still no indication that De Beers is going submit a bid, so we may be the only bidder. If our bid is accepted, there will be a lot for you to do here. I'll make sure things are running smoothly in New York."

Johannes booked a flight to London on British Airways but needed an expensive private flight to New York in order to arrive on time. Eighteen hours in the air gave him plenty of time to think about this unusual board meeting.

Consolidated Diamonds was a privately held corporation. Charles Hess, the patriarch of the Hess family, had died almost nine months ago, and his 51 percent of the company's stock was held by a trust of which his son Peter, Johannes's friend and the man who had brought him into Consolidated so many years ago, was the trustee. Various family members were trust beneficiaries. Peter and his three siblings each owned 10 percent of the company, and Johannes owned 9 percent. The board now had five members: the Hess siblings and Johannes. The members were not paid, but Johannes had a handsome salary and routinely met performance standards for a generous bonus.

They usually held quarterly meetings, which were mostly pro forma. He couldn't figure out why Peter didn't want to discuss the meeting over the phone or the meeting's urgency. The only thing that kept coming to mind was that it had something to do with the estate and trust left by Charles.

When he got to New York, Johannes had just enough time to stop by his apartment, shower, and change clothes before the meeting in Consolidated's conference room at 425 Park Avenue. The Hess family was waiting for him. After greeting his fellow board members, Johannes noted that the usual complement of refreshments was absent. There was a folder for each member. Once the greetings were completed, Peter, as chairman, called the meeting to order. They all sat, and he began.

"Luc, first, on behalf of all of us, I want to tell you how proud we are of what you did in rescuing Sarah from those criminals. We are ecstatic that she will recover fully from her ordeal. In recognition of your extraordinary actions, we have approved an additional bonus for you of one hundred thousand dollars and want to be sure the company pays for all expenses you incurred in her rescue. Additionally, we would like for you to work with counsel to devise a way for Sarah to receive a similar bonus that would be an award for personal injury or something that would not be taxable to her."

Johannes began to relax. Maybe they were feeling a little guilty about refusing the ransom request. Regardless, this was good news, but he still couldn't see the need for all the urgency to have this meeting.

Peter continued. "The reason we called you home on such short notice is that we have received a buyout offer from Bharat Patel. It's being made by a shell company that will eventually be folded into De Beers."

Johannes was taken by surprise. He thought the offer had died months ago when Patel hadn't reduced it to writing. Obviously, Patel had gone over his head directly to the decision makers. Not knowing what to say, Johannes said nothing.

Peter filled the silence. "You deserve to know why the family is willing to sell the company you have been largely responsible for building for the last four decades. There are several reasons that make this the right time for us to sell.

"First, the estate faces a substantial estate tax bill for Father's fifty-one percent interest in the company. For years, I tried to get him to give up control and do some sophisticated estate planning, but he refused, so now we must pay the government. On the bright side, the government gets only one bite at the apple because his shares got a step up in basis at his death, so there will be no capital gains tax.

"Second, Luc, you are ready to retire. Third, with the supply problem at the Golden Wattle, we are in uncharted waters. Maybe we could outbid De Beers for the Debswana interest, but at what cost? With you retiring, the family doesn't want to pile on that much debt. I know you've been grooming Sarah to step into your shoes, but your shoes are big, and she adds another element of uncertainty.

"Fourth, but perhaps most importantly, the family…" Peter looked at each of his siblings, who nodded affirmatively. "The family wants to use the proceeds to pursue their personal interests in business, investment management, and charitable endeavors. It's time for a liquidity event. Fifth, and finally, our investment bankers think the price and terms are reasonable."

Johannes was completely blindsided. At a loss for words. How could he argue against their decision? He was ready to retire. They needed the money to pay estate tax. The future was uncertain at best, and they all wanted to do something else with their inheritance. It was so sensible. He needed time to think, but there was no time, so he created some with questions.

"What will happen to our employees? Many of them have been with us for years."

"Nothing. Patel intends to operate Consolidated as an independent division for the time being. There will be no personnel cuts. He plans to offer Sarah the

CEO position at an increased salary," smiled Peter, who had obviously anticipated the question.

Johannes nodded. That was all he could do. No brilliant argument had popped into his head. Of course, with new ownership, things would change, but they did not know how or when.

"When is the closing?"

"Forty-five days from signing the agreement, which will be tomorrow. Luc, we've been friends for forty years. If you were staying with the company, things might be different. But you are ready to move on, and so are we. I truly think this is the best thing for us, the employees, and you."

"This was unexpected, but you've convinced me. I wish all of you the very best."

Hugs and handshakes followed.

As he left the room, Johannes had only one negative thought: How was he going to break this to Sarah? She had been discharged from the hospital today. What a welcome-home present.

CHAPTER 74

AS A SKY FULL of gray-black clouds moved over Gaborone, chasing away the remaining daylight, Sarah, barefoot and dressed in jeans and one of Baruti's white oxford button-down shirts with reading glasses perched on top of her head, was going over a spreadsheet that was warm out of the printer, a pencil in hand. Within a few hours of being discharged from the hospital, with Baruti's help, she had commandeered a connecting hotel room and turned it into an office. Papers were stacked on the bed. Her computer and a printer were set up on a desk that had been requisitioned from the business center on the second floor, along with a comfortable desk chair. More papers were scattered on a folding table. She had been working nonstop to catch up on what needed catching up and prepare a draft of the final bid for the partnership interest in Debswana.

Sarah checked her watch and panicked. She and Baruti were having a quiet dinner in the hotel's private dining room in an hour. She dropped the spreadsheet on her desk and rushed through the connecting door into her sleeping quarters, undressing as she went.

As she was drying off from her shower, her cell phone rang. It was Johannes. The call lasted only five minutes but turned her life upside down.

Did she want to run Consolidated? Of course; she knew Johannes had been grooming her to take over when he retired. Did she want to work for Bharat Patel? She had been upset when she had thought he had tried to bribe her, but Johannes had been proven right: he wanted her to run the company. For how long? If

Consolidated was to eventually be absorbed into De Beers, what would happen to her? Would she have to move to Johannesburg? Would the De Beers management accept her? She had hundreds of questions.

Her future, while uncertain, was wide open. Sarah had never needed to look for a job. She had been recruited out of business school by Goldman Sachs, and headhunters were still calling. A job was not the issue. She could find a challenging job in a heartbeat. The issue was what she wanted to do with the rest of her life. Maybe she should think of this as an opportunity.

Sarah got dressed, combed her hair, and rushed out to meet Baruti, forgetting to apply any makeup. She realized that at the elevator and stopped for a moment, then she chuckled. After their time in the bush, he certainly knew what she looked like without makeup.

The hotel's private dining room was an intimate space located down the hall from the public restaurant. The ebony wood table for six was set for two with fine china and crystal stemware. The lighting was low, supplemented by a candelabra on the table. Fabric-covered walls, excellent African landscape oil paintings, plush burgundy carpeting, and a glass wall overlooking the lights of downtown Gaborone created an elegant setting.

Baruti was waiting with a warm smile on his face. By the time he hugged her tightly and kissed her briefly on the lips, he knew something was wrong.

A white-jacketed waiter appeared, took their cocktail order, and disappeared.

"What is it?" Baruti asked with a genuinely concerned look on his face.

Sarah told him about the call from Johannes and the De Beers purchase of Consolidated. By the time she finished, the waiter reappeared with their drinks. When he asked for their dinner order, Sarah asked Baruti to order for her.

Baruti quickly ordered and started asking questions, which Sarah answered in as few words as possible. It did not take him long to realize that she was totally distracted.

"Sarah, forgive me, but I think you need some time alone to process what you're going to do."

The relief on her face was palpable. She hugged Baruti tightly and kissed his lips briefly.

"Thank you for understanding. I don't think I can eat right now. Maybe later I'll order room service. You're wonderful to be so understanding."

Sarah left the dining room.

Baruti was motionless for a long moment. Not much of a celebration. He went to the sideboard and removed a bottle of fine French champagne from the ice bucket, pouring himself a glass. He tasted the champagne and looked at the lights of Gaborone.

Sarah was not the only one who had to make a decision about the future. He wanted her to be part of his future, but he had nothing to offer her. She was a hard-charging American businesswoman with an unlimited future in New York City. He thought of himself as a capable businessman, but would he fit in the big city? What about his mixed blood? Did it matter one way or the other? It did not matter here in Botswana, but would it matter in race-obsessed America?

He had two more days to decide whether to go to New York for the final interview with Marriott International. What if he took the job and Sarah was transferred to Joburg? What a cruel joke that would be.

Sarah returned to her room and changed back into her jeans and white shirt before she noticed the blinking red button on the hotel phone. Bharat Patel had called, wanting to set up a Skype meeting to discuss the job he was offering her at Consolidated. Sarah began pacing the room trying to organize her thoughts. When the idea hit her, she stopped dead and dropped onto the bed.

She had done it! She had won. Patel was offering her the CEO job because of her brains and talent. It had nothing to do with the color of her skin. The world knew that Barat Patel, one of the richest men in the world, did not hire people based upon the color of their skin.

Sarah spent the next hour with a pad and pencil jotting down and organizing questions for Patel about the future of Consolidated, her exact responsibilities, to whom would she report, and her relationship with the main office and the other De Beers executives. Another half hour was spent making a list of points that her employment contract would have to cover. There was no way she would accept the job without an iron-clad five-year employment contract that would have to include a generous severance payment even if she was discharged for alleged cause. She had learned from Elon Musk's acquisition of Twitter and his firing of the executive suite for cause without paying severance.

Finally, Sarah called it a night and crawled into the hotel's nice, soft bed, eager for some sleep that had been in short supply since her kidnapping. Unfortunately, what little sleep she got came with horrible dreams about her kidnapping mixed with one where she walked in a thick mist and stepped off a cliff, dropping into nothingness.

CHAPTER 75

SARAH GAVE UP TRYING to sleep when daylight crept into her room from the window that was only partially covered by curtains. Another shower and a cup of coffee from the Keurig machine got her feeling human. Out of habit, she opened her email and found one from Bharat Patel again asking for a Skype meeting to discuss the job and review the draft employment contract that was attached to the email. Sarah ordered breakfast from room service and watched BBC News until she finished eating and called for room service to pick up her tray.

By ten, she was still reviewing the draft contract when her room phone rang. It was Mokgweetsi Masisi's administrative assistant, asking her to meet with the president for lunch at his office. He did not say why, and she did not think it polite to ask. After all, Masisi was the president of Botswana, and his time was valuable. It must be something important.

Sarah had no preconceived notion about what having lunch with the president would be like. She had enjoyed the lunch with him and Anne and the delightful dinner at their home, but this seemed to be something official. She was surprised when she was ushered into Masisi's office and discovered that lunch was to be takeout deli-style chicken sandwiches and diet sodas at the small conference table in his office.

Masisi led the conversation through the status of her recovery and the surprising purchase of Consolidated by De Beers, leaving only one bidder for the Debswana partnership interest. In passing, he mentioned that he had spent an hour on the phone with Johannes that morning, causing Sarah to wonder what they could have spoken about for so long. After they finished their sandwiches and disposed of the wrapping paper and paper plates, Masisi got down to business.

"Sarah, I've been giving a lot of thought to how to deploy the capital we're getting from the Debswana sale in a way to develop an information economy. This is a transitional concept for our country, and to be frank, it will require a level of financial sophistication that we don't have. We need people to help us do this. I need someone with financial sophistication to hire the right people, put capital in the right places, and take overall responsibility for the transition. I think that we must establish a new government department to do this."

Sarah found this conversation puzzling. If he was right that Botswana needed people with financial sophistication to get the transition moving, what did this have to do with her?

"As I mentioned, I spoke at length with Luc about you and to some contacts I have at Goldman Sachs. Needless to say, they had nothing but praise for your abilities."

Where was this going? Before she could process more, Masisi continued.

"Sarah, I want you to head this project. I know you aren't an IT person, but you'll hire IT people. I want your financial management experience. We're going to need every nickel to pull this off. We cannot have the usual government boondoggles with waste and payouts to favored people. This must be done right from inception. It is a hugely responsible job, and I want you to do it."

Sarah, obviously surprised, reacted immediately. "I don't know what to say, Mr. President. I'm honored that you are considering me, but without knowing more about your plans, I don't know if I'm the right person for the position.

"Furthermore, Mr. President, have you thought about whether a noncitizen could be a cabinet minister?"

"That won't be a problem. I have the power to make you a citizen of Botswana on the statutory grounds of special circumstances. However, under our law, that would require you to give up your US citizenship…"

Sarah was shaking her head no when he continued.

"But that is not necessary. There is currently a bill to allow dual citizenship that is buried in a legislative committee that I could push toward a hearing. In the meantime, you could be a consultant with a five-year contract…"

Again, Sarah began to shake her head, but Masisi pushed forward. "Your entire fee would be paid up front without a claw-back feature if you quit or are fired. That should protect you.

For the next two hours, they talked about his plans for Botswana. Sarah's interest in the position increased as he shared his ideas for the future development of the country.

"Mr. President," Sarah said. "My head is swimming. I sense it's a wonderful opportunity for someone, but I don't know if that someone is me. Maybe we could meet tomorrow and talk about it."

On the way back to her hotel Sarah felt that an unimaginably heavy burden had been lifted from her. She had to chose between two jobs that had been offered because of what she had done with her life. Two clean offers that had to do with who she was not her skin color. Her grandmother would be so proud. A tear leaked from her right eye and she let it run down her cheek.

EPILOGUE

A YEAR LATER, SARAH Taylor-Jones, Botswana's minister of information, married Baruti Masisi, CEO of the Masisi Hotel Group, in a ceremony at the Vumbura Plains Camp in Botswana's Okavango Delta. The fourteen luxurious tents were occupied by a select few Masisi family friends and the US ambassador to Botswana and his wife. Included among the close friends were Aiden Bekker and his wife. The man who gave away the bride was Luc Johannes, the retired former president/CEO of Consolidated Diamonds, PLC, who attended with his companion, Heidi Blomqvist, both of whom were tanned and fit after several months of sailing in the Mediterranean and hiking in Switzerland.

Some weeks prior to the wedding, during an interview with Bloomberg News, Sarah was asked what had motivated her to move from New York City, the financial capital of the world, to Botswana. Was it love, the reporter had asked?

Sarah had replied, "To borrow a phrase, it's complicated, and a number of factors came into the decision. Love was certainly one of them, but Baruti was prepared to take a job in New York to be with me. When I decided to stay in Botswana, he was overjoyed. So I had my love regardless of my decision.

"There was the opportunity to work with talented people to transition Botswana's economy. That was something very few people get a chance to accomplish. My work would have a direct impact on so many people. I love the culture of Botswana. It's a 'We are all in this together' mentality that I love."

What Sarah did not tell the interviewer was that she had found a home where she could just be Sarah.

Printed in Great Britain
by Amazon